Carol

Also by Sarah Gray

Wuthering Bites

Published by Kensington Publishing Corp.

A Vampire Christmas Carol

SARAH GRAY

KENSINGTON BOOKS
www.kensingtonbooks.com

KENSINGTON BOOKS are published by

Kensington Publishing Corp.
119 West 40th Street
New York, NY 10018

ISBN-13: 978-0-7582-6683-5
ISBN-10: 0-7582-6683-9

First Kensington Trade Paperback Printing: October 2011
10 9 8 7 6 5 4 3 2 1

Printed in the United States of America

STAVE 1

THE VAMPIRES AND
MR. SCROOGE

Marley was dead to begin with. There is no doubt whatever about that. Seven years ago that very night, on Christmas Eve, Scrooge was called to his deathbed, hours, perhaps moments, before the inevitable. And Scrooge had possessed full intention of attending said grim event. His greatcoat upon his back, his stovepipe hat upon his head, he was nearly out the door when a towering, dark-haired man, cloaked full in black, appeared at the counting house. Coal black eyes and a face as handsome as ever seen, he was not a man to be ignored, even by someone of the import of Ebenezer Scrooge.

A business proposition this gentleman, who gave his name as Mr. Wahltraud, said he had to offer, one quite profitable, one Scrooge dared not refuse. But the mysterious gentleman would not agree to return, not even in half an hour's time, giving Scrooge the opportunity to say a proper farewell to his dying partner. It was a take-or-leave proposal; the stranger had no time to dally. And so, in honor of Marley's last breath, Scrooge did what Marley would have done. He removed his coat and hat and escorted the man to his private office where, in no more than an hour's time, a fine contract was signed and sealed. In that hour of business, Marley did pass, or so was relayed to Scrooge by one of his clerks.

Proper burial arrangements were made and carried out by those who attended to such details, but Scrooge went himself to the cemetery a few nights later to be certain Marley was secure in the grave. After all, one could never leave such matters up to those with nothing to gain from completing the task. Scrooge had not achieved the place he had by leaving important matters to the less vigilant.

The night he went was dark, and a cold wind blew, driving the clouds, furiously and fast, before it. Scrooge noted that there was a black, gloomy mass that seemed to follow him, not hurrying in a wild chase, but lingering sullenly behind, and gliding darkly and stealthily on. Had he known then who it was . . . what . . . perhaps he would have turned back. He did not turn back, for he was dedicated in his pursuit, but he often looked behind him at this, and, more than once, stopped to let it pass over. But somehow, when he went forward again, it was still behind him, coming mournfully and slowly up, like a shadowy funeral train.

On his journey to Marley's final resting place, Scrooge had to pass a poor, mean burial-ground—a dismal place. It was raised a few feet above the level of the street, and parted from it by a low parapet-wall and an iron railing was a rank, unwholesome, rotten spot, where the very grass and weeds seemed, in their frowzy growth, to tell that they had sprung from paupers' bodies. The weeds struck their roots in the graves of men, sodden, while alive, in steaming courts and drunken hungry dens. And here, in truth, they lay, parted from the living by a little earth and a board or two—lay thick and close—corrupting in body as they had in mind—a dense and squalid crowd. Here they lay, cheek by jowl with life, no deeper down than the feet of the throng that passed there every day, and piled high as their throats. Here they lay, a grisly family, all these dear departed brothers and sisters of the ruddy clergyman who did his task so speedily when they were hidden in the ground! Marley's grave was beyond there—he had only to find it.

While Scrooge was thus engaged, there came toward him, with noise of shouts and singing, some fellows full of drink, followed by others, who were remonstrating with them and urging them to go home in quiet. They were in high good humor, and one of them, a little, wizened, hump-backed man, began to dance. He was a grotesque, fantastic figure, and the few bystanders laughed.

Scrooge was unmoved by the unseemly mirth, and did not so much as look upon the jester's face. When they had passed on, he turned in through the iron gates and did not have to walk far to find the earthen mound he was so intent upon inspecting.

When he found it, at last, he could not look upon the spot among such a heap of graves, but he conjured up a strong and vivid memory of the man himself, and how he looked when last he saw him draw breath. For a reason unknown to Scrooge, instead of picturing Jacob Marley, he recalled the figure of some goblin-creature he had once seen chalked upon a door, as a child. Startled by the memory, he turned to look over his shoulder, the toes of his boots in the freshly turned dead earth. The black mass he had seen before was there again, hovering just behind him.

Bah. Humbug. Scrooge turned upon Marley's fresh grave and set out for his partner's home, now his own. As he drew nearer and nearer, a sense of prickly apprehension set upon him. This feeling became so strong at last, that when he reached his door, he could hardly make up his mind to turn the key and open it.

"My condolences, Mr. Scrooge."

Scrooge whipped around, startled by the voice.

It was the stranger who had appeared at Scrooge's counting house only nights before who tipped his tall black hat, stepped out of the cloaked darkness, almost out of nothingness, for it seemed he was not there one moment, then there the next.

It was, surprisingly enough, it was Mr. Wahltraud. But where had he come from? Scrooge had not seen him when he approached the door; he seemed to appear out of nothingness. Suspicious, Scrooge took him more closely, eying him port and stern.

A handsome gentleman, he appeared, with a young face, but with an older figure in its robustness and its breadth of shoulder, say a man of eight-and-thirty, or at the utmost forty. He was so extremely pale, this Mr. Wahltraud, that the contrast between his black wool cloak and the glimpses of white throat below the neckerchief would have been almost ludicrous but for his broad temples, black eyes, clustering black hair, and ivory teeth.

"Step aside; my day has been long," Scrooge grumbled with a wave of his yellow cane, which had at the top a bone hand with the semblance of a ring on its little finger and a black ball in its grasp.

"I apologize for the intrusion, but I understand that you intend to take up residence in Mr. Marley's home." He had an accent Scrooge could not quite place, not English, though most definitely schooled in London. Germanic, perhaps? Definitely not French or Italian or Danish, nor was he reeling of the manner of speech proclaimed by the icy regions such as Norway, which left only Prussian, Austrian, or one of the lesser barbaric states. He gazed up at the red-brick house, with black outside shutters, green inside blinds, a black street-door up two white steps, a brazen door-plate, and a brazen door-handle full stop. "Considering the size of the abode, I thought you might be interested in renting the first floor and cellars."

"Renting?" Scrooge echoed. Instantly, his weariness vanished as the hope of financial gain lent strength to his countenance. And why should he not make a profit on Marley's house? It was far too big, with too many rooms for Scrooge or any single man to occupy. Would not Marley eagerly have done the same with Scrooge's home, given the opportunity?

"As a purveyor of wine and spirits, the cool darkness below street level would serve me well," said Wahltraud.

"Do you have a family?"

"A wife, sir. No children."

"Good," Scrooge muttered. "I hate children." He named a price well above what the stranger should have agreed to pay. Wahltraud took it without haggling and was on his way in less time than it took Scrooge to mount the high brick steps.

Old Marley would have complimented Scrooge on the bargain he had struck. But Marley could not because old Marley was as dead as a door-nail. Mind! I don't mean to say that I know, of my own knowledge, what there is particularly dead about a door-nail. I might have been inclined, myself, to regard a coffin-nail as the deadest piece of ironmongery in the trade. But the wisdom of our ancestors is in the simile, and my unhallowed hands shall not disturb it, or the country's done for. You will therefore permit me to repeat, emphatically, that Marley was as dead as a door-nail.

As was Wahltraud, I must inject, for I cannot withhold the information a moment longer. Scrooge, however, was unaware of this fact, though I wonder if he would have cared, considering the sum of money the tenant offered. Payment for a full year was offered in advance, due on the very next day.

But soon enough, my dear reader, I will come to Wahltraud, his queen, and his minions. As for Marley, Scrooge and he were partners for I don't know how many years. Scrooge was his sole executor, his sole administrator, his sole assign, his sole residuary legatee, his sole friend, and sole mourner. And even Scrooge was not so dreadfully cut up by the sad event, but that he was an excellent man of business on the very day of the funeral, and solemnized it with an undoubted bargain.

The mention of Marley's funeral brings me back to the point at which I began pages ago. There is no doubt that Marley was dead. This must be distinctly understood, or nothing wonderful can come of the story I am going to relate. If we were not perfectly convinced that Hamlet's Father died before the play began, there would be nothing more remarkable in his taking a stroll at night, in an easterly wind, upon his own ramparts, than there would be in any other middle-aged gentleman rashly turning out after dark in a breezy spot—say Saint Paul's Churchyard for instance—literally to astonish his son's weak mind.

2

Before I continue with the tale, I must fair warn you of the tenants Scrooge did so cleverly lay bargain with the day of Marley's funeral. That black scourge that did follow him to the cemetery and then home was none other than his new tenant, the supposed wine purveyor. He was King Wahltraud, and his wife, Queen Griselda, was waiting for him at their current abode beneath a tavern off The Strand when Wahltraud returned from making the deal with Scrooge that night.

"My dearest, my darling," Griselda greeted him exuberantly from the bottom of the dark staircase. A beauty she was, pale and white as the waxen berries of mistletoe, as beautiful as King Wahltraud was handsome. "And so the deed is done?" she asked with excitement.

"Done and buried," Wahltraud responded, plucking his gloves from his fingertips, relishing the snap of the leather and its scent of a slaughtered beast. He laughed at his jest. "And we are to take up residence in his cellars within the week."

Griselda squealed with delight and threw her arms around her husband, embracing him close. "And so Ebenezer Scrooge is ours?" she begged, looking up at her walking-dead husband in eager anticipation. This project, tedious in time and effort, had taken nearly a full human lifetime. But it would all be worthwhile for Wahltraud and Griselda if Scrooge went the way of Marley. In fact, it would be better, for they had great plans for this human.

Wahltraud brought his lips to Griselda's and they kissed. Then nipped like pups at play. She was the first to draw blood, he the first to howl with pleasure. "Tell me all," she cried. "Have we the cellars, my precious? Have you gained them for me?"

You see, Wahltraud and Griselda were not wine purveyors, Prussian brewers, or even ordinary English citizens. Unbeknownst to Scrooge and most of London, they were not even human. Wahltraud was the undisputed King of Vampires, Griselda his crowned queen, and Scrooge her pet project which had kept her busy the last half-century. But how could Scrooge have known? How could anyone have known? You might say if Scrooge had scrutinized his situation with more care, he might have realized that the events played out in his life up to this day were not of his own making. But, again, I get ahead of myself.

Back to Marley . . . Dead as a door-nail.

3

Scrooge never painted out Old Marley's name the week he died or any of the months or years that followed. There it stood, seven years afterward, above the London warehouse door: *Scrooge and Marley*. The firm was known as Scrooge and Marley even after one partner's death. Sometimes people new to the business called Scrooge Scrooge, and sometimes Marley, but he answered to both names. It was all the same to him.

Oh! But he was a tight-fisted hand at the grindstone, Scrooge. A squeezing, wrenching, grasping, scraping, clutching, covetous old sinner! He was hard and sharp as flint, from which no steel had ever struck out generous fire, secret, and self-contained, and solitary as an oyster. The cold within him froze his old features, nipped his pointed nose, shriveled his cheek, stiffened his gait, made his eyes red, his thin lips blue, and spoke out shrewdly in his grating voice. A frosty rime was on his head, and on his eyebrows, and his wiry chin. He carried his own low temperature always about with him; he iced his office in the dog-days, and didn't thaw it one degree at Christmas.

External heat and cold had little influence on Scrooge. No warmth could warm him, no wintry weather chill him. No wind that blew was more bitter than he; no falling snow was more intent upon its purpose, no pelting rain less open to entreaty. Foul weather didn't know where to have him. The heaviest rain, and snow, and hail, and sleet, could boast of the advantage over him in only one respect. They often came down handsomely, and Scrooge never did.

Ebenezer Scrooge was a cold-hearted man and everyone knew it. Nobody ever stopped him in the street to say, with gladsome looks, "My dear Scrooge, how are you? When will you come to see me?" No beggars implored him to bestow a trifle, no children asked him what it was o'clock. No man or woman ever once in all his life inquired the way to such and such a place, of Scrooge. Even the blind men's dogs appeared to know him, and when they saw him coming on, would tug their owners into doorways and up courts, and then would wag their tails as though they said, "No eye at all is better than an evil eye, dark master!" Did they know the truth of who . . . what controlled Scrooge? Do dogs have some knowledge on this subject that humans do not?

We will never know, for dogs, of course, do not speak. The point is, Scrooge did not care that no one spoke to him unless forced to do so. It was the very thing he liked. He liked to edge his way along the crowded paths of life, warning all human sympathy to keep its distance.

Or so he believed.

So he had been *trained* to believe, convinced by the events that had unfolded throughout his lifetime. It was all part of the plan, from his childhood . . . no, from his birth and before. Ebenezer Scrooge had been King Wahltraud and Queen Griselda's pet project from the very conception of his existence.

Could one take a human, born pure and good, and make him evil? Or would the innate, sickening goodness of mankind always prevail? Could a man be bribed by money or lust to disregard his innate humanness? To take advantage of the less fortunate, the hungry? It was a conversation tossed about for centuries among vampires on every continent, and one of Wahltraud and Griselda's favorites . . . Thus evolved the challenge of Ebenezer Scrooge. And so we return to the story at hand again, although I forewarn you now, I am known to skip forward and back in a good tale, relying on the notion that anyone with a little good sense and the interest will follow.

❧ 4 ❧

So, once upon a time—of all the good days in the year, on Christmas Eve—and seven years after Marley's death—old Scrooge sat busy in his counting house. It was cold, bleak, biting weather. It was foggy and he could hear the people in the court outside go wheezing up and down, beating their hands upon their breasts, and stamping their feet upon the pavement stones to warm them. The city clocks had only just gone three, but it was quite dark already—it had not been light all day—and candles were flaring in the windows of the neighboring offices, like ruddy smears upon the palpable brown air. The fog came pouring in at every chink and keyhole, and was so dense without, that although the court was of the narrowest, the houses opposite were mere phantoms. To see the dingy cloud come drooping down, obscuring everything, one might have thought that nature lived hard by, and was brewing on a large scale.

The door of Scrooge's interior office was open that he might keep his eye upon his clerks, who in a dismal little cell beyond, a sort of tank, were copying ledgers. Bob Cratchit was one. He had been with Scrooge and Marley from the early days; for how many years, Scrooge could not recollect. It seemed as if he had always been there upon his stool. And then there was Lucius Disgut, who arrived unexpectedly the very week Marley died. Willing to work long hours for miniscule wages, willing to be degraded and taken advantage of by his employer, he was practically a gift from the heavens. Or so Scrooge thought, at the time, not realizing that he was never the recipient of gifts, from the heavens or from humans.

Scrooge had a very small fire that afternoon of the anniversary of his partner's death, but the clerks' fire was so very much smaller that it looked like one coal. They couldn't replenish it, for Scrooge kept the coal-box in his own room, and so surely as one of the clerks came in with the shovel, the master predicted that it would be necessary for them to part. Wherefore the clerks put on their comforters, and tried to warm themselves at the candle, in which effort, not being men of a strong imagination, they failed. It was Cratchit who seemed to suffer more from the cold than Disgut; at times, Disgut appeared almost to enjoy the suffering.

"A merry Christmas, Bob Cratchit! God save you!" a cheerful voice cried, followed by the sound of the front door closing.

It was the voice of Scrooge's nephew, Fred, his dead sister's son, and from his perch behind his battered desk, Scrooge eyed him suspiciously. The young man was always in and out of Scrooge's place of business, talking with Cratchit, whispering, smiling. Sometimes their talk was serious, but other times there was laughter. What business did a man like Fred have with a clerk? What business did either of them have with laughter? For neither was in a good financial situation.

Fred had so heated himself with rapid walking in the fog and frost, this nephew of Scrooge's, that he was all in a glow; his face was ruddy and handsome, his eyes sparkled, and his breath smoked.

"A merry Christmas," Cratchit greeted Fred cheerfully. "Good to see you, sir." He lowered his voice so that Scrooge could not hear him. "The VSU meeting last night, I'm sorry I couldn't make it, but my Tim was feeling poorly. It went well, I trust?"

"Well, I should say, indeed. We had an excellent speaker on the use of the club and the pike. I only wish you could have been there." Fred rubbed his hands together for warmth, for it seemed colder inside his Uncle Scrooge's counting house than on the streets. "And there was a report made concerning the nest we believe has been found in Cheapside. A raid is being organized to fall between Christmas and New Year's Day."

The Vampire Slayers Union, or VSU as they were known on the streets, was a group of dedicated and courageous men, and the occasional woman, who had joined forces in London to fight the constant infestation of ghoulish vampires. The vampires had been in existence for years, centuries, perhaps since the beginning of time, not only in Transylvania and the sewers of Paris, but lurking in the very shadows of London Bridge and flying from the ramparts and windows of Buckingham Palace; but in days of strife among the common people, they became bolder. It was nothing these days in London for a vampire to swipe a grocer or shoeshine off the street in the shadows of dusk and suck the life's blood out of him and throw him on a rubbish heap; nothing to find a countess or a knight of the chamber drained to an empty husk and stuffed in a chamber pot.

"You can count me in," Cratchit whispered, glancing in Scrooge's direction.

"We know we always can, Cratchit!" Fred clapped him on the shoulder. "You're the best I know with a sharpened pike and a vampire on the loose. I want you at my side in a raid, I'll fair say that!"

"What's that? What are you talking about, Cratchit?" The other clerk peered through his round, smudged spectacles. Disgut was a short, thin, bony man with skin so ivory white that it glowed, save for the dark circles that ringed his orbs. He had an interrogative nose and little restless perking eyes, which appeared to have been given to him for the sole purpose of peeping into other people's affairs.

Cratchit looked up at Disgut, then back at Scrooge's nephew, and lowered his voice until it was barely a whisper. "Did you hear of the attack on the charwoman near Charing Cross?"

Cratchit glanced Scrooge's way, shook his head, and dipped his pen into his inkwell, pretending to concentrate on his numbers. "Found dead yesterday morning on her mother's doorstep, flat as a dead mouse swept from beneath a beer barrel."

"No," Fred murmured. "A tragedy. And there was also that lamplighter and his son only two days ago."

"No," Cratchit cried. "I had not heard." Then, upon seeing the stony-eyed gaze of Scrooge, he lowered his head, hunkering over his desk, which was less a desk and more a slab of wood than most. "Do tell. . . ."

"On Fleet Street at Ludgate Hill," Fred explained. "Only the night before last. He was doing his duty, his son at his side, when both were swept off their feet. A hackney coachman saw it all from his box, but could do nothing to save them. The poor souls. The father was dragged off his ladder and carried behind a venison shop by two beasties in red cloaks."

"So bold," cried Cratchit.

"The child, no more than six, was bitten, sucked right there at the foot of the ladder (for no one dared intervene for fear of becoming dessert), and then carried off in a pickle barrel into the tunnels to be finished off at the leisure of another."

Cratchit gasped. "Six years old? Why, he would be the age

of my Tiny Tim. The poor lamplighter. The poor family." He shook his head, his knit cap sliding this way and that. "I must say, I've never known a lamplight, but I hear they are a simple people." He peered up at the man who he truly considered a friend despite the differences in their social class. That was one thing the vampires had done for London society; it had brought the classes together in order to fight them.

"That is the third lamplight taken in the last fortnight; they seem to like them. Think you, perhaps, the vampires find them tastier than, say, a poulterer or a charmaid?"

"I don't know. Perhaps. I know that they are a strange and primitive people," Fred observed. "They rigidly adhere to old ceremonies and customs which have been handed down among them from father to son since the first public lamp was lighted out of doors. They intermarry, and betroth their children in infancy; I was told the boy was already promised to a gravedigger's daughter. They enter into no plots or conspiracies (for who ever heard of a traitorous lamplighter?), they commit no crimes against the laws of their country (there being no instance of a murderous or burglarious lamplighter). They are, in short, notwithstanding their apparently volatile and restless character, a highly moral and reflective people, having among themselves as many traditional observances as the Jews, and being, as a body, if not as old as the hills, at least as old as the streets. It is an article of their creed that the first faint glimmering of true civilization shone in the first street-light maintained at the public expense. They trace their existence and high position in the public esteem, in a direct line to the heathen mythology, and hold that the history of Prometheus himself is but a pleasant fable, whereof the true hero is a lamplighter."

"A tragedy." Cratchit sighed, glancing into the wavering light of the sputtering candle on his desk.

"Sir." Disgut interrupted quite suddenly, pouncing off his

stool (for he was trying mightily to hear every word, most of which he could not distinguish). For you see, Disgut was not what he appeared to be. But I imagine you have already deduced that morsel.

Actually, Disgut *was* what he appeared to be: a pale, nosy man with beady dark eyes and dirty spectacles, but he was no ordinary clerk. Did you take notice of my mention that he was hired the very week Marley died, coinciding with the first time Wahltraud made himself visible to Scrooge? Ah, yes, one of the King of the Vampire's minions he was. Of course! For years he had played spy for Wahltraud, and forever fearing punishment for not being able to repeat every word said in Scrooge's counting house, he interrupted the conversation between Cratchit and Scrooge's nephew, afraid they were plotting against the King of Vampires. (Which of course, they were.)

"Would you care to make your way to Mr. Scrooge's office?" Disgut cut his rodent-like eyes at Cratchit. "We've work to do, still, you see."

"Most certainly. Thank you." The nephew looked back to Cratchit, even as he made his way through the narrow doorway. "We'll speak later." And then he called cheerfully to his uncle, "A merry Christmas!"

"Bah!" said Scrooge. "Humbug!"

"Christmas a humbug, Uncle!" said Scrooge's nephew. "You don't mean that, I am sure?"

"I do," said Scrooge. "Merry Christmas! What right have you to be merry? What reason have you to be merry? You're poor enough. Not as poor as those two." He pointed an arthritic finger at his two clerks hovering over their desks. "But poor enough."

"Come, then," returned the nephew gaily. "What right have you to be dismal? What reason have *you* to be morose? You're as rich as your clerks are poor."

Scrooge, having no better answer ready on the spur of the moment, said, "Bah!" again and followed it up with "Humbug!"

"Dear me, don't be cross, Uncle," said the nephew.

"What else can I be," returned he, "when I live in such a world of fools as this? Merry Christmas! Out upon merry Christmas. What's Christmas time to you but a time for paying bills without money, a time for finding yourself a year older, but not an hour richer, a time for balancing your books and having every item in them through a round dozen of months presented dead against you? If I could work my will," said Scrooge indignantly, "every idiot who goes about with 'Merry Christmas' on his lips should be boiled with his own pudding, and buried with a stake of holly through his heart. He should!"

At the suggestion of a human being boiled in pudding, Disgut perked up his ears, for he was a tragic creature, mostly human, but not entirely, with a taste for human blood. Raw was acceptable; he liked it cooked, on occasion. But boiling a man in pudding seemed a waste, not to mention the possibility of adding unwanted sweet and fat to one's diet. Boiled in pudding? Disgusting!

Of course, no man in the counting house could have known this little tidbit about the man on the stool pretending to add his figures while listening to his employer's conversation.

"Uncle!" pleaded the nephew.

"Nephew!" returned the uncle sternly. "Keep Christmas in your own way, and let me keep it in mine."

"Keep it!" repeated Scrooge's nephew. "But you don't keep it."

"Let me leave it alone, then," said Scrooge. "Much good may it do you! Much good it has ever done you!"

"There are many things from which I might have derived good, by which I have not profited, I dare say," returned the nephew. "Christmas among the rest. But I am sure I have always thought of Christmas time, when it has come round—apart from the veneration due to its sacred name and origin, if anything belonging to it can be apart from that—as a good time. It is a kind, forgiving, charitable, pleasant time. This is the only time I know of, in the long calendar of the year, when men and women seem by one consent to open their shut-up hearts freely, and to think of people below them as if they really were fellow-passengers to the grave, and not another race of creatures bound on other journeys. And therefore, Uncle, though it has never put a scrap of gold or silver in my pocket, I believe that it has done me good, and will do me good. I say, God bless it!"

Bob Cratchit, in the tank, applauded with great gusto; Disgut screwed up his thin face and fixed his black eyes upon his companion. Becoming immediately sensible of the impropriety, Cratchit hopped off his stool, poked the fire, and extinguished the last frail spark forever.

Scrooge looked Cratchit's way. "Let me hear another sound from you," he said, "and you'll keep your Christmas by losing your situation! Disgut does twice the work of you for less coin!"

It was untrue of course, for Cratchit was a hard worker. Everyone knew it, but no one dared argue with Ebenezer Scrooge.

"You're quite a powerful speaker, sir," Scrooge added, turning back to his nephew. "I wonder you don't go into Parliament."

"Don't be angry with me, Uncle. And don't poke fun at me. I am sincere in my wishes. Come! Dine with us tomorrow."

"What are you having?"

"Sir?"

"You offer a free meal. What are you having?" Scrooge demanded.

"Well . . ." The nephew hesitated. "A roasted joint of pork

with potatoes and gravy. I . . . I believe the pork will be stuffed with sage and onion."

"No goose?" Scrooge questioned.

"No goose," Fred repeated. "But breads and cheeses and, I believe, grouse pie."

"And dessert?"

Fred nodded, not entirely sure what the intention of his uncle's questioning was, but thinking it might be a positive sign. "Desserts, to be sure. Apple and cherry tarts, and butterfly cakes with clotted cream and jam." Forever the optimist, he looked at Scrooge. "So shall we see you tomorrow?"

"Indeed," Scrooge said.

"Indeed?" Fred was so excited that he nearly reached out and clasped his uncle's hand. "We will see you?"

"In Hades!"

Taken aback but not surprised, disappointed but not discouraged, Fred drew himself to his full height. "But why?" he asked. "Why will you not join my wife and me on Christmas Day?"

"Why did you get married?" said Scrooge.

"What has that to do with anything?"

"Why?" Scrooge repeated, narrowing his gaze.

"Because I fell in love."

"Because you fell in love!" growled Scrooge, as if that were the only thing in the world more ridiculous than a merry Christmas. "Good afternoon!"

"Nay, Uncle, but you never came to see me before I married Penny. Never once, no matter what was served. Why give it as a reason for not coming now?"

"Good afternoon," repeated Scrooge, quite satisfied with himself.

Trying not to feel crushed, Fred clasped his hands in a plea. "I want nothing from you; I ask nothing of you. Why cannot we be friends?"

"Good afternoon."

"I am sorry, with all my heart, to find you so resolute. We have never had any quarrel, to which I have been a party. But I have made the trial in homage to Christmas, and I'll keep my Christmas humor to the last. So a merry Christmas, Uncle!"

"Good afternoon," replied Scrooge, drawing the sides of his coat more closely to ward off the cold . . . and perhaps, unbeknownst to him, the cold-eyed stare of his clerk Disgut.

"And a happy new year!"

"Good afternoon!" said Scrooge.

His nephew left the room without an angry word. He stopped at the outer door to bestow a final greeting of the season on the clerks. Disgut pretended not to hear the nephew, but Cratchit, who, cold as he was, was warmer than Scrooge, offered a merry smile and a word of good cheer.

"There's another fellow," muttered Scrooge, who overheard him. "My clerk, with fifteen shillings a week, and a wife and family, talking about a merry Christmas. The day I see any reason for him to be cheery, I'll retire to Bedlam."

❧ 5 ❧

Cratchit, in letting Scrooge's nephew out, had let two other people in. They were portly gentlemen, pleasant to behold, and now, with their hats off, passed through the tank. Disgut, who seemed relieved the nephew was gone, perked up with interest again.

"Whatever are they doing here?" Disgut asked Cratchit quietly, though not so quietly that they could not hear him.

"I've no idea. It's not my place to ask, nor yours," Cratchit answered, showing them to Scrooge's office and then returning to his perch.

The visitors had books and papers in their hands, and bowed to him.

"Scrooge and Marley's, I believe," said one of the gentlemen, referring to his list. "Have I the pleasure of addressing Mr. Scrooge, or Mr. Marley?"

"Mr. Marley has been dead these seven years," Scrooge replied. "He died seven years ago, this very night."

"I am so sorry," said one.

"No doubt so was he," Scrooge replied, his tone as dry and stale as bread crumbs swept across a baker's floor.

The gentlemen looked at each other and one cleared his throat as if to prod the other on.

"We have no doubt his liberality is well represented by his surviving partner," said the one presenting his credentials.

It certainly was, for they had been two kindred spirits. At the ominous word "liberality," Scrooge frowned, and shook his head, and handed the credentials back.

"At this festive season of the year, Mr. Scrooge," said the gentleman, taking up a pen, "it is more than usually desirable that we should make some slight provision for the poor and destitute, who suffer greatly at the present time. Many thousands are in want of common necessaries; hundreds of thousands are in want of common comforts, sir."

"Are there no prisons?" asked Scrooge after a blink and a pause.

"Plenty of prisons," said the gentleman, laying down the pen.

Scrooge's bushy white eyebrows rose, almost as if of their own accord. "And the union workhouses?"

"Have you ever been to a workhouse, sir?" asked the more portly of the two gentlemen, though both appeared amply fed. "Do you know what workhouses do to the body and soul? Do you know what the faces of the citizens of the workhouse look like?" Guessing at the answer, he went on before Scrooge could reply.

"While having not previously stepped foot within the walls of such a place, it was my duty last Sunday past to attend service in the chapel of a workhouse here in London, one holding near to two thousand paupers."

Scrooge looked at him without so much as a fleck of emotion.

"Among this congregation were some evil-looking young women, and beetle-browed young men, but not many—perhaps that kind of character is kept away. Generally, the faces (those of the children excepted) were depressed and subdued, and wanted color. Aged people were there, in every variety. Mumbling, blear-eyed, spectacled, stupid, deaf, lame; vacantly winking in the gleams of sun that now and then crept in through the open doors, from the paved yard, shading their listening ears, or blinking eyes, with their withered hands, poring over their books, leering at nothing, going to sleep, crouching and drooping in corners. There were weird old women, all skeletal within, all bonnet and cloak without, continually wiping their eyes with dirty dusters of pocket-handkerchiefs, and there were ugly old crones, both male and female, with a ghastly kind of contentment upon them which was not at all comforting to see. Upon the whole, it was the dragon, pauperism, in a very weak and impotent condition, toothless, fangless, drawing his breath heavily enough, and hardly worth chaining up. These are the souls I have recommitted myself to giving aid."

"So the workhouses are still in operation?" Scrooge questioned, not appearing to be the least affected by the tragic experience of the gentleman.

"They are. Still," returned the gentleman, "I wish I could say they were not."

"The Treadmill and the Poor Law are in full vigor, then?" said Scrooge.

"Both very busy, sir."

"Oh. I was afraid, from what you said at first, that something had occurred to stop them in their useful course," said Scrooge. "I'm very glad to hear it."

"Under the impression that they scarcely furnish Christian cheer of mind or body to the multitude," returned the gentleman, "a few of us are endeavoring to raise a fund to buy the poor some meat and drink, and means of warmth. We choose this time, because it is a time, of all others, when want is keenly felt, and abundance rejoices. There is one family in particular we would like to see kept warm this Christmas; a lamplighter's widow and her seven remaining children. I'm certain you heard. It was in all the papers. Her husband and child were murdered by the vampires." He whispered the last word as if fearing the very spoken word might evoke them. "On Ludgate Hill this very week. The father was dragged from his ladder, murdered, his body left behind a venison shop. The young boy was carried off in a pickle barrel. Needless to say, his body is not expected to be recovered."

"Vampires?" Scrooge spat. "Bah! Humbug!"

The other gentleman could hold his tongue no longer. "Surely a man of your education cannot doubt their existence?"

"I've seen no vampires!" Scrooge explained. "Have you?"

He said it so loudly, with such distaste, that the man stepped back. "Not . . . not with my own eyes, no. But that does not mean they don't exist. They are clever creatures that travel in the darkness and disguise themselves as ordinary citizens. Surely you know that, an educated man such as yourself?"

"I know nothing of the sort!" Scrooge lifted his pen and returned his attention to the work at hand. "Good day."

The gentleman, holding his pen poised, pressed his plump lips together. Obviously his belief was so strong in the cause that he would not give up easily. "What . . . what shall I put you down for?"

"Nothing!" Scrooge replied.

"You wish to be anonymous?" He dared a tiny smile.

"I wish to be left alone," said Scrooge. "Since you ask me what I wish, gentlemen, that is my answer. I don't make merry myself at Christmas and I can't afford to make idle people merry. I help to support the establishments I have mentioned— they cost enough, and those who are badly off must go there."

"Many can't go there and many would rather die."

"If they would rather die," said Scrooge, "they had better do it, and decrease the surplus population. Besides, I don't know that."

"But you might know it," observed the gentleman.

"It's not my business," Scrooge returned. "It's enough for a man to understand his own business, and not to interfere with other people's. Mine occupies me constantly. Good afternoon, gentlemen!"

Seeing clearly that it would be useless to pursue their point, the gentlemen tipped their hats and withdrew from Scrooge's office. Just as they were to enter the street, Disgut appeared behind them. One moment he was on his stool, the next, standing in the doorway, casting his sour breath on them. "Do not come here again," he warned, managing to hiss despite the lack of Ss in his words.

The gentlemen looked at each other in disbelief, then back at the hunched, pale clerk. Never had they heard such insolence from a clerk, or witnessed such an oddity as the man's translucent pinched face. "Sir?"

"You heard me," Disgut said. "Do not come here again, or those who plucked the lamplighter and his son from their ladder will be at your doorstep." He lifted his upper lip, baring his teeth. They were certainly not fangs, but mostly definitely oddly shaped, as if they had been filed to points . . . or perhaps he consumed rocks and had broken them off.

"Are you threatening us?" the more portly of the two gentlemen demanded.

"I am making a promise," Disgut replied with a sneer.

Both gentlemen, frightened by the sight of the sharpened

teeth and not entirely certain what to make of them, took a step back, giving little attention to the traffic in the street.

"Go!" Disgut threatened. "Run, while you are still able."

The portly gentlemen did not run, for it probably would have been difficult, considering their portly states, but they most certainly did not take their time in crossing the street and disappearing into the relative safety of the darkness.

❧ 6 ❧

Back inside his office, Scrooge resumed his labors with an improved opinion of himself, and in a more facetious temper than was usual with him.

Meanwhile the fog and darkness thickened so that people ran about with flaring links, proffering their services to go before horses in carriages and conduct them on their way. The ancient tower of a church, whose gruff old bell was always peeping slyly down at Scrooge out of a Gothic window in the wall, became invisible, and struck the hours and quarters in the clouds, with tremulous vibrations afterward, as if its teeth were chattering in its frozen head up there. The cold became intense. In the main street, at the corner of the court, some laborers were repairing the gas-pipes, and had lighted a great fire in a brazier, round which a party of ragged men and boys were gathered, warming their hands and winking their eyes before the blaze in rapture. The water-plug being left in solitude, its overflowing sullenly congealed and turned to misanthropic ice. The brightness of the shops where holly sprigs and berries crackled in the lamp heat of the windows, made pale faces ruddy as they passed. Poulterers' and grocers' trades became a splendid joke, a glorious pageant, with which it was next to impossible to believe that such dull principles as bargain and sale had anything to do. The Lord Mayor, in the stronghold of the mighty Mansion House, gave orders to his fifty cooks and butlers to keep Christmas as a Lord Mayor's household should and even the little tailor, whom he had fined five shillings on the previous Monday for being drunk in the streets, stirred up tomorrow's pudding in his garret, while his lean wife and the baby sallied out to buy the beef.

Despite their fear of the vampires that seemed to ooze from the darkness, the citizens of the town found a merriness on their tired faces and in their croaky voices. They were afraid to be certain; mothers kept their little ones by the hand, and husbands and wives walked arm in arm, but it was not enough to deter them from going about their business this Christmas Eve.

As soon as full darkness fell, it became even foggier yet, and colder. It was a piercing, searching, biting cold. Was it the vampires that brought the unearthly chill? If the good Saint Dunstan had but nipped the Evil Spirit's nose with a touch of such weather as that, instead of using his familiar weapons, then indeed he would have roared to lusty purpose.

The owner of one scant young nose, gnawed and mumbled by the hungry cold as bones are gnawed by dogs, stooped down at Scrooge's keyhole to regale him with a Christmas carol, but at the first sound of "God bless you, merry gentleman. May nothing you dismay!" Scrooge seized the ruler with such energy of action, that the singer fled in terror, leaving the keyhole to the fog and even more congenial frost.

Much to Scrooge's dismay and his employees' delight (for not even Disgut liked working for the miser), the hour of shutting up the counting house arrived. With an ill-will Scrooge dismounted from his stool, and tacitly admitted the fact to the expectant clerks in the tank, who instantly snuffed their candles out, and put on their hats.

"You'll both want all day tomorrow, I suppose?" said Scrooge.

Disgut wanted the day himself as much as Cratchit, but for entirely different reasons. While Cratchit would be spending Christ's birthday at church and dining with his family, Disgut would be sitting down to a different sort of dining experience. He had received an invitation to a Winter Solstice feast to be held in the underground tunnels beneath the city, where the vampires lived by day when not prowling the streets by night. While the Cratchits feasted on bits of fatty beef and parsnips, Disgut would be sinking his teeth into human flesh, sipping the hot, rushing blood, a thought that quite excited him. The dinner *guests* were being brought in from all over the city at that very moment and being housed in the chambers beneath the city to be kept alive for the celebration, and some, it was rumored, would be taken stumbling from ale-houses and thus highly spiced with beer and rum and other spirits. Others, he heard, who had stuffed themselves with goose or plum pudding, would be taken right off the streets to satisfy even the most particular drinkers of blood during this festive season. The beautiful Queen Griselda had invited Disgut herself . . . actually she had sent one of her hags, but it was near the same as a personal invitation, wasn't it? Obviously, her highness had singled him out as worthy. After all these years, she had finally recognized his great worth to her, and he was certain he would be rewarded at the feast, if not by coin then by a better position.

But, again, I digress. I return to the tale and what was taking place in the cold tank of Scrooge's office.

Though Disgut was eager to have the day off, he still let Cratchit be the one to step up to the hearth and press his toes to the coals with Scrooge.

"If quite convenient, sir," said Cratchit, "we would like the day off."

"It's not convenient," said Scrooge, "and it's not fair. If I was to stop half-a-crown the both of you for it, you'd think yourselves ill-used, I'll be bound?"

Cratchit smiled faintly while Disgut feigned great interest in a patch on his sleeve as he thought of all the delicious human blood pudding he would feast on upon the morrow.

"And yet," said Scrooge, "you don't think me ill-used, when I pay a day's wages for no work."

"But it is only once a year," observed Cratchit, glancing at Disgut for support.

"Once a year," Disgut repeated, half-heartedly.

"A poor excuse for picking a man's pocket every twenty-fifth of December!" said Scrooge, buttoning his greatcoat to the chin. "But I suppose you must have the whole day. Be here all the earlier the next morning."

The clerks promised that they would, and Scrooge walked out with a growl. The office was closed in a twinkling, and Cratchit and Disgut, with no love lost between them, parted ways. Cratchit, with the long ends of his white comforter dangling below his waist (for he boasted no greatcoat), went down a slide on Cornhill, at the end of a lane of boys, twenty times, in honor of it being Christmas Eve, and then ran home to Camden Town as hard as he could pelt, with one eye peering over his shoulder in fear of bloodsuckers, to play at blindman's bluff with his children.

7

On his way to dine, Scrooge had several stops to make, his first to collect the interest due on a loan he made to a baker some weeks back. Having a mind to buy a crust or two of bread, he waited impatiently in line.

As Scrooge stood inside the bake shop, the King of the Vampires walked past the foggy window, his queen upon his arm. They had been following him at a distance, one of Griselda's favorite pastimes, for two blocks. "Just a peek, my darling," Griselda begged from ruby lips.

"I have business to attend to," Wahltraud argued, but even as he spoke, he slowed his pace so that she might catch a glimpse of his wife's protégé through the streaky window as they passed the shop. "He should not see us watching him," he warned.

Griselda plucked a slender, pale hand from her rabbit-fur muff to stroke Wahltraud's cheek. "He will not see us because he is like all humans," she murmured. "He does not see what he does not wish to see. I do believe we could walk right into his counting house, devour both his clerks before his very eyes, and throw their carcasses upon his hearth, and he would not notice."

"What a foolish thing to say, my love. If we devoured Disgut, we would have to replace him. You know how difficult it is to find a human who will turn on its own, especially during this syrupy season." He leaned down to press a kiss to her cheek, and the cold of his breath made her shiver with pleasure.

To any human who passed Wahltraud and his queen on the street, the couple appeared to be a pair of discreet lovers, exchanging mellifluous words in the fog that lingered particularly thick and vaporous in front of the bake shop. Only those poor humans who had the misfortune to meet them in a dark alley or come face-to-face and have those dark, haunting eyes stare into their own would ever realize what they were. Then, fear would descend upon the unfortunate, but it would be too late, and the knowledge they had gained would be short-lived.

"Do you see your Scrooge, my precious?" Wahltraud whispered, nipping at her ear tucked inside a velvet hood, encircled with black rabbit fur.

"I cannot." She pouted her full lips. "The window is too streaked with soot and the inside foggy with condensation," she complained. "But the baker's to flavor the bread with a drop of his own blood. Everyone on the street knows what *Mr. Scrooge* gets with his nourishment."

"There, there, we can see him later as he enters our abode, if we hurry, my love. I still have a matter to attend to." He gently guided her away from the shop and its human stench of burnt butter, scorched flour, and despair. Human despair *de profundis*, was quite a gloriously revolting scent, better than sadness or fear. It filled a vampire's nostrils quite to capacity, thick and cloying, intoxicating, for it was the unhappiness of human beings that the vampires thrived upon.

"You do not think we need to keep an eye on him?" Griselda questioned. She had the blackest eyes, eyes that could see through him to the very depths of his black soul, eyes that could freeze humans in their tracks and bring them willingly, step by step, to their own undoing.

"Keep an eye on him?" Wahltraud opened the top button of his greatcoat, enjoying the chill of the night that slipped through the gap in the wool like icy bones.

"So no one might assuage his sour countenance with their gelastic wishes of happy Christmas and such." She hissed the words, despising the taste of them. "You know how these humans are with their wishes of good health and prosperity in the new year, and other such piffle."

"He's already yours, my darling. I swear to you on the rotting carcass of my beloved mother. You have done an excellent job with him. Nothing could persuade him to see any goodness in his human world. He is long past that."

"I suppose you are right," she conceded, allowing him to bustle her along. "But we might send one of those disgusting creatures to watch over him just the same." With a rise of her lovely chin, she indicated one of the stinking urchins hanging back a reasonable distance from the king and the queen. Some were vampires; others, humans who, like Disgut, had acquired, over time, a taste for human blood and were willing to do whatever was asked of them to taste of it.

"As you wish, my love." Wahltraud had only to raise a finger, indicating someone was to stay behind and watch the bakery, and one of the dirty, stinking minions stepped out from the group and rushed to do his bidding.

The sound of carol singers from the street corner near the butcher shop brought a scowl to Griselda's lovely lips as they left the shop.

"Oh come all ye faithful, joyful and triumphant,
Oh come ye, O come ye to Bethlehem.
Come—"

"Come, and let me sink my teeth into your flesh," Griselda threatened.

Unaware there were vampires so near, the carol singer's lusty voices filled the air:

"Born the King of—"

"That sound," Griselda cried, clasping her hands over her head. "Sweet Hades! That sound! It makes my brain ache. I think we should kill them all and decorate the snow with Christmas red."

"Griselda. Griselda, my love." Wahltraud halted, covering her hands with his and hushing her. He gazed into her black, heartless eyes. "When on the streets, you must take care not to draw attention to yourself. Remember that incident at King's Cross last year? We ended up with twenty-seven bodies to dispose of. We live so freely among the humans because they are not smart enough to see us, but we must rely on our own cleverness to keep that true."

"Oh, pooh, you've become so conventional! You never let me have any fun anymore. Remember Kiev, the summer of the Black Death? We left hundreds of bodies in the streets and you never cared a fig."

"Long ago," he sighed. "We were young and drunk on love, and that was before the prophecy of the birth of the Scion of the Great Culling."

"Scion of the Great Culling." She laughed, lowering her hands, but cringing at the sound of the carol singers launching into another refrain. "I've taken care of that, haven't I?" She brushed her hair with her fingertips. "Am I bleeding from my ears, love? Christmas carols sometimes make me bleed from my ears."

Wahltraud kissed her lips. "You are not bleeding from the ears." He then grasped her hand and led her forward again. "Now, come along. Let me check in with my minions to be certain that arrangements have been made for the feast tomorrow, and we'll go home and I'll pour you a fine glass of Belgian blood."

"Ah, the feast tomorrow! Perhaps it is worth waiting for. But could we have one of those?" Griselda asked as he rushed her past the carol singers.

"One of what?"

"Why, one of those." She pointed at a child in the crowd of singers. "I like the little one with the red nose and lips. He looks delicious."

"Not tonight, my love. But perhaps I can add a carol singer or two to the menu." Wahltraud smiled indulgently at his wife, and led her down the street.

❧ 8 ❧

Scrooge left the baker's and went to a tavern. Once having read all the newspapers and beguiled the rest of the evening with his banker's-book, he set out for home. He took the same route as he did each night, a creature of habit as we all are, but tonight somehow felt different and twice he turned to gaze behind. In the feeble lamplight, he saw nothing but a gloomy gray mass, a trick of the eyes in the fog, no doubt.

Only a few blocks from home, he halted in front of a clean white house, of a staid and venerable air, with a quaint old arched door, choice little long, low lattice-windows, and a roof of three gables. The silent street was full of gables, with old beams and timbers carved into strange faces. It was oddly garnished with a queer old clock that projected over the pavement out of a grave red-brick building, as if Time carried on business there, and hung out his sign. Abandoned to the centuries of weather, which have so defaced the dark apertures in its walls, that the ruin looked as if the rooks and daws had pecked its eyes out. Above the arched door hung a carved sign:

RICHARD WATTS, Esq. by his Will, dated 22 Aug. 1579,
FOUNDED THIS CHARITY FOR SIX POOR TRAVELERS,
WHO NOT BEING ROGUES, OR PROCTORS,
MAY RECEIVE GRATIS FOR ONE NIGHT,
LODGING, ENTERTAINMENT, AND FOUR PENCE EACH.

He had passed this abode a hundred times, a thousand, but had never noticed the ridiculous sign. A preposterous concept, to offer poor travelers a roof! While he was yet surveying the shoddy place, he espied, at one of the upper lattices which stood open, a decent body, of a wholesome slender appearance, whose eyes he caught inquiringly addressed to his.

So shocked by the blue-eyed gaze that met his, he stumbled back and then set out along the street again.

He almost thought he made his escape, but then heard her steps behind him. She called out and yet he continued on, wondering what had so addled him as to cause him to linger in the first place.

"Ebenezer!"

Still he did not turn. Not until she caught the sleeve of his coat and voiced him to halt or drag her through the frozen slush of the street.

"Ebenezer," she repeated, more softly this time, her voice as haunting as the black and gray glooms that followed him each day and night.

When he turned, for the briefest moment, he did not see a woman of the age she was (younger than he but not by many years), but as she had been in past. He remembered Belle at about twenty, when her hair was not tucked matronly upon her head but fell free in natural ringlets. A lovely girl, with a frank face, and wonderful eyes, eyes so large, so soft, so bright, set to such perfection in her kind good head. He remembered once saying that he was certain the blue of her eyes must have been the very color of heaven. Belle had been round then, and fresh and dimpled and spoilt, and there was in her an air of timidity and dependence, which was the best weakness in the world, and gave her the only crowning charm a girl so pretty and pleasant could have been without.

He did not see the timidity nor dependence in her face today, and found himself wanting nothing but to escape her presence.

"Ebenezer, were you looking for me?"

He found himself stuttering and then stammering. "Certainly . . . m-m-most certainly not."

She gazed into his eyes, not seeming in the least bit fearful of him, or angry, as most were. Which was quite miraculous, actually, considering that she of all people might have thought she had the most reason to hold a grudge against him.

"But I saw you standing at my doorstep," she said with rosy lips. Her breath came in great white puffs of frost, for the temperature was still dropping. "I thought, perhaps, you had decided to accept my invitation for Christmas breakfast tomorrow after church, and you were stopping to tell me yourself." There was hope in her voice that seemed to blossom as a rose opened to the summer sunshine.

"You send me an invitation every year," he grumbled.

"And every year I wait for you, and every year you do not come."

The gray gloom that had been following him since he left the tavern seemed to creep closer, gliding along the filthy gutter. He did not know if Belle saw it or just sensed it, but she glanced over her shoulder and drew her cloak, hastily thrown on, tighter around her neck, lifting the hood. The cloak appeared quite worn out and very old; the crushed remains of a bonnet on her head seemed as if it had been picked up from a ditch or dunghill.

"Then you would be better not to waste the pen and ink, would you not?" he demanded.

"I will not give up on you, Ebenezer," she cried, her voice quite full of a passion for a woman dressed so poorly. "I never will. I told you that. I told you that from the beginning. I will not let them have you."

He ignored her words, which made him uncomfortable in the pit of his stomach. She would not let *who* have him? "So that is where you live?"

"You know it is," she said in a soft, earnest voice. "I have seen you walk by. You have stood gazing in my windows. I know you have seen me, though you pretend you do not."

"And you give respite to poor travelers?"

"It is my calling, that among *other things*." She looked into his eyes, putting emphasis on those last words.

Scrooge had no idea what she referred to and did not wish to know. "Good evening, then," he said, striding away.

"Must you go so quickly? Could you not come in for a hot drink?"

"Certainly not."

Belle remained on the street until he disappeared in the darkness, the gray gloom following close behind.

⚜ 9 ⚜

Inside her front door, Belle removed her cloak, shook it out, and left it in the entryway. Inside her parlor, a quaint room with a snug fireplace at the upper end, a glimpse of the snowy street shone through the low mullioned window and beams over the window.

She found one of her *travelers*, wrapped in a quilt, seated before the fire, a cup of mulled cider in his hand. He was no traveler at all, in actuality, but a native Londoner, come to Belle to seek asylum and medical care. Belle had purchased the meager property many years ago under the guise of continuing the intentions of the original owner, Richard Watts, when in fact it was a haven for vampire slayers.

Any slayer in trouble could come to Belle's door, be he running from a particularly nasty vampire, or injured in a fight against one of the beasts. Belle hid the men, patched them up, fed them, clothed them, and sent them back onto the streets when they were ready to fight another day against the infestation that threatened the very existence of Londoners.

"Who was that man? Come closer and warm yourself. You

should not be going out on the street on a night like this," said Mortimer Ginsby. The young man had been with Belle near a fortnight. Vampires had killed his parents and little brother and left Mortimer for dead in his burning house. Slayers returning from a meeting had found his nearly drained body and brought him to Belle. He was already looking pink-cheeked again and was eager to return to the streets and avenge the death of his family.

Belle thrust her chapped hands out to the warmth of the fire. She needed to return upstairs to check on the gentleman she had been nursing when she spotted Ebenezer from the window. He had a child, his daughter, with him. But she would linger for a moment to warm herself and then take the gentleman a cup of tea.

"I knew him once."

"Miss?" The gentleman had a cheerful face, still possessing two rows of white teeth, and bright hazel eyes that reached out with compassion.

Belle worked her chilly hands before the fire, as if by warming the flesh, she could warm her heart. "We were once engaged to be married, Mr. Scrooge and I. We were very much in love." She smiled at the memory of it.

"What happened?" Ginsby asked.

"Quite simply, sir?" She gazed over her shoulder to him. "The vampires."

"But . . . but he is still alive."

She exhaled. "He is, indeed, for the vampires have never touched his flesh, to my knowledge."

"Never bitten him? Then how . . ." He let his sentence drift into silence, sensing she needed a moment before telling the tale.

"No one knows but me, and I cannot even tell you how I know, but . . . the vampires have, for years, been trying to make him one of their own," she said softly, gazing into the fire.

"Why, I do not know, but they have . . . swayed him. He was once a good-hearted man. Kind, loving, but somehow they have convinced him to turn away from those he loves, from all mankind."

"How is that possible?" Ginsby asked, unable to contain himself, for he had never heard such a tale. All he knew of the vampires was what he had experienced. They attacked humans, sucked their blood until they were dead, and then cast their bodies aside. If you challenged them, they fought wildly. The only way to kill a vampire was to put a pike through his heart, or decapitate him. And once they discovered you were a slayer, they could be unrelenting in their pursuit of you, if they chose to do so. It was for this reason that Ginsby's family was dead, his home burned out, and he was living here out of the kindness of Belle.

"I do not know how they have done it," Belle said. "I . . . I have no proof. I only know it to be true in my heart."

"Is . . . is there hope for Mr. Scrooge, then, or is he lost?"

Belle stood, a tiny smile up the curve of her lips, for she was still a pretty woman. Her eyes shone. "Oh, Mr. Ginsby, there is always hope. I only wish I knew how to help him before his soul is lost."

"Is there a way?"

As he spoke, Belle turned her head toward the window. "Did you hear that?"

"Hear what?"

"That sound. That howl?"

"A howl?" Mr. Ginsby turned to look in the direction Belle stared. "I hear nothing but the shift of coal in the fire, miss."

It was at that moment that Belle realized what she heard was most definitely real, but not being entirely earthly; it could not be heard by every ear. She had a caller, but not of human flesh.

"Might you excuse me, Mr. Ginsby? I think I'll put another pot of water on for tea."

But instead of going into the kitchen, Belle donned her cloak and stepped out onto the dark, deserted street. The fog was so thick now that it would have been hard to say what lurked there. She looked one way and then the other, for you see, she was one of those who had the *gift* of being able to see and hear the dead almost as easily as the living. It was not a gift exactly, and most assuredly sometimes a curse, but an ability she had learned to live with since she was a child.

Holding her hood with numbing fingers, she called out into the darkness, praying she did not call to a vampire rather than a spirit. "Are you there?" she called. "Have . . . have you need of assistance?" She asked this because it was rare that the dead contacted the living, except when in dire need of aid. "Good evening?" Still, there was no answer.

Belle was just about to turn and run back up her steps when suddenly an apparition appeared before her, so ghastly to the view that despite having encountered many spirits through the years, she shrieked aloud, and recoiled in horror. "Do I know you, sir?" she asked in a shaking voice.

He could not answer because his chin was bound up with a kerchief, which was odd, but not as odd as his pigtail hair bristling out from his head or the heavy chain he wore bound around his waist and dragging behind him. Tangled in the chain's links were what appeared, in the mist of his semi-opaque body, to be keys, paddocks, and purses. With horny hands bound by the chain, and glassy eyes, the spook traced a finger in the very drops of sweat upon his brow, one word—Marley.

"Marley?" she questioned, taking a closer look at the horrid face. "Not . . . Mr. Jacob Marley?" She gave a little laugh, for once upon a time she had known a Jacob Marley well; he had been Ebenezer's partner and his friend before that. But Jacob had been dead many years, and this . . . this apparition did not much resemble him.

"How can I help you, Mr. Marley?" she asked earnestly, sensing it really was him. As she spoke, she kept an eye on the street; apparitions sometimes drew vampires. (They seemed as fascinated by them as humans were.) In her eagerness to waylay the spirit that called, she had not brought with her the pike she often toted at night for protection; she now considered going back for it. It would be of no protection against this spirit (they were rarely threatening, anyway), but it might save her life should one of the beasties choose the moment to show himself.

The spirit untied the handkerchief, his jaw fell open, and he spoke to her then, in something of his own voice, but sharpened and made hollow, like a dead man's face. What he said, God knows. He seemed to utter words, but they were such as man or woman had never heard. And this was the most fearful circumstance of all, to Belle, to see Jacob Marley standing there, gabbling in an unearthly tongue.

"I am sorry," she said firmly, willing away her fear (for no matter how many times she encountered these unearthly specters, they still gave her unease). "You'll have to speak English. I cannot understand your tongue."

There was more garbling, then, "You seek me?"

She shook her head, surprised by the notion. Did anyone *seek* such ghastly spirits as this? "No, no, I'm sorry. I did not call you."

He nodded grimly, but in disagreement.

"No, no, I'm sure I did not." Then she looked at him more closely. "Wait . . . when I said to Mr. Ginsby, I wished there was a way I could help Ebenezer, did you hear my words?"

He nodded, this time in the affirmative.

"And you've come on his behalf?"

Again, he nodded, the chains making a racket that she thought certain could be heard clearly to the tailor's shop on the next block. "On your behalf and his."

"His? You mean Ebenezer's?"

"Do you love him?" the ghost of Jacob Marley demanded, seeming to fight the weight of the chains bound around him. "Still after all these years? After all he has done to turn you, to turn all of mankind away?"

Tears filled Belle's eyes. It had been a very long time since she and Ebenezer had been in love, so long that she could barely remember them as they had been, young and full of hope. But the love was still there deep in her heart. "I do love him," she told the specter, shivering now not just from the cold, but for fear that maybe Ebenezer truly was now lost. "Is there anything you can do?" she begged. "Anything any of us can do? I never married, but have instead devoted my life to fighting the vampires, caring for those who fight them, perhaps because I could not help Ebenezer."

"Ask," Marley howled, lifting his feet off the ground, chains rattling.

"What?" She drew her cloak closer, truly afraid now.

"You must ask me to go to him," Marley cried. "I cannot save myself. I am lost, but that which threatens him is far worse even than my fate."

"What do you mean?" she cried. "Whatever could be worse than your fate?" She motioned to his clanging, chain-ridden form.

"They wish to make him one of them."

"No!" she cried. But she knew it was true. Somehow, she had always known it was true. She heard a dog bark in the distance and flinched. "Oh, please, Jacob, do come inside. The streets are dangerous at night. We are not safe."

"I do not have *time!*" he cried. "The request for a spirit such as myself must be made out of true love. Only true and abiding love can carry me through the veil to Ebenezer Scrooge."

Realizing what he was saying, Belle clasped her hands together as if in the front pew of a cathedral. Her hood fell away and her dark hair, streaked only lightly with silver, came down round her shoulders. "Please, Jacob, I beg of you. Go to him. Help him see the error of his ways. Save him from the vampires! Can you do that?" Tears filled her eyes. "I do not know how the vampires have controlled him and turned his heart sour. I only know that they have. If . . . if it is possible, please help him. Save him from their clutches. Save him from his fate."

The ghost of Jacob Marley rose up with a cry and a howl so loud, so frightening, that Belle covered her ears with her hands, squeezed her eyes shut, and fell to her knees in the wet, muddy snow. When she opened her eyes a moment later, she was alone in the street.

❧ 10 ❧

Perhaps there is always hope, perhaps there is not, for as Belle was begging the ghost of Marley to save Scrooge, Scrooge, having finished a dismal dinner in a dismal tavern, did approach his home, where his tenants were waiting for him (of which of course he was not aware). He lived in the chambers upstairs, which had once belonged to his deceased partner. They were a gloomy suite of rooms, in a lowering pile of building up a yard, where it had so little business to be, that one could scarcely help fancying it must have run there when it was a young house, playing at hide-and-seek with other houses, and forgotten the way out again. The structure was old enough now, and dreary enough, perfect for a vampire couple. The yard was so dark that even Scrooge, who knew its every stone, was fain to grope with his hands. The fog and frost so hung about the black old gateway of the house, that it seemed as if the genius of the weather sat in mournful meditation on the threshold.

Now, it is a fact that there was nothing at all particular about the knocker on the door, except that it was very large. It is also a fact that Scrooge had seen it, night and morning, during his whole residence in that place; also that Scrooge had as little of what is called fancy about him as any man in the city of London, even including—which is a bold word—the corporation, aldermen, and livery. Let it also be borne in mind that Scrooge had not bestowed one thought on Marley, since his last mention of his seven-years-dead partner that afternoon. And then let any man explain to me, if he can, how it happened that Scrooge, having his key in the lock of the door, saw in the knocker, without its undergoing any intermediate process of change—not a knocker, but Marley's face.

Marley's face. It was not in impenetrable shadow as the other objects in the yard were, but had a dismal light about it, like a bad lobster in a dark cellar. It was not angry or ferocious, but looked at Scrooge as Marley used to look with ghostly spectacles turned up on its ghostly forehead. The hair was curiously stirred, as if by breath or hot air; and, though the eyes were wide open, they were perfectly motionless. That, and its livid color, made it horrible; but its horror seemed to be in spite of the face and beyond its control, rather than a part of its own expression.

As Scrooge looked fixedly at this phenomenon, it was a knocker again.

To say that he was not startled, or that his blood was not conscious of a terrible sensation to which it had been a stranger from infancy, would be untrue. But he put his hand upon the key he had relinquished, turned it sturdily, walked in, and lighted his candle.

He did pause, with a moment's irresolution, before he shut the door; and he did look cautiously behind it first, as if he half expected to be terrified with the sight of Marley's pigtail sticking out into the hall. But there was nothing on the back of the door, except the screws and nuts that held the knocker on, so he said, "Pooh, pooh," and closed it with a bang.

The sound resounded through the house like thunder. Every

room above, and every cask of the wine merchant's wine, did shudder at the assault and appeared to have a separate peal of echoes of its own. Scrooge was not a man to be frightened by echoes. He fastened the door, and walked across the hall.

Just as Scrooge was to take the stairs, his tenants appeared at the open door of the cellar. Odd that he had not noticed the door ajar a moment before, or the shadow of their forms in the alcove.

"Mr. Scrooge." Mr. Wahltraud was dressed for dinner in black, his coat, as always, impeccable, his face as pale as moonlight.

"Mr. Wahltraud. Mrs. Wahltraud." Scrooge removed his hat. He did not care to be sociable with the wine dealer or his wife, but he collected enough rent from them that he could not deny them at least a good evening, which was precisely what he offered. Nothing more. Nothing less.

"I trust your day was profitable?"

"Profitable enough." Scrooge continued on his way to the staircase that led to the rooms he occupied above, his cane striking soundly on the hardwood floor.

The missus was an attractive woman with long black hair twisted high on her head and lips a ruby red, but her face was as pale as his, perhaps paler. It was no wonder, of course, that she did not have more color in her cheeks, as much time as they spent in the cellar, minding their inventory.

"Plans for the morrow?" she sang as sweetly as a songbird sings in springtime . . . but with an edge to that sweet melody that gave Scrooge discomfort somewhere in the recesses of his mind. "Christmas Day and all?"

"Bah, humbug," Scrooge mumbled. And with a final good evening, he made his way up the steps.

❦ 11 ❦

Griselda grasped Wahltraud's sleeve as they watched her pet project march upward. "You do not think he will go to the nephew's for dinner tomorrow, do you? I do not want him near that young man. He is too full of *good cheer*. There will be laughter and dancing and smiles and talk of giving gifts to the poor. It is revolting!"

"Why would he go? The invitation has been extended for years, and never has it been accepted. Thanks to your well-orchestrated meddling." He nuzzled her slender white neck.

She ran her hand the length of his sleeve, nearly purring with pleasure. "I know. Is it not pleasing that he has such a weak constitution? That he has become so . . . malleable?" She sighed. "But I am concerned about the woman. Belle. She seems made of stronger stuff, and growing stronger with each year that passes. We've not been able to get to her. No one can. She is one of those rare humans who is truly good to the core of her soul." She made a gagging sound.

"You have no need to be concerned with her," Wahltraud scoffed, turning to take his wife, his queen, into his arms. "She had her chance long ago with him. You had your way. She is nothing."

"Nothing now, but once his true love," she reminded him with a pout. "And, therefore, dangerous. Always dangerous. You never know when a woman like that might lead a man like Scrooge down the path of truth. What if she revealed to him what we have been doing all these years? The sheer knowledge of what we do could weaken my position with him, and I am so very close to having him, for surely he cannot live too many years longer."

"She cannot warn him, my love, because she does not know."

Griselda frowned. "I think it is time we rid ourselves of her. She is a pest. She has taken another slayer in, you know. It was reported to me today." She peered into his black eyes. "The trouble, of course, is that she is difficult to reach, the way those spirits surround her, *protecting* her from us."

"There, there, my dearest. Do not fret yourself." He kissed her cheek and then drew his mouth down along her jawline.

Griselda lengthened her neck, closing her eyes. "Just a nibble," she whispered.

He kissed her neck and then drew his fangs along the sweet, pale flesh. "Not here."

"Below stairs?" She looked up at him with longing.

"It will be a quiet night, tonight, I think." He offered his arm. "And I am all yours."

Scrooge went up the stairs, trimming his candle as he went, paying no mind to his tenants who watched him from the shadows. You may talk vaguely about driving a coach-and-six up a good old flight of stairs, or through a bad young Act of Parliament, but I mean to say you might have got a hearse up that staircase, and taken it broad-wise, with the splinter-bar toward the wall and the door toward the balustrades, and done it easy. There was plenty of width for that, and room to spare, which is perhaps the reason why Scrooge thought he saw a locomotive hearse going on before him in the gloom. Half-a-dozen gas-lamps out of the street wouldn't have lighted the entry too well, so you may suppose that it was pretty dark with Scrooge's dip.

Up Scrooge went, not caring a button for that. Darkness was cheap, and Scrooge liked it. But before he shut his heavy door, he left his can in the corner, and walked through his rooms to see that all was right. He had just enough recollection of the face in the knocker to desire to do that.

As he opened the door to the sitting room, he heard a strange noise, a thump and a scrape across the floor, and froze, hand on the doorknob, door open a crack. The room was dark inside and he lifted the candlestick high, but it cast a measly yellow light. He cleared his throat. The only reply he received was a silence quieter than a graveyard at midnight.

It was on the tip of his tongue to call out to Marley, but that would have been ridiculous, of course. His partner was door-nail dead and could not be in the sitting room . . . or on the front door, for that matter. Scrooge, having near convinced himself of those truths, was just about to close the door when he heard a scrape against the wooden floor again.

"Who's in here?" he demanded, pushing the door full open, but not making the leap of faith to enter.

What Scrooge saw in the far corner of the room was his housemaid, Gelda, and her more-than-a-little-odd son, Tag. Gelda was a woman of thirty years, or perhaps fifty. One could not say; life had not been kind to her. Short and lumpy in stature, she had a long, hooked nose, centered in a face so wrin-kled as it could be mistaken for a large rotten apple upon her shoulders. Worse even than her unfortunate face was the foul stench that clung to her, following her from room to room, a scent that reminded Scrooge of beef left too many days in the cupboard and riddled with maggots . . . or perhaps a potato that had rolled from the bag and lain forgotten on the floor until the slime it produced trickled through the floorboards, creating such a foul stench that it would offend even a tanner's apprentice.

"What are you doing in here?" Scrooge demanded, plucking a handkerchief from his pocket to cover his nose; her scent was that fetid.

"Mr. Scrooge," she exclaimed.

The son, with the same hooked nose as his mother, held his hands behind his back. "M-M-Mr. S-S-Scrooge." A string of drool slowly stretched from the corner of his mouth, down-ward to the floor.

The housekeeper tucked her hands behind her back as her son had done.

Scrooge looked to Gelda, too impatient to wait on the addle-pated boy, who could take up to ten minutes' time to speak any sensible thought. "Why are you still here?" Scrooge was very clear as to what he paid the maid to do in the home, and standing in the dark was not among her duties.

"Jes tidyin' up, sir." She looked a bit like an alley cat that had just swallowed a brightly colored bird. "Before we make our way home, sir," she sniveled.

"W . . . way h . . . h . . . home," the boy repeated, for he always repeated what his mother said, quite an annoying habit. More like an affliction, Scrooge supposed.

"In the dark?"

"Ye told me to quit usin' yer candles. Wastin' 'em." She didn't wait for him to lay comment. "Left gruel on the hob, I did, sir."

"O . . . on the h . . . h . . . hob, sir."

Without responding, Scrooge stepped back and closed the door, leaving them in darkness. They had obviously found their way in there in the dark; they could find their way out and, as she pointed out, not waste one of his candles. His movement was so swift that he did not see the thing that Tag was holding behind his back slip out of his filthy hands and hit the floor with a soft thud. It should have been a louder thud, but the orphan child, snatched off the street only an hour ago, weighed no more than a small man's waistcoat. The child was a Christmas gift for the king and queen.

Scrooge heard the muffled thud, but gave it no mind as he went on to the next room and then the next, checking to be certain all was as it should be. He found nobody under the table, nobody under the sofa, a small fire in the grate; spoon and basin ready, and the little saucepan of gruel Gelda had left upon the hob. Nobody under the bed, nobody in the closet, nobody in

his dressing-gown, which was hanging up in a suspicious attitude against the wall. Lumber-room as usual. Old fire-guard,
old shoes, two fish-baskets, washing-stand on three legs, and a
poker.

Quite satisfied, he closed his door and locked himself in;
double-locked himself in, which was not his custom. Thus secured against surprise, he took off his cravat, put on his dressing-
gown and slippers, and his nightcap, and sat down before the
fire to take his gruel.

It was a very low fire, indeed, of little consequence on such a
bitter night. He was obliged to sit close to it, and brood over it,
before he could extract the least sensation of warmth from such
a handful of fuel. The fireplace was an old one, built by some
Dutch merchant long ago, and paved all round with quaint
Dutch tiles, designed to illustrate the Scriptures. There were
Cains and Abels, Pharaoh's daughters, Queens of Sheba, An-
gelic messengers descending through the air on clouds like
feather-beds, Abrahams, Belshazzars, Apostles putting off to
sea in butter-boats, hundreds of figures to attract his thoughts,
and yet that face of Marley, seven years dead, came like the ancient Prophet's rod, and swallowed up the whole. If each
smooth tile had been blank at first, with power to shape some
picture on its surface from the disjointed fragments of his
thoughts, there would have been a copy of old Marley's head
on every one.

"Humbug!" said Scrooge and walked across the room.

After several turns, he sat down again. As he threw his head
back in the chair, his glance happened to rest upon a bell, a dis-
used bell that hung in the room, and communicated for some
purpose now forgotten with a chamber in the highest story of
the building. It was with great astonishment, and with a
strange, inexplicable dread, that as he looked, he saw this bell
begin to swing. It swung so softly in the outset that it scarcely

made a sound, but soon it rang out loudly, and so did every bell in the house.

This might have lasted half a minute, or a minute, but it seemed an hour. The bells ceased as they had begun, together. They were succeeded by a clanking noise, deep down below, as if some person were dragging a heavy chain over the casks in the wine merchant's cellar. Scrooge then remembered to have heard that ghosts in haunted houses were described as dragging chains.

One of the doors downstairs flew open with a booming sound, and then he heard the noise much louder, on the floors below, then coming up the stairs, then coming straight toward his door.

Could it be the tenants, he wondered. It was not like them to make such a racket, though he did, on occasion, believe he heard a scream from their rented floor or the cellar below. But this sound that approached his door was like no other sound he had heard before.

"It's humbug still!" said Scrooge. "I won't believe it."

His color changed though, when, without a pause, that which created the horrendous racket came through the heavy door, and passed into the room before his eyes. Upon its coming in, the dying flame leaped up, as though it cried, "I know him, Marley's ghost!" and fell again.

It was the same face, the very same as he had seen on the knocker. Marley in his pigtail, usual waistcoat, tights, and boots, the tassels on the latter bristling, like his pigtail, and his coat-skirts, and the hair upon his head. The chain he drew was clasped about his middle. It was long, and wound about him like a tail, and it was made (for Scrooge observed it closely) of cash-boxes, keys, padlocks, ledgers, deeds, and heavy purses wrought in steel. His body was transparent, so that Scrooge, observing him, and looking through his waistcoat, could see the two buttons on his coat behind.

Scrooge had often heard it said that Marley had no bowels, but he had never believed it until now.

No, nor did he believe it even now. Though he looked the phantom through and through, and saw it standing before him. He felt the chilling influence of its death-cold eyes and marked the very texture of the folded kerchief bound about its head and chin, which wrapper he had not observed before. He was still incredulous, and fought against his senses.

"How now!" said Scrooge, caustic and cold as ever. "What do you want with me?"

"Much." It was Marley's voice, no doubt about it. "I have been sent by one who loves you."

"No one loves me," Scrooge scoffed. "Who are you?"

"Ask me who I was."

"Who were you, then?" said Scrooge, raising his voice. "You're particular, for a shade." He was going to say "to a shade," but substituted this, as more appropriate.

"In life I was your partner, Jacob Marley."

"Can you—can you sit down?" asked Scrooge, looking doubtfully at him.

"I can."

"Do it, then."

Scrooge asked the question, because he didn't know whether a ghost so transparent might find himself in a condition to take a chair, and felt that in the event of it being impossible, it might involve the necessity of an embarrassing explanation. But the ghost sat down on the opposite side of the fireplace, as if he were quite used to it.

"You don't believe in me," observed the ghost. "Or the love someone still bears for you."

"I don't," said Scrooge. "In one or the other."

Marley seemed to settle in the chair. "What evidence would you have of my reality beyond that of your senses?"

"I don't know," said Scrooge.

"Why do you doubt your senses?"

"Because," said Scrooge, "a little thing affects them. A slight disorder of the stomach makes them cheat. You may be an undigested bit of beef, a blot of mustard, a crumb of cheese, a fragment of an underdone potato. There's more of gravy than of grave about you, whatever you are!"

Scrooge was not much in the habit of cracking jokes, nor did he feel, in his heart, by any means, waggish then. The truth is, that he tried to be smart, as a means of distracting his own attention, and keeping down his terror; for the specter's voice disturbed the very marrow in his bones.

To sit, staring at those fixed glazed eyes, in silence for a moment, would play, Scrooge felt, the very deuce with him. There was something very awful, too, in the specter's being provided with an infernal atmosphere of its own. Scrooge could not feel it himself, but this was clearly the case, for though the ghost sat perfectly motionless, its hair, and skirts, and tassels, were still agitated as if by the hot vapor from an oven.

"You see this toothpick," said Scrooge, returning quickly to the charge, for the reason just assigned, and wishing, though it was only for a second, to divert the vision's stony gaze from himself.

"I do," replied the ghost.

"You are not looking at it," said Scrooge, observing Marley's gaze still upon him.

"But I see it," said the ghost, "notwithstanding."

"Well," returned Scrooge, "I have but to swallow this, and be for the rest of my days persecuted by a legion of goblins, all of my own creation."

"And love is a bit of undigested beef?" demanded the ghost.

"Less tangible even that you, Spirit. And more useless. Humbug, I tell you. Humbug!"

At this the spirit raised a frightful cry, and shook its chain with such a dismal and appalling noise, that Scrooge held on tight to his chair, to save himself from falling in a swoon. But how much greater was his horror, when the phantom taking off the bandage round its head, as if it were too warm to wear indoors, its lower jaw dropped down upon its breast (far further than when he had spoken to Belle, for he had not wished to frighten her).

Scrooge fell upon his knees, and clasped his hands before his face.

"Mercy!" he said. "Dreadful apparition, why do you trouble me?"

"Man of the worldly mind!" replied the ghost. "Do you believe in me or not?"

"I do," said Scrooge with a shudder. "I must. I believe more in your existence than love's, for certain. But why do spirits walk the earth, and why do they come to me?"

"It is required of every man," the ghost returned, "that the spirit within him should walk abroad among his fellow men, and travel far and wide, and if that spirit goes not forth in life, it is condemned to do so after death. It is doomed to wander through the world—oh, woe is me—and witness what it cannot share, but might have shared on earth, and turned to happiness. And your fate, Ebenezer Scrooge, threatens worse yet thanks, thanks be to the creatures that live below your stairs and below this fine city."

"Worse how?" Marley was daft, Scrooge was certain of it. Then he wondered if that was even possible. His partner had been many things in life, but that trait had not been one of them. "What creatures living below my stairs? Rats? Do you mean rats?"

"I mean your tenants," the ghost bellowed. "Where are your eyes to see, your ears to hear? Your *tenants* mean to make you one of their own. All these years they have blackened your heart, and when you die, there will be no humanity left within you. You will not have the wretched opportunity I have been given. Your fate will be worse, Ebenezer Scrooge. You will become one of them!"

"One of who? One of what?"

"One of the vampires."

Scrooge rocked back and gave a low chuckle, despite the proximity of the frightening specter. "Vampires? My tenant, the wine purveyor, and his wife? Bah, humbug!"

Again the ghost raised a cry, and shook its chain and wrung its ghastly hands.

"You are fettered," said Scrooge, trembling as he tried not to consider the fate Marley had suggested. "Tell me why."

"I wear the chain I forged in life," replied the ghost. "I made it link by link, and yard by yard. I girded it of my own free will, with the help of King Wahltraud and Queen Griselda and others, and of my own free will I wore it."

Scrooge trembled more and more.

"Would you know," pursued the ghost, "the weight and length of the strong coil you bear yourself? It was full, as heavy and as long as this, seven Christmas Eves ago. You have labored on it, since. It is a ponderous chain!"

Scrooge glanced about him on the floor, in the expectation of finding himself surrounded by some fifty or sixty fathoms of iron cable, but he could see nothing. "A chain," he said. "So I will be bound as you are now, to carry the links."

The ghost shook its ghastly head. "Your chain will rob you of what is left of your humanity and you will walk the streets of London taking blood, taking the lives of those you should have served in life! You will not be dead. You will wish that you were!"

Scrooge shuddered at the thought of drinking blood, for it was never a taste he had acquired; he did not even eat blood pudding. "Jacob," he said imploringly. "Old Jacob Marley, tell me more. Speak comfort to me, Jacob."

"I have none to give," the ghost replied. "It comes from

other regions, Ebenezer Scrooge, and is conveyed by other ministers, to other kinds of men. Nor can I tell you what I would. A very little more is all permitted to me. I cannot rest, I cannot stay, I cannot linger anywhere. My spirit never walked beyond our counting house. Mark me in life, my spirit never roved beyond the narrow limits of our money-changing hole, and weary journeys lie before me."

It was a habit with Scrooge, whenever he became thoughtful, to put his hands in his pockets. Pondering on what the ghost had said, he did so now, but without lifting up his eyes, or getting off his knees.

"You must have been very slow about it, Jacob," Scrooge observed, in a business-like manner, though with humility and deference.

"Slow!" the ghost repeated.

"Seven years dead," mused Scrooge. "And traveling all the time?"

"The whole time," said the ghost. "No rest, no peace. I carry the incessant torture of remorse. And this fate I consider far better than yours will be."

"You travel fast?" said Scrooge.

"On the wings of the wind," replied the ghost.

"You might have got over a great quantity of ground in seven years," said Scrooge.

The ghost, on hearing this, set up another cry, and clanked its chain so hideously in the dead silence of the night, that the Ward out on the street would have been justified in indicting it for a nuisance.

"Oh! captive, bound, and double-ironed," cried the phantom, "not to know, that ages of incessant labor by immortal creatures, for this earth must pass into eternity before the good of which it is susceptible is all developed! Not to know that any Christian spirit working kindly in its little sphere, whatever it may be, will find its mortal life too short for its vast means of usefulness! Not to know that no space of regret can make amends for one life's opportunity misused! Yet such was I! Oh! such was I!"

"But you were always a good man of business, Jacob," faltered Scrooge, who now began to apply this to himself.

"Business!" cried the ghost, wringing its hands again. "Mankind was my business. The common welfare was my business; charity, mercy, forbearance, and benevolence, were all my business. The dealings of my trade were but a drop of water in the comprehensive ocean of my business!"

It held up its chain at arm's length, as if that were the cause of all its unavailing grief, and flung it heavily upon the ground again. "At this time of the rolling year," the specter said, "I suffer most. Why did I walk through crowds of fellow-beings with my eyes turned down, and never raise them to that blessed star which led the Wise Men to a poor abode? Were there no poor homes to which its light would have conducted me? How did I not see the vampires as they tread in our tracks, yours and mine?"

Scrooge was very much dismayed to hear the specter going on at this rate, and began to quake exceedingly. Vampires in their tracks? What did he speak of? He made no sense, this phantom.

"Hear me!" cried the ghost. "My time is nearly gone. It is only by the heart of Belle that I have been able to linger this long. Will you listen?"

"Belle? I do not understand why you speak her name, though I will listen, indeed, for I have little choice," said Scrooge. "But don't be hard upon me. Don't be flowery, Jacob! Pray!"

"I have sat invisible beside you many and many a day, and I have watched the Queen of Vampires control your every move, your every thought."

It was not an agreeable idea, not of Marley or vampires,

though which was worse he could not say at this moment. Scrooge shivered, and wiped the perspiration from his brow.

"That is no light part of my penance," pursued the ghost. "But as I have told you, my fate is not as execrable as yours will be. I am here tonight to warn you, that you have yet a chance and hope of escaping your providence, which first came to be before your birth."

"My providence? Before my birth? Whatever do you speak of?"

"There is a chance and hope of my procuring your salvation, Ebenezer."

"You were always a good friend to me," said Scrooge. "Please do not do this to me. Your talk of vampires and providence, it frightens me more than the presence of your ghost here before me."

"You have no choice in this matter, Ebenezer. You will be haunted," resumed the phantom, "by three spirits."

Scrooge's countenance fell almost as low as the ghost's had done. "Is that the chance and hope you mentioned, Jacob?" he demanded, in a faltering voice.

"It is."

"I—I think I'd rather not," said Scrooge.

"Without their visits," said the ghost, "you cannot hope to avoid the path before you. Expect the first tomorrow, when the bell tolls one."

"Couldn't I take them all at once, and have it over, Jacob?" hinted Scrooge, tugging at the sleeve of his night robe.

"Expect the second on the next night at the same hour. The third upon the next night when the last stroke of twelve has ceased to vibrate. Look to see me no more, and look that, for your own sake, you remember what has passed between us!"

When it had said these words, the specter took its wrapper from the table, and bound it round its head, as before. Scrooge knew this, by the smart sound its teeth made when the jaws were brought together by the bandage. He ventured to raise his eyes again, and found his supernatural visitor confronting him in an erect attitude, with its chain wound over and about its arm.

The apparition walked backward from him, and at every step it took, the window raised itself a little, so that when the specter reached it, it was wide open.

It beckoned Scrooge to approach, which he did. When they were within two paces of each other, Marley's ghost held up its hand, warning him to come no nearer. Scrooge stopped. It was not so much in obedience, as in surprise and fear, for on the raising of the hand, he became aware of confused noises in the air: incoherent sounds of lamentation and regret, wailings inexpressibly sorrowful and self-accusatory. The specter, after listening for a moment, joined in the mournful dirge and floated out upon the bleak, dark night.

Scrooge followed to the window, desperate in his curiosity. He looked out.

The air was filled with phantoms, wandering hither and thither in restless haste, and moaning as they went. Every one of them wore chains like Marley's ghost. Some few (they might be guilty governments) were linked together; none were free.

Many had been personally known to Scrooge in their lives. He had been quite familiar with one old ghost, in a white waistcoat, with a monstrous iron safe attached to its ankle, who cried piteously at being unable to assist a wretched woman with an infant, whom it saw below, upon a doorstep. The misery with them all was, clearly, that they sought to interfere, for good, in human matters, and had lost the power forever.

Below them on the street ran creatures black and shrouded with mist, something like the thing that had followed Scrooge home the night he had gone to Marley's grave almost seven years ago. They came and went, scuttling along the dark street, and while he watched, one snatched a child from a mother's arms and disappeared into the night, leaving the mother a weeping heap upon the snow.

Whether these creatures faded into mist, or mist enshrouded them, he could not tell. But they and their spirit voices faded together, and the night became as it had been when he walked home from the tavern.

Scrooge closed the window, and examined the door by which the ghost had entered. It was double-locked, as he had locked it with his own hands, and the bolts were undisturbed. He tried to say "Humbug!" but stopped at the first syllable. And being from the emotion he had undergone, or the fatigues of the day, or his glimpse of the invisible world, or the dull conversation of the ghost, or the lateness of the hour, or the absurd talk of vampires, he found himself much in need of repose. He went straight to bed, without undressing, and fell asleep upon the instant.

STAVE 2

THE FIRST OF THE THREE
SPIRITS AND MORE VAMPIRES

❦ 13 ❦

When Scrooge awoke, it was so dark that looking out of bed, he could scarcely distinguish the transparent window from the opaque walls of his chamber. He was endeavoring to pierce the darkness with his eyes, when the chimes of a neighboring church struck the four quarters. He listened for it to strike the hour.

To his great astonishment the heavy bell went on from six to seven, and from seven to eight, and regularly up to twelve, then stopped. Twelve. It was past two when he went to bed. The clock was wrong. An icicle must have got into the works. Twelve o'clock.

He touched the spring of his repeater, to correct this most preposterous clock. Its rapid little pulse beat twelve and stopped.

"Why, it isn't possible," said Scrooge, "that I can have slept through a whole day and far into another night. It isn't possible that anything has happened to the sun, and this is twelve at noon."

The idea being an alarming one, he scrambled out of bed, and groped his way to the window. He was obliged to rub the frost off with the sleeve of his dressing-gown before he could see anything, and could see very little then. All he could make out was that it was still very foggy and extremely cold, and that there was no noise of people running to and fro, and making a great stir, as there unquestionably would have been if night had beaten off bright day, and taken possession of the world. This was a great relief, because "Three days after sight of this First of Exchange pay to Mr. Ebenezer Scrooge on his order," and so forth, would have become a mere United States security if there were no days to count by.

Scrooge went to bed again, and thought, and thought, and thought it over and over, and could make nothing of it. The more he thought, the more perplexed he became, and the more he endeavored not to think, the more he thought.

Marley's ghost bothered him exceedingly. Every time he resolved within himself, after mature inquiry, that it was all a dream, his mind flew back again, like a strong spring released, to its first position, and presented the same problem to be worked all through. Was it a dream or not?

Surely Belle, the woman he had foolishly engaged himself to all those years ago, had actually not summoned a ghost for the benefit of a man who had left her an old maid, an old maid who boarded travelers to keep herself in bread and coal. It was as outrageous as the suggestion that Mr. Wahltraud and his wife were vampires . . . vampires that were trying to control Scrooge's life. Unthinkable!

"Vampires! Bah, humbug," he muttered loudly, just to hear the sound of his own voice in the cold, empty chamber that was a dismal darkness. Pure and utter nonsense. Of course, one did hear rumors, but not anything that need concern him. Mind your own business and let others mind theirs was his motto, and his business was making money. Vampires, so it was said, desired only human blood, not coin or bank notes, and thus he and his interests were safe enough, he was quite certain.

It occurred to Scrooge that he should rise and stoke the dying coals on the brazier, but felt as his muscles would not, *could not* move, and so he lay in this state until the chime had gone three-quarters more. He then remembered suddenly that the ghost had warned him of a visitation when the bell tolled one. He resolved to lie awake until the hour was passed and, considering that he could no more go to sleep than go to heaven, this was, perhaps, the wisest resolution in his power.

The quarter was so long that he was more than once convinced he must have sunk into a doze unconsciously, and missed the clock. At length it broke upon his listening ear.

Ding, dong!

"A quarter past," said Scrooge, counting.

Ding, dong!

"Half past," said Scrooge.

Ding, dong!

"A quarter to it," said Scrooge.

Ding, dong!

"The hour itself," said Scrooge triumphantly, "and nothing else!"

He spoke before the hour bell sounded, which it now did with a deep, dull, hollow, melancholy *one*. Light flashed up in the room upon the instant, and the curtains of his bed were drawn open.

The curtains of his bed were drawn aside, I tell you, by a hand. It was not the curtains at his feet, nor the curtains at his back, but those to which his face was addressed. The curtains of his bed were drawn aside and Scrooge, starting up into a half-recumbent attitude, found himself face-to-face with the unearthly visitor who drew them, as close to it as I am now to you, and I am standing in the spirit at your elbow.

It was a strange figure, like a child, yet not so like a child as like an old man, viewed through some supernatural medium, which gave him the appearance of having receded from the view, and being diminished to a child's proportions. Its hair, which hung about its neck and down its back, was white as if with age, and yet the face had not a wrinkle in it, and the most tender bloom was on the skin. The arms were very long and muscular, the hands the same, as if its hold were of uncommon strength. Its legs and feet, most delicately formed, were, like those upper members, bare. It wore a tunic of the purest white, and round its waist was bound a lustrous belt, the sheen of which was beautiful. It held a branch of fresh green holly in its hand, and, in singular contradiction of that wintry emblem, had its dress trimmed with summer flowers. But the strangest thing about it was, that from the crown of its head there sprung a bright clear jet of light, by which all this was visible, and which was doubtless the occasion of its using, in its duller moments, a great extinguisher for a cap, which it now held under its arm.

Even this, though, when Scrooge looked at it with increasing steadiness, was not its strangest quality. For as its belt sparkled and glittered now in one part and now in another, and what was light one instant, at another time was dark, so the figure itself fluctuated in its distinctness, being now a thing with one arm, now with one leg, now with twenty legs, now a pair of legs without a head, now a head without a body, of which dissolving parts, no outline would be visible in the dense gloom wherein they melted away. And in the very wonder of this, it would be itself again, distinct and clear as ever.

"Are you the spirit, sir, whose coming was foretold to me?" asked Scrooge. A foolish question, perhaps, when speaking to a phantom standing at the side of your bed, but how else did one begin a conversation with a phantom?

"I am." The voice was soft and gentle. It was singularly low, as if instead of being so close beside him, it were at a distance.

"Then who, and what are you?" Scrooge demanded. He was still frightened, but put out as well.

"I am the Ghost of Christmas Past."

"Long past?" inquired Scrooge, observant of its dwarfish stature.

"*Your* past."

Perhaps Scrooge could not have told anybody why, if anybody could have asked him, but he had a special desire to see the spirit in his cap, and begged him to be covered.

"What," exclaimed the ghost, "would you so soon put out, with worldly hands, the light I give? Is it not enough that you are one of those whose passions made this cap, and force me through whole trains of years to wear it low upon my brow?"

Scrooge reverently disclaimed all intention to offend or any knowledge of having willfully bonneted the spirit at any period of his life. He then made bold to inquire what business brought the spirit there and how long he intended to stay.

"Your welfare," said the ghost. "I come at the bequest of a woman called Belle. There are few humans who can reach out to spirits; it is fortunate she was able to do so for your benefit. Another spirit, that belonging to a Jacob Marley, made these arrangements. As to how long we will remain together, I cannot answer that on human terms. As long as it takes must, therefore, be my answer."

Scrooge expressed himself much obliged, but he wanted no part of Belle's bequest and he could not help thinking that a night of unbroken rest would have been more conducive to that end.

The spirit must have heard him thinking, for it said immediately, "Your reclamation, then. Take heed." It put out its strong hand as it spoke, and clasped him gently by the arm. "Rise and walk with me."

It would have been in vain for Scrooge to plead that the weather and the hour were not adapted to pedestrian purposes, that bed was warm, and the thermometer a long way below freezing, that he was clad but lightly in his slippers, dressing-gown, and nightcap, and that he had a cold upon him at that time. The grasp, though gentle as a woman's hand, was not to be resisted. He rose, but finding that the spirit made toward the window, clasped his robe in supplication.

"I am mortal," Scrooge remonstrated, "and liable to fall."

"Bear but a touch of my hand there," said the spirit, laying it upon his heart, "and you shall be upheld in more than this."

14

As the words were spoken, they passed through the wall, and Scrooge found himself upon an open country road, with fields on either hand. The city had entirely vanished. Not a vestige of it was to be seen. The darkness and the mist had vanished with it, for it was a clear, cold, winter twilight, with snow upon the ground.

"Good Heaven!" said Scrooge, clasping his hands together, as he looked about him. "I was bred in this place. I was a boy here."

The spirit gazed upon him mildly. Its gentle touch, though it had been light and instantaneous, appeared still present to the old man's sense of feeling. He was conscious of a thousand odors floating in the air, each one connected with a thousand thoughts, and hopes, and joys, and cares long, long, forgotten.

"What is this place?" the ghost asked, gazing down on the stone house nestled quaintly on a moor not far from London, but far enough to make idyllic.

"My boyhood home where I was born," Scrooge murmured, feeling lightness in his head that he could not, at first, recognize, it had been so long since it had come upon him. *Nostalgia.*

A very regular feature on the face of the country, the Scrooge family's stone house was, and not the least disguise toned down or shaded off that uncompromising fact in the landscape. A great square house with a heavy portico darkening the principal windows, as its master's heavy brows overshadowed his eyes, it was. A calculated, cast-up, balanced, and proved house. Three windows on this side of the door, three on that side; a total of six in this wing, a total of six in the other wing, two and ten carried over to the back wings. A lawn and garden and an infant avenue, all ruled straight like a botanical account-book. Gas and ventilation, drainage and water-service, all of the best quality. Iron clamps and girders, fireproof from top to bottom, mechanical lifts for the housemaids, with all their brushes and brooms, everything that one's heart could desire. It was a fine house, a sturdy house, Scrooge recalled, lacking only in one thing; the love of a mother.

"Your lip is trembling," said the ghost. "And what is that upon your cheek?"

Scrooge muttered, with an unusual catching in his voice, that it was a pimple and begged the ghost to lead him where he would and get it over with.

"It appears to me to be a tear. Can it be that somewhere lurking in that shriveled heart there lies a crumb of sentiment for what is past and lost to you?"

"A pimple, I tell you!"

"Clear and wet, certainly more tear than inflammation."

"A dripping from a tree branch, perhaps, but all the same some liquid of a natural origin and no tear of mine. I am not a man given to weeping or any other public display of emotion."

"Tear or not, weeping or not, inside we must go."

Scrooge shook his head. "Not . . . not inside. Seeing this

place from here, it is enough. It . . . it is not necessary to walk within its walls."

"But it is."

Against his will, Scrooge felt himself propelled forward. As they drew closer, drifting first above the house, then suddenly standing in a hallway, he heard the sounds of great commotion, a household turned on end; dogs barked, maids whispered and shrieked, and there was talk of a midwife who had taken her leave too soon.

"A birth?" Scrooge asked.

The ghost smiled kindly, a hint of pity on its face.

"Whose?"

The ghost did not answer and Scrooge became anxious, twisting his hands in the long sleeves of his dressing-gown. It was a ridiculous question, of course; he knew the answer, for they were at his childhood home and this journey was into his past, was it not? "Mine?"

The ghost nodded.

"Mine and Fan's?" he asked for further clarification, though there was no need for that question either, for he and Fan were born on the same Christmas Eve, twins. "Why must I see this? What is the point in my being present to see myself become the death of my mother?" Scrooge demanded, sounding bolder than he felt, for a part of him wanted to lay his gaze upon the face he had never seen, but a part of him feared the sight.

Scrooge saw behind him a man and recognized the face at once. The gentleman was rusty to look at, reputed to have made good thrift out of aristocratic marriage settlements and aristocratic wills, and to be very rich. He was, even in those days, of what was called the old school—a phrase generally meaning any school that seems never to have been young—and wore knee breeches tied with ribbons, and gaiters or stockings. One peculiarity of his black clothes and of his black stockings, be they silk or worsted, was that they never shone. Mute, closed, irresponsive to any glancing light, his dress was like himself.

But there was something in the face at that moment that it took a moment for Scrooge to recognize, having never recalled seeing it on his father's face: pity . . . and fear.

"Where is the wet nurse?" bellowed Scrooge's father. "The babes do not do well. They've need of a wet nurse immediately! And why has the midwife taken her leave so quickly! A midwife should still be with Mrs. Scrooge. I do not know of these women's things, but by heaven I will have an answer!"

A maid in a dingy mobcap, apparently the bravest of the gaggle, approached Mr. Scrooge and bent her head low. "The midwife, Agnes, was called away, sir. I do not know why. The nature of her calling results in people calling for her in a rush. Another emergency birth, perhaps. But the wet nurse has just arrived, accompanied by another midwife. They say they were sent by Agnes, to care for Mrs. Scrooge. Good references, they say."

At that moment, Scrooge heard the feeble cry of an infant, and he turned to gaze down the hall as something long dead seemed to waken and stir within his chest. At the end of the hall was the master bedchamber of the house, and the place where he knew his mother lay dying.

"These are but shadows of the things that have been," said the ghost, as if knowing what thoughts raced through Scrooge's mind. "They cannot be altered, and those you see have no consciousness of us."

"They cannot see us?" begged Scrooge.

"They cannot," said the ghost kindly.

Somewhere in the house, as the shadows of evening settled in, a door slammed. Feet pattered on the stone floor and three women rushed by, the first being the maid who had spoken to Scrooge's father shortly before.

Scrooge turned on his slippered feet. "Wait. I know that one

woman. You . . . you said this is my past, but that cannot be."
He gestured lamely to one of the two women just arrived.
"*That* woman is of my present."

If the ghost heard, he made no reply.

"That is my . . . my tenant's wife," Scrooge insisted, unable
to comprehend what he was seeing. He followed the women
down the hall. "That is not a wet nurse or a midwife, that is
Mrs. Wahltraud, the wine purveyor's wife."

"Name's Mrs. Grottweil, mum, wet nurse sent by Agnes,"
said the woman accompanying the supposed new midwife, the
one who looked like Mrs. Wahltraud.

Now, Mrs. Grottweil, she looked as she should have. She
was a fat old woman with a husky voice and a moist eye, which
she had a remarkable power of turning up, and only showing
the white of it. Having very little neck, it cost her some trouble
to look over herself, if one may say so, at those to whom she
talked. She wore a very rusty black gown, rather the worse for
snuff, and a shawl and bonnet to correspond. In these dilapi-
dated articles of dress she had, on principle, arrayed herself,
time out of mind, on such occasions as the present when she
was greatly needed. Arriving just in time to save a babe from
starvation, she often invited the proud parents to present her
with a fresher suit of clothing, an appeal so frequently successful, that the very fetch and ghost of Mrs. Grottweil, bonnet and
all, might be seen hanging up, any hour in the day, in at least a
dozen of the secondhand clothes shops about town. The face of
Mrs. Grottweil—the nose in particular—was somewhat red
and swollen, and it was difficult to enjoy her society without
becoming conscious of a smell of spirits. Like most persons
who have attained great eminence in their profession, she took
to hers very kindly, insomuch that, setting aside her natural
predilections as a woman, she went to a birth with zest and
relish.

Mrs. Grottweil took one of the two babes nestled in Mrs.

Scrooge's arms, the female child. It began to squeal, much like a piglet removed from suckling, when she dislodged it from its mother's arm.

Emma Scrooge lifted heavy eyelids. "Nurse, why do you not take my son?" she asked, her exhaustion heavy in her speech.

Mrs. Grottweil made no reply except to see the household maid out of the room. "Mrs. Scrooge must have her rest." She closed the bedchamber door, wood panels moving right through the ghost standing in the doorway, barely missing Scrooge. There was light in the room now, but the light that came from a few lamps burning, lamps Mrs. Grottweil now turned down.

"My son must be fed," said Mrs. Scrooge, gazing lovingly at the infant in her arms that was not much bigger than a pint of ale. "We will call him Ebenezer."

"So you will," said Mrs. Wahltraud, moving closer to the bed as Mrs. Grottweil withdrew to the far side of the room, where a rocking chair and a large cradle awaited. "So it has been foretold."

"Foretold? What do you mean?" asked Mrs. Scrooge.

The midwife sighed. "You know very well what I mean. I know you bred him for the purpose of the prophecy," she hissed.

Scrooge, the Scrooge of the future, grown to manhood and beyond, not the infant Scrooge or the father Scrooge, could not take his eyes off the new midwife. She looked just like the wine purveyor's wife with her black hair and pale skin . . . and yet she did not. And she certainly did not have the appearance of any midwife Scrooge had ever seen!

The inky black hair of Mrs. Wahltraud was carefully smoothed down, and waved away under a trim tidy cap, in the most exact and quiet manner imaginable. Her neatly flowered skirts—red and white, like the bed-curtains hanging from the master bed—were as composed and orderly, as if the very wind that blew so hard out of doors could not disturb one of their folds. Her little bodice was so placid and neat, that there should have been protection for her in it, had she needed any, with the roughest people.

"I know nothing of a prophecy," Scrooge's mother said. "These children were conceived of love, as all children should be."

Scrooge felt a strange twist in his chest and wondered if indigestion was upon him again.

"Who are you?" Scrooge's mother asked, gazing up from the bed that was becoming wet with blood to the woman who stood over her.

"Are they not going to do something for her?" asked Scrooge of the spirit. "Are they not going to try to save her life?"

"This shouldn't take long," said Mrs. Wahltraud, glancing from the pool of blood on the bed to Mrs. Grottweil and smiling a most unsettling smile, one that gave Scrooge the watcher chills down his spine and made his breath come in deep, strangled gasps. "This will not even require my intervention." She clasped her ivory hands. "Excellent. Have we brought bottles to collect some of the blood?"

"Wait," said Scrooge, looking upon the black-haired woman again. "Ghost, this makes no sense. This woman looks precisely like my tenant's wife, but it cannot be her, for this woman is no older than the one who lives in the lower apartments of my house. You said this is my past. She would be much older by now. An old woman, older than myself." He shook his head, searching his brain for some explanation. Perhaps this was his tenant's wife's mother or grandmother, but the likeness was uncanny. That had to be it. "A relative?" he asked his ghostly guide. "One carrying the same lineage?" (He had first thought to use the term "bloodline" but had been unable to utter the word.)

The spirit looked on at the scene unfolding, offering no explanation.

"John?" Even with her fair hair, wet to her face with her perspiration, and her skin pale from the exertion of the birth and blood loss, she was a beautiful woman, Emma Scrooge. Fan had looked so much like her; Scrooge could see that now in her high cheekbones and arched brows.

"John, where are you?" she pleaded, reaching out. Emma opened her eyes. They were blue, the same color Scrooge's had been when he was a younger man. The same color as Fan's.

"You have your orders, Mrs. Grottweil. Are you clear as to what you must do?" Mrs. Wahltraud asked, plucking the baby Ebenezer right from his mother's arms.

"Wet nurse? Are you going to feed my little Ebenezer?" Mrs. Scrooge begged, beginning to lose consciousness. "You'll care for him. Tell me you will. . . ." Her voice faded as she closed her eyes again, her time on earth growing quickly to an end.

"I understand perfect," said Mrs. Grottweil, settling down to put the baby Fan to her enormous breast. The babe shook tiny fists, turning away, but the wet nurse forced her teat into the little mouth. "A drop of blood a day to the boy, but not the girl. Just milk for this one."

"That's right. A drop of blood a day for Ebenezer Scrooge."

"Blood?" Ebenezer shuddered. "You do not give infants *blood*. Even I know that, and I have never known an infant in my life."

"And I'm to keep it in the mister's head after the missus is dead that it was that one's fault she went the way she did." The wet nurse lifted her chin in the direction of the baby boy. "Killed his mother, he did, the worthless mite."

"A good start," Mrs. Wahltraud crooned to the baby in her arms, looking into its innocent blue eyes. "Killing your mother.

Scion of the Great Culling?" she scoffed, her tone turning bitter. "We shall see."

"But I didn't kill her. Look!" Ebenezer cried, running to his mother's bedside. "She still breathes. But someone must help her!" He turned expectantly to see the ghost watching him with sad eyes. "She is bleeding to death. Surely someone can do something for her. She wants to live; I see it in her face, in her eyes. We cannot simply stand and watch while life seeps from her drop by drop."

The spirit said nothing.

"But I cannot help her, can I?" asked Ebenezer, feeling as if all the air were suddenly gone from the room. He spoke then in a small voice. "None of us can, because these are the shadows of what is done."

The phantom nodded.

"But what I don't understand, Queen Griselda, if I might say, is why you just wouldn't kill that little one and be done with him," Mrs. Grottweil was saying.

"Don't call me that. Not here!" ordered Mrs. Wahltraud.

Mrs. Grottweil bobbed her head and continued. "If the prophecy says Ebenezer Scrooge will be the father of the Scion of the Great Culling, if the prophecy says he will father the man who will be the greatest vampire slayer of all time, why do we not snap his little neck, or drop him in a well, or tuck him into a riding boot and cast him into the sea now and be done with him?"

"Because that would be too easy," said Mrs. Wahltraud.

" 'Twould be easy for certain. I done it before, when a woman couldn't feed a babe or she just didn't care for a twelfth."

"You don't understand. How could you, you worthless hunk of dung? I want Ebenezer Scrooge for myself," Mrs. Wahltraud said. She held him before her to gaze into his blue eyes. "It would be easy to kill him, but to train him, to make him one of my own, now *that* would be a feat!"

"Good plan, mum. I'll do as I'm told, do you right," Mrs. Grottweil promised from the corner of the room where she rocked the female child. "And like you told me, you'll not suck my children dry and hang 'em on the clothes-line, will you?" she asked hopefully.

"You do have a great many," Mrs. Wahltraud mused. "Perhaps you have one or two to spare for one who has always done well by you and yours?"

"Nay, my queen, you promised that I should keep them all. I have your word, sworn and sealed in blood on the night of the full moon."

"Yes, yes, yes, I know all that, but it is most tiresome when you have so many to spare and they are so sweet and tasty in appearance."

"Not so sweet when they must sleep in the pigsty or pigeon coop to keep them safe from roaming vampires who might be tempted to snatch one or two, not sweet at all with the mess the swine and pigeons do make and—"

"Do not trouble me with your domestic trifles," Queen Griselda warned crossly. "Twenty-seven, twenty-eight if one counts the dumpy one with the bald head, twenty-eight screaming, quarreling offspring, and you deny your mistress even one. It is most distressing."

"But they are all so dear to me, gracious lady, and all will grow to serve you and yours."

"Better some serve me now by quenching my insatiable thirst. You are a woman without heart or pity or the faintest scrap of gratitude."

"Still, my lady, you have promised, and I shall hold it to you. Surely so much time in the sty and coop have soured their blood and given it a most unwholesome flavor that you—"

At that moment, Emma Scrooge opened her eyes. "Give me

my son," she whispered. Though already half-dead, she still had a certain strength of conviction to her voice. "You cannot have him."

"You fool," Queen Griselda said. "He is already mine, and there is nothing you can do about it!" She leaned over Emma and drew back her pale lips, revealing long, fanged incisors.

Scrooge flinched, for even though these were merely images of the past, the fangs, and what they indicated, were quite startling. He had never believed there really were vampires, not in all these years. He had discounted the rumors as so much lower-class drivel and never wasted his time in pondering their reality or purpose; he'd never believed they could touch him.

Emma Scrooge, however, did not flinch. Instead, she looked Queen Griselda in the eyes and whispered, "You will never get away with this. I lied. I know the prophecy and I know what will come to pass. My grandson will fulfill the prophecy. He will hunt you down. He will take your life and the life of the King of the Vampires!"

The queen threw back her head and laughed, gnashing her great pearly fangs. "We will see about that, won't we?"

Scrooge turned to the phantom. "I do not fully understand." He shook from the top of his bedcap to the toes of his slippers. "The vampire queen thinks I will father a son who will be the Scion of the Great Culling? She thinks that my child will become a great vampire slayer? That is preposterous! Particularly considering my present state. I am too old to father a child!"

"Time will tell," the ghost said cryptically. "A child could still come to you."

"A child," Scrooge grumbled. "Why would I ever burden myself with a squalling, troublesome addition to my household? Any fool knows that a child must be fed once, even twice a day until they are at least seven before gainful employment can be found for them. There are shoes to buy, and even secondhand, which can be found at any stand on Trotters Row, are a good h'pence apiece, and in winter, it must have a coat or at least a blanket of some kind to wear against the wind and cold. Not to mention the cost of an education and the constant coming and going of young ones, leaving doors ajar and wasting candles. Why indeed would a sensible man of business such as I ever bring a child into the world?"

But the spirit only regarded him with that long and mournful stare and then suddenly, the room changed. They were no longer in his mother's bedchamber but in the second-best parlor of the house, a cozy room not far from the kitchen where Ebenezer and Fan had taken their lessons as young children.

Without the spirit saying so, Scrooge knew that time had passed.

❦ 15 ❧

Standing in a far corner, near a bookshelf of his father's books, Scrooge watched himself, as a lad, enter with his books, and an exercise-book and a slate. Fan was ready at her writing desk, but not half so ready as Ebenezer's father in his easy-chair by the window (though he pretended to be reading a book), or as Mrs. Grottweil, sitting near Ebenezer's father stringing steel beads. (She had never been dismissed though the Scrooge children at seven were well past the age of needing a wet nurse.) The very sight of the two who had such an influence over Scrooge brought back all the fear and sadness he had felt as a child.

"I was not a good student," Scrooge said to the spirit to cover his own feelings of anxiety. "Though I know that must greatly surprise you, I did not even have a head for numbers in those days. I would study, know my recitation, and then when forced to perform for my father, I do not know where the word and numbers went. I wonder where they do go, by-the-by?"

If the ghost had an opinion, he did not offer it.

Scrooge watched as he handed a book to Fan, for she was far

quicker in her studies than he had ever been. Perhaps it was a grammar, perhaps a history, or geography. The lad took a last drowning look at the page as he gave it into her hand, and started off aloud at a racing pace while he thought he still had it fresh. The young Ebenezer tripped over a word and the elder Mr. Scrooge looked up. He tripped over another word. Mrs. Grottweil looked up. He reddened, tumbled over half-a-dozen words, and stopped.

Scrooge remembered the day well. At the time, he had thought Fan would have shown him the book if she dared, but she did not dare, and she said softly:

"Oh, Ebenezer, Ebenezer!"

"Now, Fan," said Mr. Scrooge, "be firm with your brother. Don't say, 'Oh, Ebenezer!' That's childish. He knows his lesson, or he does not know it."

Scrooge's father's eyes then lighted on his son's. "Now, Ebenezer," he said, "you must be far more careful today than usual." He gave the cane he carried a poise and a switch, and having finished his preparation of it, laid it down beside him, with an expressive look, and took up his book.

This was a good freshener to young Ebenezer's memory, as a beginning. The lad's words of his lessons slipped off, not one by one, or line by line, but by the entire page. The boy tried to lay hold of them, but they seemed, as Scrooge recalled, to have put skates on, and to skim away with a smoothness there was no checking.

The seven-year-old Scrooge began badly, and went on worse. Book after book was added to the heap of failures, Mrs. Grottweil being firmly watchful of them all the time. And when they came at last to a question about five thousand cheeses, Fan burst out crying.

"Fan!" said Mrs. Grottweil, in her warning voice.

Scrooge then watched as his father rose and said, taking up a cane, "Why, Mrs. Grottweil, we can hardly expect Fan to bear, with perfect firmness, the worry and torment that her brother has caused today. Fan is quite bright and greatly strengthened and improved in her lessons, but we can hardly expect her to teach him day in and day out when he clearly has put in no effort to learn."

"You are quite right, sir," said Mrs. Grottweil, looking up from her beading. "I know not what else to do with him. 'Tis time, perhaps"—she peered up at him—"to send him on his way as we have discussed."

"Ebenezer, you and I will go upstairs, boy."

As Mr. Scrooge took his son out the door, Fan ran toward them. Mrs. Grottweil said, "Fan Scrooge! Are you a perfect fool?" and interfered. Fan stopped up her ears then, and began to cry.

"Please," Scrooge begged of the spirit. "Do not make me see this."

But the ghost said nothing, and Scrooge felt himself gliding behind the boy and the father.

Mr. Scrooge took his son to his room slowly and gravely—a delight in that formal show of doing justice, for surely his mind had been poisoned by Mrs. Grottweil's lies. Then when they got there, suddenly he twisted the boy's head under his arm.

Scrooge stiffened in anticipation of what was to come.

"Father! Sir!" the boy cried to him. "Don't! Pray don't beat me! I have tried to learn, sir, but I can't learn while you and Mrs. Grottweil are watching me. I can't indeed!"

"Can't you, indeed, Ebenezer?" he said. "We'll try this, then."

He had his head as in a vise, but he twined round him somehow, and the boy stopped him for a moment, entreating him not to beat him. It was only for a moment that he stopped him, for he cut him heavily an instant afterward, and in the same instant the boy caught the hand with which Mr. Scrooge held his mouth, between his teeth, and bit it through.

Mr. Scrooge beat Ebenezer then, as if he would have beaten him to death. Above all the noise they made, Scrooge heard Fan running up the stairs, and crying out. Then Mr. Scrooge was gone, at last, and the door was locked outside. At Scrooge's feet lay his former self, fevered, and hot, and torn, and raging in a puny way, upon the floor.

Tears glistened in Scrooge's eyes as the child before him became quiet and an unnatural stillness seemed to reign through the whole house. How well he remembered, when his smart and passion began to cool, how wicked he began to feel! He hated them at that moment; his father, Mrs. Grottweil, even Fan. Even his long-lost mother. Damn them all!

Scrooge watched as the boy sat listening for a long while, but there was not a sound. He then crawled up from the floor, and saw his own face in the glass, so swollen, red, and ugly that it almost frightened him. (It certainly frightened Scrooge now.) His stripes were sore and stiff, and made him cry afresh, when he moved, but they were nothing to the guilt he felt for damning his own sweet mother, who had given her life to give him his. The guilt lay heavier on his breast than if he had been a most terrible criminal, and the longer he thought of it, the greater the offense seemed.

Scrooge watched as it began to grow dark, knowing there was no need to tell the ghost he had seen enough. Only the spirit could determine when enough was enough, and so he would be further tortured by these memories. The young boy shut the window (he had been lying, for the most part, with his head upon the sill, by turns crying, dozing, and looking listlessly out), when the key was turned, and Mrs. Grottweil came in with some bread and meat and milk.

"Please tell me there is no blood in that milk," Scrooge said in horror.

If the ghost knew the answer, he did not provide one.

Mrs. Grottweil put the nourishment down upon the table

without a word, glaring at her charge all the while, and then retired, locking the door after her.

It grew light again and Scrooge watched himself wake the next morning, being cheerful and fresh for the first moment, and then being weighed down by the stale and dismal oppression of remembrance. Mrs. Grottweil came again before he was out of bed, told him he was free to walk in the garden for half an hour and no longer, retired, leaving the door open, that he might avail him of that permission.

The boy did so, and did so every morning of his imprisonment, which lasted five days. If he could have seen his sister alone, he would have gone down on his knees to her and besought her forgiveness for the way he had cursed at her and their dear mother. But he saw no one except Mrs. Grottweil during the whole time.

The length of those five days Scrooge (as a boy or a man) could convey no idea of to anyone. They occupied the place of years in his remembrance.

On the last night of his restraint, Scrooge watched as he was awakened by hearing his own name spoken in a whisper. The boy started up in bed, and, putting out his arms in the dark, said, "Is that you, Fan?"

There was no immediate answer, but presently he heard his name again, in a tone so very mysterious and awful, that he thought he had gone into a fit.

"The keyhole, you silly boy," Scrooge urged his younger self.

The boy groped his way to the door, and, putting his own lips to the keyhole, whispered, "Is that you, Fanny, dear?"

"Yes, my own precious Ebenezer," she replied. "Be as soft as a mouse, or the cat'll hear us."

He understood this to mean Mrs. Grottweil, and knew that he must be careful and quiet; her room being close by.

"How are you, dear Fanny? Are you very angry with me?"

Scrooge could hear his sister crying softly on her side of the keyhole, and he turned to the ghost. "Must we be here, still? It is no longer even Christmas Eve."

"The event began on Christmas Eve and becomes a cornerstone to who you have become, Ebenezer," responded the spirit.

With a sigh, Scrooge turned back to the children.

"I'm not so very angry with you, brother," said Fan. "Not very. I only wish you had not angered Father so again, is all."

"What is going to be done with me, Fan, dear? Do you know?"

"School. Near London," was Fan's answer. The boy was obliged to get her to repeat it, for she spoke it the first time quite down his throat in consequence of him having forgotten to take his mouth away from the keyhole and put his ear there; and, though her words tickled him a good deal, he didn't hear them.

"School? Perhaps that would be better, for both of us," he said cheerfully for a lad who had been near beaten to death by his father. "Perhaps Father will be kinder to you, then."

"No, no, this is not good, Ebenezer. How will I be able to protect you then?"

"You won't have to protect me from Father, there."

"It is not Father I worry about. It's *them.*"

"Them *who?*" the boy asked.

Scrooge turned to the ghost. "Fan knew? She knew what Mrs. Grottweil was? What Mrs. Wahltraud . . . or whatever her name is, was trying to do? But how is that . . . was it possible? She was a newborn babe that day, the same as I."

The ghost said nothing.

"When, Fan? When shall I go?" asked the young Ebenezer.

"Tomorrow."

"Is that the reason why Mrs. Grottweil took the clothes out of my drawers?"

"Yes," said Fan.

"Shan't I see you before I go?"

"Yes," she said. "In the morning."

Then Fan fitted her mouth close to the keyhole, and spoke these words through it with as much feeling and earnestness as a keyhole has ever been the means of communicating, shooting in each broken little sentence in a convulsive little burst of its own.

"Ebenezer, dear, please promise me you will take care. Please promise me you will be the good boy I know you can be and always see to those who are less fortunate. Fight them. You must fight them!"

"What are you talking about, Fan? Fight who?"

"The vampires," she whispered.

Scrooge, who had been leaning over the boy to hear every word, stood abruptly and turned to the spirit. "I do not recall her saying that. Not in all these years," he murmured.

"Oh, Fan. I'm frightened. Please don't talk of such things anymore. Please write to me at school. Promise me."

The kind soul promised, and the two kissed the keyhole with the greatest affection. The young Ebenezer patted it with his hand as if it had been her honest face—and parted.

16

With the blink of Scrooge's eye, then, he was no longer in his childhood home, he and the ghost, but on a country road.

"Wait," Scrooge begged, looking back over his shoulder, the hem of his gown tangling around his bony ankles.

The spirit looked up the road they now followed. "You recollect the way?"

"Remember it," cried Scrooge with fervor, thankful to be away from that frightful deathbed and a past he could not change. "I could walk it blindfolded."

As they walked along, Scrooge recognized every gate, and post, and tree until a little market town appeared in the distance, with its bridge, its church, and winding river. Some shaggy ponies now were seen trotting toward them with boys upon their backs, who called to other boys in country gigs and carts, driven by farmers. All these boys were in great spirits, and shouted to each other, until the broad fields were so full of merry music, that the crisp air laughed to hear it.

The jocund travelers came on, and as they came, Scrooge knew and named them every one. Why was he rejoiced beyond all bounds to see them? Why did his cold eyes glisten, and his heart leap up as they went past? Why was he filled with gladness when he heard them give each other merry Christmas, as they parted at crossroads and bye-ways, for their several homes? What was merry Christmas to Scrooge? Out upon merry Christmas. What good had it ever done to him? "They've all gone off on holiday," he remarked.

"Not all of them. The school is not quite deserted," said the ghost. "A solitary child, neglected by his family and friends, is left there still."

They left the high road, by a well-remembered lane, and soon approached a mansion of dull red brick, with a little weathercock-surmounted cupola, on the roof, and a bell hanging in it. It was a large house, but one of broken fortunes, for the spacious offices were little used, their walls were damp and mossy, their windows broken, and their gates decayed. Fowls clucked and strutted in the stables, and the coach-houses and sheds were overrun with grass. Nor was it more retentive of its ancient state within, for entering the dreary hall, and glancing through the open doors of many rooms, they found them poorly furnished, cold, and vast. There was an earthy savor in the air, a chilly bareness in the place, which associated itself somehow with too much getting up by candle-light, and not too much to eat.

They went, the ghost and Scrooge, across the hall, to a door at the back of the house. It opened before them, and disclosed a long, bare, melancholy room, made barer still by lines of plain benches and desks. At one of these, a lonely boy was reading near a feeble fire, and Scrooge sat down upon a bench, and wept to see his poor forgotten self as he used to be.

Not a latent echo in the house, not a squeak and scuffle from the mice behind the paneling, not a drip from the half-thawed water-spout in the dull yard behind, not a sigh among the leafless boughs of one despondent poplar, not the idle swinging of an empty store-house door, no, not a clicking in the fire, but fell upon the heart of Scrooge with a softening influence, and gave a freer passage to his tears.

"The place where my father sent me that day."

The phantom pointed to a foggy window, left open a crack so that the voices outside carried within. Beyond the window, standing not in the schoolyard, but the yard of his home was Scrooge's father and sister. Scrooge didn't know how such a thing was possible and, at this point, cared little, for it seemed less a feat than the time travel he was experiencing or less incredible than the presence of vampires in England or anywhere on earth, for that matter.

"But why cannot we not go to fetch Ebenezer on our way to church?" his twin sister begged.

She was a blooming schoolgirl, now, with flowing brown hair tied with a blue ribbon beneath her white bonnet, her beauty remarkable for her age. Upon her face, Scrooge could already see the young woman she would become.

"Get into the carriage and do not question my authority," Mr. Scrooge said harshly. "I will not speak of this again, child!"

"But, Father, why?" cried Fan, tears filling her eyes, eyes like her mother's . . . like Scrooge's. "Why must Ebenezer stay at school alone when I am able to live here in the comfort of our home?"

"You know why," the elder Scrooge said.

"But it's not true." She dabbed prettily at her tears. "It was not Ebenezer's fault that Mother died! And he has become a fine scholar. You have listened too long to Mrs. Grottweil and her lies! I tell you, I do not need a wet nurse or a nursemaid or whatever it is she calls herself, and I want her dismissed. The truth of my mother's day she hides from you is far darker than simple death in childbirth. Far more sinister."

"Get into the carriage," ordered Mr. Scrooge, taking his

daughter's arm roughly. "And I will hear no more on the matter. Ebenezer will stay in school!"

"Fan," Scrooge called out, reaching for his long-lost sister. But the image faded until he was no longer certain it had ever been there.

The spirit touched Scrooge on the arm, and pointed to his younger self inside the schoolroom, intent upon his reading.

"What Queen Griselda said came to pass. My father believed I was responsible for my mother's death. That was really why he sent me away. Not because I did poorly in my lessons that day." Tears welled in Scrooge's eyes again. "I see it all. I did not understand, but all becomes clear to me."

"Look forward now," the ghost said.

Suddenly, a man, in foreign garments, wonderfully real and distinct to look at, stood outside the window, with an axe stuck in his belt, and leading by the bridle an ass laden with wood.

"Why, it's Ali Baba," Scrooge exclaimed in ecstasy. "It's dear old honest Ali Baba. Yes, yes, I know. One Christmas time, when yonder solitary child was left here all alone, he did come, for the first time, just like that. Poor boy. And Valentine," said Scrooge, "and his wild brother, Orson; there they go. And what's his name, who was put down in his drawers, asleep, at the Gate of Damascus? Don't you see him? And the Sultan's Groom turned upside down by the Genii, there he is upon his head. Serves him right. I'm glad of it. What business had he to be married to the Princess?"

To hear Scrooge expending all the earnestness of his nature on such subjects, in a most extraordinary voice between laughing and crying, and to see his heightened and excited face would have been a surprise to his business friends in the city, indeed.

"There's the parrot," cried Scrooge. "Green body and yellow tail, with a thing like a lettuce growing out of the top of his head, there he is. Poor Robin Crusoe, he called him, when he came home again after sailing round the island. 'Poor Robin Crusoe, where have you been, Robin Crusoe?' The man thought he was dreaming, but he wasn't. It was the parrot, you know. There goes Friday, running for his life to the little creek. Halloa. Hoop. Hallo."

Then, with a rapidity of transition very foreign to his usual character, Scrooge said, in pity for his former self, "Poor boy," and cried again. "I wish . . . ," he muttered, putting his hand in his pocket, and looking about him, after drying his eyes with his cuff. "But it's too late now."

"What is the matter?" asked the spirit. "Surely you can see what a burden he must have been to his father . . . the cost he must have been . . . the shoes . . . the books . . . the quills and ink and slates . . . all wasted on one who had killed his own mother."

"But I didn't kill her. I was an innocent babe," Scrooge whispered.

"What? What do you say?"

"Nothing," said Scrooge, hanging his head. "Nothing."

The ghost waited.

"It is only that there was a boy singing a Christmas carol at my counting house door last night. I should like to have given him something, that's all. After all, if it is true that vampires roam our streets, then he took great risk to sing that carol in the hopes of brightening my day."

The ghost smiled thoughtfully, and waved its hand, saying as it did so, "Let us see another Christmas."

17

Scrooge's former self grew larger at the words, and the room became a little darker and dirtier. The panels shrunk, the windows cracked, fragments of plaster fell out of the ceiling, and the naked laths were shown instead, but how all this was brought about, Scrooge knew no more than you do. He only knew that it was quite correct, that everything had happened so, that there he was, alone again, when all the other boys had gone home for the jolly holidays.

"I do not know why no one ever invited me home with them," Scrooge said sadly. He saw himself not reading now, but walking up and down despairingly, occasionally glancing at the window at the commotion in the yard. Through a crack in the window the joyous sounds of families being reunited could be heard. There was laughter and the sound of sleigh bells as students set off to spend the holidays with their families.

"If only, in all those years, just one boy would have asked me," Scrooge murmured, feeling quite sorry for himself, at that point. "If only just one had cared."

The spirit turned with a sweeping hand, and a door opened.

From inside, Scrooge heard the sound of his headmaster's voice, only it was not the pleasant voice he recalled from his years there.

"You most certainly will not invite him home with you," hissed the headmaster. "Take that boy home with you and you will regret the day you ever met Ebenezer Scrooge."

At the mention of his name, Scrooge moved closer to the door. It was the headmaster's office. Inside, the man held Joshua Cuttleman, Scrooge's school chum, by the throat, up against a paneled wall.

"Sir?" cried Joshua, who was a short boy with a long face, but nice enough in manners. He was not brainy, and not the cleanliest of boys, but he had always seemed to have a good heart and had often shared treats sent from home with Ebenezer . . . until the headmaster had caught him and punished poor Joshua. Sharing of sweets was particularly frowned upon at school, though why, Scrooge had never known.

"You . . . you cannot tell me I cannot take a friend home with me, sir," Joshua crowed boldly.

"I can and I will." The schoolmaster wrapped his hands more tightly around Joshua's stringy throat and the boy's pinched face went red, then purple.

As Scrooge watched from the doorway, the headmaster, a tall, thin man with a slight hare-lip, drew back said malformed lip and bared a set of tiny incisors. They were not so nearly as impressive as Queen Griselda's, and appeared homemade, but were still startling. Scrooge had had no idea!

"He-he's l-like Mrs. Grottweil," Scrooge stuttered in shock. "My schoolmaster, he was working for her, wasn't he? For Queen Griselda?" He rushed forward and tried to enter the schoolmaster's office, but it seemed he could not, for when he stepped through the threshold, the office seemed to move another step away, and then another step away and another and so forth.

"Attempt to offer an invitation, Cuttleman," the headmaster threatened, "and I will sink my fangs into you, I will bite you and drink your blood. I will come to you at night and have a taste of you, and then when you are too weak from blood loss to fight, I will give you up to the true bloodsuckers, who will drink you dry and toss your bones into the outhouse hole so that your mother and father will have nothing to bury."

"So he is not actually a vampire?" Scrooge observed. "Like Mrs. Grottweil, he . . . ," he searched for the right phrase, "works for the vampires? But *they* are not vampires, are they?"

"They are humans who have acquired a taste for human blood, thanks to the vampires," the spirit said. "They are called *minions*. They are at the beck and call of the vampires. Queen Griselda and King Wahltraud have many minions."

"My . . . my father," the boy Joshua dared bravely, gaining Scrooge's attention again. "I will tell my father that you have tried to intimidate me, and he will tell the other boys' fathers and they will see you dismissed." His face was growing brighter red by the moment, his thin cheeks now shiny. "They will see you thrown in prison for aiding and abetting the vampires."

The headmaster, still holding tightly to Joshua's throat, threw back his head and laughed heartily. The sound came out slightly garbled due to his facial affliction. "And then I will go to your family home in the dark of night and I will pluck your little sisters, one by one, out of their beds and hand them out the window to one of my accomplices. Do you know how much vampires will pay for fresh, young, rosy-cheeked English girls on the auction block in Transylvania?"

"My sisters?" Joshua sobbed. "You would murder a little girl?"

"The lass missing from the village last week?" The headmaster lifted a bushy brow. "Drained and tucked beneath a rain barrel on the high street. She will be nothing but a crust by the time she is found. Unless you'd like to go looking for her body now. We could go together."

A tear slipped down Joshua's face. "Let me go," he whispered, "and I will say nothing to Ebenezer. I will not extend the invitation."

"And you will suggest to the other lads they follow your lead," the headmaster warned as he slowly released him.

"Yes," the boy agreed, defeat on his red face. "Ebenezer will not be invited anywhere by any of us."

Scrooge recalled that, sadly, after that Christmas holiday, Joshua did not return to school. His one friend, gone. And Scrooge had never known why; now he knew that the poor boy had been forced to run for his life because he had wanted to show a schoolmate a little kindness.

Scrooge turned to the ghost, with a mournful shaking of his head, and a tear upon his cheek that matched Joshua's those many years ago. "I thought they simply did not like me. I had no idea the headmaster threatened them."

"It was not the schoolmaster's intention for you to know, nor was it the intention of the vampires," the spirit responded as he turned to point to another door off the classroom. "Another Christmas . . ."

❧ 18 ❧

The paneled door opened and Scrooge's sister Fan darted in, and put her arms about his neck, and kissed him and addressed him as her "Dear, dear brother." She was taller than he had seen her a few moments before . . . and more beautiful. She was so like their mother that a lump rose in Scrooge's throat.

"I have come to bring you home, dear brother," said the girl, clapping her hands, and reaching out to grasp his cheeks between her hands. "To bring you home, home, home."

She was dressed in shot-silk of the richest quality and smelled of dried lavender. Upon her head she wore a beaver bonnet, and over her shoulders, a red cloak of fine worsted wool, embroidered at the hem with green leaves and vines and other such ornamentation. In her ears sparkled earbobs.

The younger Scrooge did not seem to believe his good fortune for, no doubt, he thought his fate sealed by men such as the schoolmaster and women such as his wet nurse. "Home, Fan?" returned the boy. "But what of Mrs. Grottweil? She swore she would not see me cross the threshold again. Our father—"

"Mrs. Grottweil is gone!" Fan cried, brimful of glee. "I sent her packing myself, with Father's blessing. He caught her drinking blood from the milkmaid who delivers Tuesdays and Thursdays. I do not know that he believed she was a bloodsucker, but he agreed she no longer had a place in our home."

"And now I shall come home?" the boy repeated, still in disbelief.

"Yes. Home, for good and all. Home, forever and ever. Father is so much kinder than he used to be, that home's like heaven. He spoke so gently to me one dear night when I was going to bed, that I was not afraid to ask him once more if you might come home. I think that once Mrs. Grottweil was gone, and he no longer under her influence, he began to see the truth of what happened to our mother. He understands now that you were not responsible for Mother's death and that the vampires are the ones to be held accountable. He intends to see the magistrate and have Mrs. Grottweil questioned, if they can find her. We heard that she had fled after Father let her go."

"Such good news, Fan! I can hardly believe your words!"

"Well, you should, because he sent me in a coach to bring you. And you're to be a man," she said, opening her bright blue eyes wide, "and you are never to come back here, but first, we're to be together all the Christmas long, and have the merriest time in all the world."

"You are quite a woman, Fan," exclaimed the boy.

She clapped her hands and laughed, and tried to touch his head, but he had shot up and was now much taller than his twin, so she laughed again, and stood on tiptoe to embrace him. Then she began to drag him, in her eagerness, toward the door and he, with no reason not to go, accompanied her.

A terrible voice in the hall cried, "Bring down Master Scrooge's box, there," and in the hall appeared the schoolmaster himself, who glared on Master Scrooge with a ferocious condescension, and threw him into a dreadful state of mind by shaking hands with him. "No one is displeased with the education we have provided here?"

The young Scrooge looked up at him. "No, sir. It's only that my father has need of me."

He then conveyed him and his sister into the veriest old well of a shivering best parlor that ever was seen, where the maps upon the wall, and the celestial and terrestrial globes in the windows, were waxy with cold. Here he produced a decanter of curiously light wine, and a block of curiously heavy cake, and administered installments of those dainties to the young people. At the same time, sending out a meager servant to offer a glass of something to the postboy, who answered that he thanked the gentleman, but if it was the same tap as he had tasted before, he had rather not. Master Scrooge's trunk being by this time tied on to the top of the chaise, the children bade the schoolmaster good-bye right willingly, and getting into it, drove gaily down the garden sweep, the quick wheels dashing the hoar frost and snow from off the dark leaves of the evergreens like spray.

"My dear, dear sister, Fan." Scrooge sighed, watching as Fan and his younger self drove away.

"Always a delicate creature, whom a breath might have withered," said the ghost. "Particularly because the wet nurse who became her nursemaid, Mrs. Grottweil, saw her bled regularly while she slept so as to keep her weak. But she had a large heart."

Saddened to hear such a revelation, Scrooge felt the tears well in his eyes again. "But she had such a large heart," he repeated in agreement.

"And you know what followed next."

Scrooge hung his head. "Please tell me we do not need to return to my childhood home. I am an old man, and there is no point to revisiting the past."

"Oh, but we must return, because there is a point to all this in the end, Ebenezer Scrooge."

19

And once again, Scrooge, still in his nightclothes, was propelled through time; one moment he sat in a carriage with Fan, driving away from the school, the next he was in the front hall of his father's home. He followed Fan and the boy into the house. The spirit brought up the rear, closing the front door soundly behind them.

"Father! Father!" Fan called, her merriness still bright on her cheeks and dancing in her blue eyes. "We are here! Ebenezer is home! I have brought my dear brother home to us!"

Her words echoed in the big hall, empty and hollow, and the hair rose on the back of Scrooge's neck as he recalled the incident from long ago. The house had smelled of blood, he recalled, as it did now.

"Where is everyone?" Fan tossed her rabbit-fur muff on a side table, carved with elegant legs. "Father! We're home, Ebenezer and I! Have you not heard? I've brought your son home to you."

Fan turned into the parlor and screamed.

"Not this again," Scrooge murmured, trying to cover his ears with his hands, for he could not stand to hear her terror.

The spirit gently pulled his hands away.

Blood. There was blood everywhere. Upon the polished wood floor, the fine woolen carpet, and the horsehair settee. In front of the fireplace, in his favorite chair, sat Mr. Scrooge, awaiting his children's arrival. Dead, his throat torn out. All the servants dead, too, in the kitchen hanging from the pothooks, in an upstairs bedchamber dangling from a closet nail, and yet another suspended from the attic window, his dry husk of a skin blowing in the wind like some faded flag of carnage. The authorities had said it was wild animals that had set upon the house, possibly the same pack of vicious hedgehogs that had earlier ravaged the town of Hogs-Wallow-Upon-Upwald.

"It was not wild animals, was it?" Scrooge asked, turning to the ghost as the bloody parlor scene slowly faded and Fan seemed to grow farther away from him. "I never believed the hedgehog story, but I thought it might have been wolves," he said hopefully.

"It was not wild animals that murdered your father," the phantom agreed kindly.

"My poor Fan," cried Scrooge. "I do not think she was ever the same after she witnessed that bloodshed. The only survivor in the house was the cook's small spit dog, and it was said that he suffered from nightmares ever after."

"Did anyone ever think to examine that spit dog's canine teeth?" the spirit asked. "Or to wonder if perhaps the evil creature was a minion of the vampires who might have opened the back door and invited them in?"

"The dog?"

"Any stranger that a dog should be caught up in such betrayal and massacre than that hedgehogs should suffer mass insanity and overrun three villages and a convent before throwing themselves over a cliff and swimming en mass for the Black Sea on a rainy Tuesday?"

"I suppose not, but the dog was very old," Scrooge mused. "I wouldn't suppose he had many teeth left."

"One needs only paws and a tall stool to unlatch a kitchen door."

"That my poor, dear Fan had once fed that cur scraps of her own bread."

"Speaking of your sister, may I remind you that she lived for some years. She died a woman," said the ghost, "but had, as I think, children."

"One child," Scrooge returned, shivering, not so much from cold as the memories he had so long buried.

"True," said the ghost. "Your nephew."

Scrooge seemed uneasy in his mind and answered briefly, "Yes. Fred."

20

Although they had but that moment left the Scrooge country house behind them, they were now in the busy thoroughfares of a city, where shadowy passengers passed and repassed, where shadowy carts and coaches battled for the way, and all the strife and tumult of a real city were. It was made plain enough, by the dressing of the shops, that here, too, it was Christmas time again, but it was evening, and the streets were lighted up.

The ghost stopped at a certain warehouse door, and asked Scrooge if he knew it.

"Know it?" said Scrooge, wiping at his eyes. "Why, I was apprenticed here. My father had made the arrangements prior to his untimely death."

They went in. At the sight of an old gentleman in a Welsh wig, sitting behind such a high desk that if he had been two inches taller, he would have knocked his head against the ceiling, Scrooge cried in great excitement, "Why, it's old Fezziwig. Bless his heart, it's Fezziwig alive again!"

Old Fezziwig laid down his pen, and looked up at the clock,

which pointed to the hour of seven. He rubbed his hands, adjusted his capacious waistcoat, laughed all over himself, from his shows to his organ of benevolence, and called out in a comfortable, oily, rich, fat, jovial voice, "Yo ho, there. Ebenezer. Dick."

Scrooge's former self, now grown a young man, came briskly in, accompanied by his fellow-'prentice. "Dick Wilkins, to be sure," said Scrooge to the ghost. "Bless me, yes. There he is. He was very much attached to me, was Dick. Poor Dick. Dear, dear."

"Poor Dick?" questioned the ghost.

"He was kind to me. Dear. The only friend I had after Joseph Cuttleman, but—"

"But he died young, your friend Dick? Of a bleeding ailment?" pressed the spirit.

Scrooge looked up at him. "How did you know?"

"A *bleeding* disease," the ghost repeated.

"Not the vampires!" Scrooge exclaimed. "I cannot believe it. I won't."

"Then do not. Your belief will not make it all the more or less true," observed the ghost. Then he pointed to the scene unfolding in the warehouse and Scrooge was drawn into a happier time, a time before Dick was bitten by vampires and left on his pallet to waste away.

"Yo ho, my boys," said Fezziwig. "No more work tonight. Christmas Eve, Dick. Christmas, Ebenezer. Let's have the shutters up," cried old Fezziwig, with a sharp clap of his hands, "before a man can say Jack Robinson."

You wouldn't believe how those two fellows went at it. They charged into the street with the shutters—one, two, three—had them up in their places—four, five, six—barred them and pinned them—seven, eight, nine—and came back before you could have got to twelve, panting like race-horses.

"Hilli-ho!" cried old Fezziwig, skipping down from the

high desk, with wonderful agility. "Clear away, my lads, and let's have lots of room here. Hilli-ho, Dick. Chirrup, Ebenezer."

Clear away. There was nothing they wouldn't have cleared away, or couldn't have cleared away, with old Fezziwig looking on. It was done in a minute. Every movable was packed off, as if it were dismissed from public life forevermore, the floor was swept and watered, the lamps were trimmed, fuel was heaped upon the fire. The warehouse was as snug, and warm, and dry, and bright a ballroom, as you would desire to see upon a winter's night.

In came a fiddler with a music-book, and went up to the lofty desk, and made an orchestra of it, and tuned like fifty stomachaches. In came Mrs. Fezziwig, one vast substantial smile. In came the three Miss Fezziwigs, beaming and lovable. In came the six young followers whose hearts they broke. In came all the young men and women employed in the business. In came the housemaid, with her cousin, the baker. In came the cook, with her brother's particular friend, the milkman. In came the boy from over the way, who was suspected of not having board enough from his master, trying to hide himself behind the girl from next door but one, who was proved to have had her ears pulled by her mistress. In they all came, one after another, some shyly, some boldly, some gracefully, some awkwardly, some pushing, some pulling, in they all came, anyhow and everyhow. Away they all went, twenty couples at once, hands half round and back again the other way. Down the middle and up again they danced, round and round in various stages of affectionate grouping; old top couple always turning up in the wrong place, new top couple starting off again, as soon as they got there, all top couples at last, and not a bottom one to help them. When this result was brought about, old Fezziwig, clapping his hands to stop the dance, cried out, "Well done!" and the fiddler plunged his hot face into a pot of porter, especially provided for that purpose. But scorning rest, upon his reappearance, he instantly began again, though there were no dancers yet, as if the other fiddler had been carried home, exhausted, on a shutter, and he were a brand-new man resolved to beat him out of sight, or perish.

There were more dances, and there were forfeits, and more dances, and there was cake, and there was negus, and there was a great piece of cold roast, and there was a great piece of cold boiled, and there were mincemeat pies, and plenty of beer. But the great effect of the evening came after the roast and boiled, when the fiddler (an artful dog, mind. The sort of man who knew his business better than you or I could have told it to him) struck up "Sir Roger de Coverley." Then old Fezziwig stood out to dance with Mrs. Fezziwig. Top couple, too, with a good stiff piece of work cut out for them; three or four and twenty pair of partners; people who were not to be trifled with, people who would dance, and had no notion of walking.

But if they had been twice as many—ah, four times—old Fezziwig would have been a match for them, and so would Mrs. Fezziwig. As to her, she was worthy to be his partner in every sense of the term. If that's not high praise, tell me higher, and I'll use it. A positive light appeared to issue from Fezziwig's calves. They shone in every part of the dance like moons. You couldn't have predicted, at any given time, what would have become of them next. And when old Fezziwig and Mrs. Fezziwig had gone all through the dance, advance and retire, both hands to your partner, bow and curtsey, corkscrew, thread-the-needle, and back again to your place, Fezziwig cut—cut so deftly that he appeared to wink with his legs, and came upon his feet again without a stagger.

When the clock struck eleven, this domestic ball broke up. Mr. and Mrs. Fezziwig took their stations, one on either side of the door, and shaking hands with every person individually as he or she went out, wished him or her a merry Christmas. When everybody had retired but the two 'prentices, they did the same to them; and thus the cheerful voices died away, and the lads were left to their beds, which were under a counter in the back-shop.

During the whole of this time, Scrooge had acted like a man out of his wits. His heart and soul were in the scene, and with his former self. He corroborated everything, remembered everything, enjoyed everything, and underwent the strangest agitation. It was not until now, when the bright faces of his former self and Dick were turned from them, that he remembered the ghost, and became conscious that it was looking full upon him, while the light upon its head burned very clear.

"A small matter," said the ghost, "to make these silly folks so full of gratitude."

"Small," echoed Scrooge.

The spirit signed to him to listen to the two apprentices, who were pouring out their hearts in praise of Fezziwig, and when he had done so, said, "He has spent but a few pounds of your mortal money, three or four perhaps. Is that so much that he deserves this praise?"

"It isn't that," said Scrooge, heated by the remark, and speaking unconsciously like his former, not his latter, self. "It isn't that, Spirit. He has the power to render us happy or unhappy, to make our service light or burdensome, a pleasure or a toil. Say that his power lies in words and looks, in things so slight and insignificant that it is impossible to add and count them up, what then? The happiness he gives, is quite as great as if it cost a fortune."

He felt the spirit's glance, and stopped.

"What is the matter?" asked the ghost.

"Nothing in particular," said Scrooge.

"Something, I think," the ghost insisted.

"No," said Scrooge, "no. I should like to be able to say a word or two to my clerks just now. That's all."

His former self turned down the lamps as he gave utterance

to the wish, and Scrooge and the ghost again stood side by side in the open air.

"There was something else Fezziwig gave you," observed the ghost. "Another opportunity."

"An opportunity in what?" asked Scrooge.

The ghost turned and the warehouse was again filled with bright light, the heavenly smells of a feast and the bright laughter of those making merry. At once, Scrooge spotted himself, leaning over a young woman, offering her a cup of punch.

"Belle," Scrooge murmured, unable to resist a smile.

"You met her here for the very first time."

"Her mother was an acquaintance of Mrs. Fezziwig's," Scrooge explained. "Mrs. Fezziwig invited her because she thought Belle might . . ."

"Belle might?"

"Like me," Scrooge said, watching the young couple intently.

Belle was laughing and Scrooge, the young man, smiling.

"She had a bit of a scare that night," Scrooge recalled aloud. "I was trying to make her feel better. She told me she was followed to Fezziwig's by vampires."

"Did you believe her?"

"I did not," he said sadly. "I thought it a ploy to get a young man's attention. Mine in particular." Again he smiled. "She was like that, Belle, fanciful, always full of suspicion. Even paranoid at times. She saw the vampires on every street corner."

"What if I told you what she saw was real?"

"I would say 'Bah, humbug!'"

The ghost smiled in a way that made Scrooge feel very small and insignificant.

"She told me the vampires followed me, too, that they watched me, but I didn't believe her."

"Why not?" the spirit inquired.

"Because she was full of all sorts of nonsense. It wasn't just the vampires she talked about all the time. Her mother was the same way. Some said they were touched. Belle claimed she saw spirits, too." Again, he laughed. "She said she could talk to them!" Scrooge eyed the ghost, realizing his own present circumstances, and his laughter died away.

"You did not believe her."

"I did not," Scrooge confirmed. "But I liked her, anyway. She was sweet and bright and so full of life. Despite her paranoia, she was intelligent. She made me laugh."

"You loved her?"

Scrooge did not answer as he gazed sadly upon the couple, remembering what it had felt like to hold her hand in his, to feel her lips upon his own. She'd always had the smoothest skin. The prettiest blue eyes. "I loved her," he murmured, almost choking on the words. "And I suppose she loved me . . . once."

"Come, my time grows short," observed the spirit. "Quick." This was not addressed to Scrooge, or to anyone whom he could see, but it produced an immediate effect, for again Scrooge saw himself. He was older now, a man in the prime of life. His face had not the harsh and rigid lines of later years, but it had begun to wear the signs of care and avarice. There was an eager, greedy, restless motion in the eye, which showed the passion that had taken root, and where the shadow of the growing tree would fall.

From the main street Scrooge entered, itself little better than an alley, a low-browed doorway led into a blind court, or yard, profoundly dark, unpaved, and reeking with stagnant odors. Into this ill-favored pit he strode, then struck thrice upon an iron grating with his foot.

"Do you know where we are?" asked the spirit.

"Of course I do. It was a gentlemen's club I belonged to many years ago."

"A gentlemen's club?" the ghost questioned. "And who brought you into this *gentlemen's club?*"

"A colleague. Another businessman."

Scrooge scratched the recesses of his mind for recollection of the man who had brought him here the very first time he attended. "I . . . cannot recall his name, but I fear he looked much like my tenant Mr. Wahltraud."

"The King of Vampires," the spirit reminded him.

"That's not possible. Please tell me my recollection is wrong."

"I wish that I could," said the spirit, pointing into the alley.

The younger Scrooge became impatient, and struck the grating thrice again.

A further delay ensued, but it was not of long duration. The ground seemed to open at his feet, and a ragged head appeared.

"Is that you, Mr. Scrooge?" said a voice as ragged as the head.

"Yes," replied Scrooge haughtily, descending as he spoke, "who should it be?"

Scrooge in his nightdress and the Ghost of Christmas Past descended behind him, as undetected as on the previous Christmas Eves.

"It's so late, we gave you up," returned the voice, as its owner stopped to shut and fasten the grating. "You're late, sir."

"I had business to attend to. A man to send to the workhouse for non-payment," said Scrooge, then still a handsome man, but with a gloomy majesty. "Make remarks when I require you," he said in the hoarsest voice he could assume and led the way, with folded arms and knitted brows, to the cellar down below, where there was a small copper fixed in one corner, a chair or two, a form and table, a glimmering fire, and a truckle-bed, covered with a ragged patchwork rug.

"Welcome, Mr. Scrooge!" cried a lanky figure, rising as from a nap.

Scrooge nodded. Then, throwing off his outer coat, he stood composed in all his dignity, and eyed his follower over.

"What news tonight?" he asked, when he had looked into his very soul.

"Nothing particular," replied the other, stretching himself—and he was so long already that it was quite alarming to see him do it.

"I do not like this place," said the older Scrooge to the ghost. "Please. Take me from here."

"This is but a shadow of your past. Whatever you did here is done."

"I was young," Scrooge argued. "These men, they brought me very profitable business deals. They introduced me to Jacob Marley. It was harmless what we did in that room. A game."

"Harmless," the spirit repeated, gazing beyond the present Scrooge to the past.

"Is the room prepared?"

"It is," replied the follower.

"The comrade—is he here?"

"Yes. And a sprinkling of the others—you hear 'em?"

"Playing skittles," said younger Scrooge moodily, referring to an ancient game involving a ball and pins to be knocked down. "Light-hearted revelers!"

There was no doubt respecting the particular amusement in which these heedless spirits were indulging, for even in the close and stifling atmosphere of the vault, the noise sounded like distant thunder. It certainly appeared, at first sight, a singular spot to choose, for that or any other purpose of relaxation, if the other cellars answered to the one in which this brief colloquy took place, for the floors were of sodden earth, the walls and roof of damp bare brick tapestried with the tracks of snails and slugs; the air was sickening, tainted, and offensive. It seemed, from one strong flavor which was uppermost among the various odors of the place, that it had, at no very distant period, been used as a store-house for cheeses, a circumstance which, while it accounted for the greasy moisture that hung about it, was agreeably suggestive of rats. It was naturally damp besides, and little trees of fungus sprung from every moldy corner.

The proprietor of this charming retreat, and owner of the ragged head before mentioned—for he wore an old tie-wig as bare and frowzy as a stunted hearth-broom—had by this time joined them. He stood a little apart, rubbing his hands, wagging his hoary bristled chin, and smiling in silence. His eyes were closed, but had they been wide open, it would have been easy to tell, from the attentive expression of the face he turned toward them—pale and unwholesome as might be expected in one of his underground existence—and from a certain anxious raising and quivering of the lids, that he was blind.

"Mr. Wahltraud, he was responsible for all of this, was he not?" Scrooge felt a flutter in his chest, one of fear and loathing . . . and regret. "It was he who arranged the business deals. These men—"

"His minions," the spirit offered.

"His minions," Scrooge whispered. "Hers . . . Queen Griselda's."

"You were her project . . . it was natural that he would aid when he could."

"What does my Mr. Scrooge drink?" asked the blind man. "Is it brandy, rum, usquebaugh? Is it soaked gunpowder, or blazing oil?"

"Or blood?" cackled a voice from the corner.

The elder Scrooge backed his way up in the dark room, taking refuge closer to the spirit. "Not blood. I never drank blood."

"Perhaps not of your own accord," was all the ghost said.

"See that it's something strong, and comes quick," cried the younger Scrooge. "And so long as you take care of that, you may bring it from the devil's cellar, if you like."

"Truer words could not have been spoke," said the spirit softly into Scrooge's ear.

A man called Stagg filled a glass with an unrecognizable dark liquid and offered it up. "Drink, sir. Death to the poor, life to all men such as yourself, and love to all fair damsels. Drink, Mr. Scrooge, and warm your gallant heart!"

Scrooge cowered near the ghost. "They were poisoning me. I came merely because they asked me to, because of the business they sent my way, but they took advantage of me. They—"

"I yearn to be abed. Lead on. To business!" With these words, Scrooge folded his arms, and frowning with a sullen majesty, passed with his companion through a little door at the upper end of the cellar.

The spirit and Scrooge followed.

The vault they entered, strewn with sawdust and dimly lighted, was between the outer one from which they had just come, and that in which the skittle-players were diverting themselves, as was manifested by the increased noise and clamor of tongues, which was suddenly stopped, however, and replaced by a dead silence, at a signal from the long comrade. Then, a young gentleman, going to a little cupboard, returned with a thigh-bone, which in former times must have been part and parcel of some individual at least as long as himself, and placed the same in the hands of Scrooge who, receiving it as a scepter and staff of authority, cocked his three-cornered hat fiercely on the top of his head, and mounted a large table, whereon a chair of state, cheerfully ornamented with a couple of skulls, was placed ready for his reception.

"And this you thought to be business?" questioned the spirit.

"It . . . it seemed harmless at the time. I . . . I killed no one."

The young Scrooge had no sooner assumed this position, than another young gentleman appeared, bearing in his arms a huge clasped book, who made him a profound obeisance, and delivering it to the long comrade, advanced to the table, and turning his back upon it, stood there. Then the long comrade got upon the table, too, and seating himself in a lower chair than Scrooge with much state and ceremony, placed the large book on the shoulders of their mute companion as deliberately as if he had been a wooden desk, and prepared to make entries therein with a pen of corresponding size.

When the long comrade had made these preparations, he looked toward the younger Scrooge, and Scrooge, flourishing the bone, knocked nine times therewith upon one of the skulls. At the ninth stroke, a third young gentleman emerged from the door leading to the skittle ground, and bowing low, awaited his commands.

"Who waits without?" barked Scrooge.

The man answered that a stranger was in attendance, who claimed admission into that secret society of Golden Knights, and a free participation in their rights, privileges, and immunities. A man called Jacob Marley. Thereupon Scrooge flourished the bone again, and giving the other skull a prodigious rap on the nose, exclaimed, "Admit him!"

"Enough! I have seen enough," Scrooge cried, gripping his sleeping gown and twisting it in his fingers.

"What purpose did this society possess?" the spirit pressed.

"To . . . to protect our interests. The interests of businessmen such as myself. To see those who could not pay sent to prison, to the workhouses."

"That night," the spirit said, "Jacob Marley made his pledge. What oath did he give?"

Scrooge closed his eyes and then slowly opened them, knowing he had no choice but to give a response. "Every member of that small remnant of a noble body took an oath to gain what he could, to take advantage where he saw benefit, and never to waver in the pursuit of wealth. We vowed not to suffer from weakness, not to accept the excuses of the poor, the sick, the unfortunate." He hung his head.

"Another night, in this chamber, you had a conversation with a man. The same man who brought you here. Do you remember?"

"I did not know him as Mr. Wahltraud, or as the King of Vampires or anything of the sort," Scrooge exclaimed. "You confuse me with tricks and fancy talk so that my head aches and I cannot be certain or what was or what is or is not."

"What did the King of the Vampires say to you that night?"

"What night?" Scrooge cried.

"You know the night. What did he say to you of Belle?"

"He . . . he said she did not really love me. He said . . . I could never make her happy. That I was a businessman, not a husband. He said that she would be a poor choice for a man such as I, that she would burden me with wailing, wet-nappied brats and that I would be a poor father. Worse than my own."

The spirit smiled sadly. "And so . . ."

❧ 22 ❧

Scrooge felt himself again swept up in time, and a moment later he saw himself seated on a bench in the park. Beside him sat Belle. She was wearing a bright green morning dress and matching green cloak and he a fine black overcoat and wool top hat. It was another Christmas Eve, but he was no longer in the employ of Fezziwig; he was a man of his own wits, his own financial success. Scrooge should have been happy to see himself so successful, but recollection of the moment brought a sadness he had not felt in more years than he could count. The sadness came from the sight of Belle's eyes, for in her eyes there were tears, which sparkled in the light that shone out of the Ghost of Christmas Past.

"I think it best, Belle, don't you?"

"It matters little," she said softly. "To you, very little. Another idol has displaced me, and if it can cheer and comfort you in time to come, as I would have tried to do, I have no just cause to grieve."

"What idol has displaced you?" he rejoined.

"A golden one. Or perhaps one more sinister."

"Please, I will hear no more of your tales of vampires! This is the even-handed dealing of the world," he said. "There is nothing on which it is so hard as poverty, and there is nothing it professes to condemn with such severity as the pursuit of wealth."

"You fear the world too much," she answered gently.

"Me? You are the one looking for vampires behind every coal bin."

"All your other hopes have merged into the hope of being beyond the chance of its sordid reproach. I have seen your nobler aspirations fall off one by one, until the master-passion, gain, engrosses you.

"I have been expecting you to end our engagement." When he said nothing, she went on. "But it is not what I want, and I do not believe it is what you want. Do you not see, Ebenezer?" she cried passionately, taking his gloved hand in hers. "You are being influenced by those who do not wish for your well-being as I do."

"More talk of vampires, I suppose. Bah!" He checked his timepiece. "I have but learned the ways of the world. Even if I have grown so much wiser, what then? Our contract is an old one. It was made when we were both poor." He took his hand from hers. "It is plain you do not approve of me or my ways. You will be happier with someone else. You . . . deserve another. Someone . . . more to your liking."

"You loved me once," she said softly.

His response was one of impatience. "I was a boy! I knew nothing of marriage. Of the world."

"And you will not reconsider?" Belle asked. "You will not give us a chance?"

"It is best that you marry while you still can. You are younger than I." He cleared his throat. "You should have children . . . you would be good at that. Rearing children. It is not a pursuit that I have the slightest interest in. So, I release you."

"Have I ever sought release?"

"In words. No. Never. But you have made it plain that you do not approve of the way I live my life."

"Because I am afraid for you, Ebenezer! You are turning your back on mankind ... and on yourself. It is true, but I would gladly think otherwise if I could," she told him. "Heaven knows. When I have learned a truth like this, I know how strong and irresistible it must be. I only hope repentance and regret will find you one day, and I will wait for that day with a full heart, for the love of him you once were."

"You will wait for me?" He rose, for he was late to a business luncheon. "That is ridiculous, Belle. I release you from our engagement, and go you must." He tipped his hat. "Good day."

"Merry Christmas," she said through tears.

He left her, and they parted.

"I saw her today, Spirit. I see her from time to time. She kept her word and never married; she is an old maid who gives refuge to poor travelers to keep herself in bread. She has learned nothing of business sense in all these years, never had two pence to put together."

"And still, after all these years, she is kind to you, as she is kind to others."

"I think I was right from the beginning. I think she is touched. Now, come," said Scrooge. "Show me no more. Conduct me home. Why do you delight to torture me?"

"One shadow more," exclaimed the ghost.

"No more," cried Scrooge. "No more! I don't wish to see it. Show me no more."

But the relentless ghost pinioned him in both his arms, and forced him to observe what happened next.

They were in another scene and place, a room, not very large or handsome, but full of comfort. Near to the winter fire sat a beautiful young woman with a babe in her arms.

"My sister, Fan," Scrooge observed.

The noise in this room was perfectly tumultuous, for there were more children there than Scrooge in his agitated state of mind could count, and, unlike the celebrated herd in the poem, they were not forty children conducting themselves like one, but every child was conducting itself like forty. The consequences were uproarious beyond belief, but no one seemed to care; on the contrary, the mother laughed heartily.

"Her nieces and nephews," Scrooge muttered. "Her husband had a large family. They were always having them to dine; so many mouths to feed!"

"She is ill, your sister," the ghost observed.

"After the birth of the boy. She was never well again. She died because of him, like my—"

"Like your mother?" the ghost questioned.

Scrooge gazed at his sister, who was still beautiful, but her face was pale, her eyes lacking some of the spark he had once known. "I intended to visit more often. She invited me, she and her husband, for Christmas and other such events, but I was busy. And they always had so many people in the house, so many children. I am not good with children."

A knocking at the door was heard, and such a rush immediately ensued that she with laughing face and plundered dress was borne toward the center of a flushed and boisterous group, just in time to greet Fan's husband, who came home attended by a man laden with Christmas toys and presents. Then the shouting and the struggling, and the onslaught that was made on the defenseless porter! The scaling of him with chairs for ladders to dive into his pockets, despoil him of brown-paper parcels, hold on tight by his cravat, hug him round his neck, pommel his back, and kick his legs in irrepressible affection. The shouts of wonder and delight with which the development of every package was received!

And now Scrooge looked on more attentively than ever, when the children were ushered out the door to their homes, and the master of the house took his infant son in his arms and sat down with Fan at his own fireside.

"Fan," said the husband, turning to his wife with a smile. "I have found another doctor who will see you. I am certain this one will make you stronger."

She smiled, leaning back in her chair to rest. "I am certain you are right, dear husband."

"He says those marks on your neck, he knows what they are."

"We know what they are, my love," she said softly.

Scrooge, standing beside the spirit, stiffened. "She has marks on her neck? Vampires? He let the vampires get to her?"

"I thought you did not believe in vampires," the spirit observed with more sarcasm than one might think such a figment of one's imagination should have. (And Scrooge was still not entirely certain that was not all that the Ghost of Christmas Past was.)

"Let us talk of something else, my love," Fan said, closing her eyes. "What did you do today? Who did you see?"

"Funny you should ask. I saw your brother," he said.

She opened her eyes, and Scrooge felt a strange tightness in his chest.

"Did you invite him to Christmas dinner? I sent a note, but it came back without reply again."

"I passed his office window, and as it was not shut up, and he had a candle inside, I could scarcely help seeing him. I tapped on the door and the window. I know that he saw me and recognized me, but he would not grant me admittance."

"Poor Ebenezer," she said, closing her eyes again.

"Yes, poor Ebenezer," agreed the husband. "Since he turned Belle away, he is quite alone in the world, I do believe."

"Spirit," said Scrooge in a broken voice, "remove me from this place."

"I told you these were shadows of the things that have been," said the ghost. "That they are what they are, do not blame me."

"They kill her, don't they? The vampires, they kill my sister, Fan. They killed my mother and then my sister."

"You did not even attend her bedside when her husband sent word that she was dying."

"Remove me," Scrooge exclaimed. "I cannot bear it."

He turned upon the ghost, and seeing that it looked upon him with a face, in which in some strange way there were fragments of all the faces it had shown him, wrestled with it.

"Leave me. Take me back. Haunt me no longer."

In the struggle, if that can be called a struggle in which the ghost with no visible resistance on its own part was undisturbed by any effort of its adversary, Scrooge observed that its light was burning high and bright, and dimly connecting that with its influence over him, he seized the extinguisher-cap, and by a sudden action pressed it down upon its head.

The spirit dropped beneath it, so that the extinguisher covered its whole form, but though Scrooge pressed it down with all his force, he could not hide the light, which streamed from under it, in an unbroken flood upon the ground.

He was conscious of being exhausted, and overcome by an irresistible drowsiness; and, further, of being in his own bedroom. He gave the cap a parting squeeze, in which his hand relaxed, and had barely time to reel to bed, before he sank into a heavy sleep.

STAVE 3

THE SECOND OF THE THREE
SPIRITS AND MORE VAMPIRES

❧ 24 ❧

Awaking in the middle of a prodigiously tough snore, and sitting up in bed to get his thoughts together, Scrooge had no occasion to be told that the bell was again upon the stroke of one. He felt that he was restored to consciousness in the nick of time, for the particular purpose of holding a conference with the second messenger dispatched to him through Belle's and Jacob Marley's ghost's intervention. But finding that he turned uncomfortably cold when he began to wonder which of his curtains this new specter would draw back, he put every one aside with his own hands, and lying down again, established a sharp look-out all round the bed. He decided he wished to challenge the spirit on the moment of its appearance, and did not wish to be taken by surprise, and made nervous.

Gentlemen of the free-and-easy sort who plume themselves on being acquainted with a move or two, and being usually equal to the time of day, express the wide range of their capacity for adventure by observing that they are good for anything from pitch-and-toss to manslaughter, between which opposite extremes, no doubt, there lies a tolerably wide and comprehensive range of subjects. Without venturing for Scrooge quite as hardily as this, I don't mind calling on you to believe that he was ready for a good broad field of strange appearances, and that nothing between a baby and a rhinoceros would have astonished him very much. Not after the vampires.

Scrooge still could barely believe the truth of what he had seen at the side of the previous spirit. All those past events Scrooge had watched with the Ghost of Christmas Past! Could they really have taken place as the ghost had shown him, rather than the way he had experienced them... or remembered them? The vampires at his birth, in the school, following him as he climbed the ladder of success... Could the vampires truly have been there all along, as the spirit suggested? Could they have manipulated his life as the ghost had demonstrated? Could Scrooge really have been right about so many things in his lifetime (at least in matters of business and investment) and yet so wrong about this? Or was what the ghost had shown him all untrue? Was this "visiting of spirits" some monstrous hoax perpetrated on him for who-knew-what reason? Perhaps a business rival thought to throw his ventures into chaos, or it might be that the quality of gruel at Mother Chow's cook shop had taken a turn for the worse and all this madness was the result of too much Thames water and sawdust stirred into the cook pot and passed on to unsuspecting customers.

It was a question so enormous to ponder that it made Scrooge's head ache to think of it.

Which brings the question to light, dear reader, as to whether or not the same vampires exist in our lives. Are they there as they were in Scrooge's life and we merely do not see them? What choices have you made, paths have you taken, not of your own free will, as you assumed, but due to control by the vampires? Are you—are our government leaders—merely puppets of scheming vampires seeking to control the human world? And taking into consideration the outlandish and costly boondoggles that our elected officials put into play in direct conflict with the wishes of those who put them into office and the manner in which perfectly sane-appearing individuals seem to lose all reason once they are in power, do vampires not seem the most logical answer? The idea makes my head ache, as well. But back to the story at hand.

Now, being prepared for almost anything there in his bed-chamber, Scrooge was not by any means prepared for nothing, and, consequently, when the bell struck one, and no shape appeared, he was taken with a violent fit of trembling. Five minutes, ten minutes, a quarter of an hour went by, yet nothing came. All this time, he lay upon his bed, the very core and center of a blaze of ruddy light, which streamed upon it when the clock proclaimed the hour, and which, being only light, was more alarming than a dozen ghosts, as he was powerless to make out what it meant, or would be at, and was sometimes apprehensive that he might be at that very moment an interesting case of spontaneous combustion, without having the consolation of knowing it. At last, however, he began to think—as you or I would have thought at first, for it is always the person not in the predicament who knows what ought to have been done in it, and would unquestionably have done it too—at last, I say, he began to think that the source and secret of this ghostly light might be in the adjoining room, from whence, on further tracing it, it seemed to shine. This idea taking full possession of his mind, he got up softly and shuffled in his slippers to the door.

The moment Scrooge's hand was on the doorknob, a strange voice called him by his name, and bade him enter. He obeyed.

It was his own parlor, the one where he had found his housekeeper, Gelda, and the boy lurking in the dark. There was no doubt it was his own place. But it had undergone a surprising transformation. The walls and ceiling were so hung with living green, that it looked a perfect grove, from every part of which, bright gleaming berries glistened. The crisp leaves of holly, mistletoe, and ivy reflected back the light, as if so many little mirrors had been scattered there; and such a mighty blaze went roaring up the chimney, as that dull petrifaction of a hearth had never known in Scrooge's time, or Marley's, or for many and many a winter season gone. Naturally, considering the cost of faggots or even the poorest grade of coal, what reasonable businessman would throw money into a fireplace merely for the purpose of heating a room when, if one had patience, summer would come, and the sun would give the same results? Nevertheless, what Scrooge saw he saw, and here, in his own parlor, a reckless squandering of hard-earned pounds and shillings went on before his eyes. Heaped up on the floor, to form a kind of throne, were turkeys, geese, game, poultry, brawn, great joints of meat, suckling pigs, long wreaths of sausages, mince pies, plum puddings, tubs of pickled eels, barrels of oysters, red-hot chestnuts, cherry-cheeked apples, juicy oranges, luscious pears, immense twelfth-cakes, and seething bowls of punch, that made the chamber dim with their delicious steam. In easy state upon this couch, there sat a jolly giant, glorious to see, who bore a glowing torch, in shape not unlike plenty's horn, and held it up, high up, to shed its light on Scrooge, as he came peeping round the door.

"Come in," exclaimed the ghost. "Come in, and know me better, man."

"Are you alone?" Scrooge dared.

"Alone?"

"No . . . vampires? It has been suggested to me by a previous visitor that vampires may reside in my own home."

"There are no vampires here at present time," the ghost said kindly. "Join me."

Scrooge entered timidly, and hung his head before this spirit. He was not the dogged Scrooge he had been, and though the spirit's eyes were clear and kind, he did not like to meet them.

"I am the Ghost of Christmas Present," said the spirit.

"Of course you are. I should have known." He glanced around. "You are certain you have not let any vampires into my parlor?" The hairs on the back of his neck prickled as if by chill, although the artificial heat of the parlor due to the excess of fire should have prevented that same sensation.

"I am certain. Now look upon me."

Scrooge reverently did so. It was clothed in one simple green robe, or mantle, bordered with white fur. This garment hung so loosely on the figure, that its capacious breast was bare, as if disdaining to be warded or concealed by any artifice. Its feet, observable beneath the ample folds of the garment, were also bare, and on its head it wore no other covering than a holly wreath, set here and there with shining icicles. Its dark brown curls were long and free. They were as free as its genial face, its sparkling eye, its open hand, its cheery voice, its unconstrained demeanor, and its joyful air. Girded round its middle was an antique scabbard, but no sword was in it, but rather a long, vicious-looking pike.

"What is that for?" Scrooge asked suspiciously. He had seen such similar weapons in the corners of shops and offices, set amongst umbrellas and walking sticks. When he had inquired to the owners of the pikes what purpose they served, he had always gotten queer looks and quick answers that had never made great sense: to chase away stray dogs, to support the clothes-line on wash day, to brace up a leaning May Pole, to fish stray buckets from the well.

The spirit glanced at the pike he carried. "It is a symbol of what we all battle."

"Stray dogs and wayward buckets?"

The spirit chuckled, but did not answer the question. Instead, he pursued his own agenda. "You have never seen the like of me before?"

"Never," Scrooge made answer to it.

"Have never walked forth with the younger members of my

family, meaning (for I am very young) my elder brothers born in these later years?" pursued the phantom.

"Are they in any way related to the vampires?" Scrooge asked suspiciously.

"They are not."

"Then I don't think I have," said Scrooge. "I am afraid I have not. Have you had many brothers, Spirit?"

"More than eighteen hundred," said the ghost.

"A tremendous family to provide for," muttered Scrooge.

The Ghost of Christmas Present rose.

"Spirit," said Scrooge submissively, "conduct me where you will. I went forth last night on compulsion, and I learned a lesson, which is working now. Tonight, if you have aught to teach me, let me profit by it. My only request is that we avoid the vampires . . . if at all possible. If, that is, they truly exist."

"Oh, they exist." His eyes twinkled. "Touch my robe."

Scrooge did as he was told, and held it fast.

Holly, mistletoe, red berries, ivy, turkeys, geese, game, poultry, brawn, meat, pigs, sausages, oysters, pies, puddings, fruit, and punch, all vanished instantly. So did the room, the fire, the ruddy glow, the hour of night, and they stood in the city streets on Christmas morning, where (for the weather was severe) the people made a rough, but brisk and not unpleasant kind of music, in scraping the snow from the pavement in front of their dwellings, and from the tops of their houses, whence it was mad delight to the boys to see it come plumping down into the road below, and splitting into artificial little snow-storms.

The house fronts looked black enough, and the windows blacker, contrasting with the smooth white sheet of snow upon the roofs, and with the dirtier snow upon the ground, which last deposit had been plowed up in deep furrows by the heavy wheels of carts and wagons. There were furrows that crossed and recrossed each other hundreds of times where the great streets branched off, and made intricate channels, hard to trace in the thick yellow mud and icy water. The sky was gloomy, and the shortest streets were choked up with a dingy mist, half-thawed, half-frozen, whose heavier particles descended in shower of sooty atoms, as if all the chimneys in Great Britain had, by one consent, caught fire, and were blazing away to their dear hearts' content. There was nothing very cheerful in the climate or the town, and yet was there an air of cheerfulness abroad that the clearest summer air and brightest summer sun might have endeavored to diffuse in vain.

For the people who were shoveling away on the housetops were jovial and full of glee; calling out to one another from the parapets, and now and then exchanging a facetious snowball—better-natured missile far than many a wordy jest—laughing heartily if it went right and not less heartily if it went wrong. The poulterers' shops were still half-open, and the fruiterers' were radiant in their glory. There were great, round, pot-bellied baskets of chestnuts, shaped like the waistcoats of jolly old gentlemen, lolling at the doors, and tumbling out into the street in their apoplectic opulence. There were ruddy, brown-faced, broad-girthed Spanish onions, winking from their shelves in wanton slyness at the girls as they went by, and glanced demurely at the hung-up mistletoe. There were pears and apples, clustered high in blooming pyramids; there were bunches of grapes, made, in the shopkeepers' benevolence, to dangle from conspicuous hooks, that people's mouths might water *gratis* as they passed. There were piles of filberts, mossy and brown, recalling, in their fragrance, ancient walks among the woods, and pleasant shuffling, ankle-deep, through withered leaves; there were Norfolk Biffins, squab and swarthy, setting off the yellow of the oranges and lemons, and, in the great compactness of their juicy persons, urgently entreating and beseeching to be carried home in paper bags and eaten after dinner. The very gold and silver fish, set forth among these choice fruits in a bowl, though members of a dull and stagnant-blooded race, appeared to know that there was something going on, and, to a fish, went gasping round and round their little world in slow and passionless excitement.

The grocers', oh the grocers'! Nearly closed, with perhaps two shutters down, or one, but through those gaps such glimpses! It was not alone that the scales descending on the counter made a merry sound, or that the twine and roller parted company so briskly, or that the canisters were rattled up and down like juggling tricks, or even that the blended scents of tea and coffee and nutmeg and ginger were so grateful to the nose, or even that the raisins were so plentiful and rare, the almonds so extremely white, the sticks of cinnamon so long and straight, the other spices so delicious, the candied fruits so caked and spotted with molten sugar as to make the coldest lookers-on feel faint and subsequently bilious. Nor was it that the figs were moist and pulpy, or that the French plums blushed in modest tartness from their highly decorated boxes, or that everything was good to eat and in its Christmas dress, but the customers were all so hurried and so eager in the hopeful promise of the day, that they tumbled up against each other at the door, crashing their wicker baskets wildly, and left their purchases upon the counter, and came running back to fetch them, and committed hundreds of the like mistakes, in the best humor possible; while the grocer and his people were so frank and fresh that the polished hearts with which they fastened their aprons behind might have been their own, worn outside for general inspection, and for Christmas jackdaws to peck at if they chose.

But soon the steeples called good people all, to church and chapel, and away they came, flocking through the streets in their best clothes, and with their gayest faces. And at the same time there emerged from scores of bye-streets, lanes, and nameless turnings, innumerable people, carrying their dinners to the bakers' shops. The sight of these poor revelers appeared to interest the spirit very much, for he stood with Scrooge beside him in a baker's doorway, and taking off the covers as their bearers passed, sprinkled incense on their dinners from his torch. And it was a very uncommon kind of torch, for once or twice when there were angry words between some dinner-carriers who had jostled each other, he shed a few drops of water on them from it, and their good humor was restored directly. For they said, it was a shame to quarrel upon Christmas Day. And so it was. God love it, so it was.

In time the bells ceased, and the bakers were shut up, and yet there was a genial shadowing forth of all these dinners and the progress of their cooking, in the thawed blotch of wet above each baker's oven, where the pavement smoked as if its stones were cooking, too.

"We saw no vampires," Scrooge remarked. "If this is present day and vampires are roaming the streets of London, surely we should have—"

"It is daylight. They are below ground until darkness falls."

"Below ground?"

"In their tunnels. Dug under the city an entirely other city. There are entrances everywhere. There is one in your cellar."

"My cellar?" murmured Scrooge. "Upon my word! In my cellar? I do not believe you."

"Look yourself one day," said the spirit. "If you dare."

Scrooge gave a little shiver, cleared his throat, and searched for a safer topic of conversation. The thought that vampires might have slept beneath his own floors, beneath his own bed-chamber, vampires with their bloodstained fingers and foul breath caused by a singular diet and less than sanitary hygiene customs, was one that he did not wish to dwell on. "Is there a peculiar flavor in what you sprinkle from your torch?"

"There is. My own."

"Would it apply to any kind of dinner on this day?" asked Scrooge.

"To any kindly given. To a poor one most. Or to one who

has given refuge or aid to those who battle the vampires. Often they are one and the same."

"Why to a poor one most?" asked Scrooge.

"Because it needs it most."

"Spirit," said Scrooge, after a moment's thought, "I wonder you, of all the beings in the many worlds about us, should desire to cramp these people's opportunities of innocent enjoyment."

"I," cried the spirit.

"You would deprive them of their means of dining every seventh day, often the only day on which they can be said to dine at all," said Scrooge. "Wouldn't you."

"I," cried the spirit.

"You seek to close these places on the Seventh Day," said Scrooge. "And it comes to the same thing."

"I seek?" exclaimed the spirit.

"Forgive me if I am wrong. It has been done in your name, or at least in that of your family," said Scrooge.

"There are some upon this earth of yours," returned the spirit, "who lay claim to know us, and who do their deeds of passion, pride, ill-will, hatred, envy, bigotry, and selfishness in our name, who are as strange to us and all our kith and kin, as if they had never lived. Remember that, and charge their doings on themselves, not us."

Scrooge promised that he would, and they went on, invisible, as they had been before, into the suburbs of the town. It was a remarkable quality of the ghost (which Scrooge had observed at the baker's), that notwithstanding his gigantic size, he could accommodate himself to any place with ease and that he stood beneath a low roof quite as gracefully and like a supernatural creature, as it was possible he could have done in any lofty hall.

And perhaps it was the pleasure the good spirit had in showing off this power of his, or else it was his own kind, generous, hearty nature, and his sympathy with all poor men, that led him straight to Scrooge's clerk's hovel, for there he went, and took Scrooge with him, holding to his robe, and on the threshold of the door the spirit smiled, and stopped to bless Bob Cratchit's dwelling with the sprinkling of his torch. Think of that. Bob had but fifteen bob a week himself he pocketed on Saturdays, but fifteen copies of his Christian name, and yet the Ghost of Christmas Present blessed his four-roomed house.

Then up rose a woman, dressed out, but poorly, in a twice-turned gown, but brave in ribbons, which are cheap and make a goodly show for sixpence which might deceive the casual eye. She laid a cloth upon their rickety table.

"Mrs. Cratchit?" asked Scrooge. "Bob Cratchit's wife? I have not had the . . . *pleasure*, of making her acquaintance."

"That is not Mrs. Cratchit. It is her sister Maena, a childless widow, who lives here and cares for the Cratchit children since their mother's death three years ago."

"Cratchit's wife died three years ago?" Scrooge looked at the ghost, genuinely startled. "I do not recall that event. He must not have spoken of it."

"He asked to take a day's leave from your employment to bury her. You denied him his request."

"Did I?" Scrooge could not, for the life of him, recall the incident. Surely, Cratchit had not explained the severity of his situation, for what employer, no matter how shrewd in the ways of business, could not see his way through to permit at least a half-day's leave, without pay, of course, for a clerk to bury his poor, dead wife? Scrooge considered questioning the ghost further, certain the phantom had his information incorrect (for surely even spirits cannot be right all the time), but the look on the ghost's face suggested that line of questioning might not be pleasing to him. Instead, he chose a different topic.

"What did she die of? Childbirth?" Scrooge chuckled at his own small jest as he looked down on the many Cratchit children spilling into the tiny room that served as kitchen, parlor, and bedchamber to some of the children as well, apparently. There seemed to be dozens of them; perhaps twenty or more, much alike in appearance, and all bearing the same pitiful appearance of their father.

"She was killed by vampires while coming home from the grocer one evening when Mr. Cratchit was working later than usual." The spirit eyed him, the look upon his face clearly accusatory. "Two of the girl children barely escaped. It was only Mrs. Cratchit's brave struggle that gave the wee ones time to run away and saved them."

"Surely you don't think me responsible for her death? Killed by vampires, indeed. Is Cratchit certain she didn't just run off to find a better life than this miserable one?" And who could blame her, he thought. Bedlam must be calm compared to the Cratchit household of a Monday morning. He could not even fathom what the cost in porridge must run his clerk to feed so many hungry mouths.

"She was not dead upon the attack. Cratchit brought her home to die in this very room. She bled to death . . . much as I believe your mother did."

Scrooge looked at the spirit, hesitated, and then turned to take in the scene in the Cratchit kitchen as it unfolded.

Belinda, the second of Cratchit's daughters, also brave in ribbons, gave her aunt assistance, while Master Peter Cratchit plunged a fork into the pitifully small saucepan of potatoes, considering the multitude that would assault the table, and getting the corners of his monstrous shirt collar (Cratchit's private property, conferred upon his son and heir in honor of the day) into his mouth, rejoiced to find himself so gallantly attired, and yearned to show his linen in the fashionable parks. And now two smaller Cratchits, boy and girl, came tearing in, screaming that outside the baker's they had smelt the goose, and known it for their own, and basking in luxurious thoughts of sage and onion, these young Cratchits danced about the table, and exalted Master Peter Cratchit to the skies, while he (not proud, although his collars nearly choked him) blew the fire, until the slow potatoes bubbling up, knocked loudly at the saucepan lid to be let out and peeled.

"What has ever got into your father then?" said the sister-in-law to Cratchit. "And your brother, Tiny Tim? That they should not be home by now on this day of all days?"

"Mayhap he stopped at the VSU meeting on the way home from church," Belinda suggested.

"A waste of time, foolery," said Maena. "What with us all here waiting on him. What difference does it make, these meetings, the patrols? It didn't save my dear sister's life, did it? They cannot eradicate them." She smoothed the wrinkled tablecloth. "We'd be better off to try to reconcile with them. Get along. It's what the good Lord taught us, is it not?"

"She has a point," Scrooge observed, crossing his arms over his chest. "If there are vampires out there—which I am not utterly convinced of—perhaps we should all try to make peace. My tenant, Mr. Wahltraud, is an excellent businessman. Perhaps—"

"Enough," the spirit interrupted. "You are here to learn, not to give advice."

Peter looked at Belinda, and the two laughed. "Get along with the vampires, Aunt Maena? Surely you do not mean that?" Peter exclaimed. "I am no Bible scholar, but I do not believe the good Lord ever suggested we should *get along* with the vampires that threaten our lives."

"I am only a woman. I know nothing of politics," said Maena with a sweep of her little hand. "I mind my business, as should you, Belinda. And you, Peter, should be thinking on how you can bring more coin to the table." She glanced around. "Martha wasn't as late last Christmas Day as this, was she?"

"Here's Martha, Aunt Maena," said a girl, appearing as she spoke.

"Here's our Martha, Aunt Maena," cried two young Cratchits. "Hurrah. There's such a goose, Martha."

"Why, bless your heart alive, my dear, how late you are," said the girl's aunt, kissing her a dozen times, and taking off her shawl and bonnet for her with officious zeal. "Surely you were not at a vampire slayers meeting, which made you late?"

"Oh, no. I attended earlier in the week." She offered a mischievous smile to her brother and sister.

Apparently this was an ongoing game between the children and their aunt. Disrespectful, in Scrooge's eyes. And uncalled for. If the girl had time to attend *meetings* of any sort, she had time to work more hours and contribute further to the family, did she not? She seemed a healthy girl, if a bit thin and bony, but as his father had always said, a rangy hound covers the most miles. Fat dogs and fat servants cost more to maintain, worked slower, and fatigued sooner.

"We'd a deal of work to finish up last night at the home of my employment," replied the girl, "and had to clear away this morning."

"Well, never mind so long as you are home," said the aunt. "Sit ye down before the fire, my dear, and have a warm cup of water, Lord bless ye."

"No, no. There's Father coming," cried the two young Cratchits, who were everywhere at once. "Hide, Martha, hide."

So Martha hid herself, and in came Bob, the father, with at least three feet of comforter exclusive of the fringe hanging down before him, and his threadbare clothes darned up and brushed to look seasonable, and Tiny Tim upon his shoulder. Alas for Tiny Tim, he bore a little crutch, and had his twisted limbs supported by an iron frame.

"Why, where's our Martha?" cried Bob Cratchit, looking

round. "I thought she would be here by now. I had hoped she might stop by the VSU meeting. There were many who asked for her, but alas, we did not see her."

"She is not coming," said Maena.

"Not coming?" said Bob, with a sudden declension in his high spirits, for he had been Tim's blood horse all the way from church, and had come home rampant. "Not coming upon Christmas Day? Please tell me she is well. And that nothing bad has befallen her." He paled considerably, obviously fearing she had met the same fate as his wife.

Martha didn't like to see him frightened, if it were only in jest, so she came out prematurely from behind the closet door, and ran into his arms. At the same time, the two young Cratchits hustled Tiny Tim, and bore him off into the wash-house that he might hear the pudding singing in the copper.

"And how did little Tim behave?" asked the sister-in-law, when she had rallied Bob on his credulity, and Bob had hugged his daughter to his heart's content.

"As good as gold," said Bob, "and better. Somehow, he gets thoughtful, sitting by himself so much, and thinks the strangest things you ever heard. He told me, coming home, that he hoped the people saw him in the church, because he was a cripple, and it might be pleasant to them to remember upon Christmas Day, who made lame beggars walk, and blind men see. He talked long and hard of the future and what it will bring him, what it will bring all of us." Bob chuckled. "He has it in his head that he will regain his strength one day and become a fine vampire slayer. The best there is."

"Like his father," said Martha, giving him another hug.

"No." He chuckled again, this time self-consciously. "I make do as necessary with my pike, but Tim dreams of being truly gifted. He imagines giving aid to the Scion of the Great Culling, who he believes will be born soon. He thinks he will stand at the Scion's side one day and see the eradication of these devils from the earth once and for all."

" 'Tis a good dream," said Martha. "An honorable one."

" 'Tis a bunch of nonsense," argued Maena. She lowered her voice. "And the two of you should not encourage him. None of you should." She pointed. "He is unwell. A cripple. He will be lucky if he survives another winter, and we all know it. We should not be filling his head with such impossibilities, not with him so soon bound for the grave."

"But he has a good heart," said Bob. "Greater than most." His voice was tremulous when he told them this, and trembled more when he said that Tiny Tim was growing strong and hearty.

Tiny Tim's active little crutch was heard upon the floor, and back he came before another word was spoken. He was escorted by his brother and sister to his stool before the fire and while Bob, turning up his cuffs—as if, poor fellow, they were capable of being made more shabby—compounded some hot mixture in a jug with gin and lemons, and stirred it round and round and put it on the hob to simmer. Master Peter, and the two ubiquitous young Cratchits went to fetch the goose, with which they soon returned in high procession.

Such a bustle ensued that you might have thought a goose the rarest of all birds, a feathered phenomenon, to which a black swan was a matter of course—and in truth it was something very like it in that house. Maena made the gravy (ready beforehand in a little saucepan) hissing hot; Master Peter mashed the potatoes with incredible vigor. Miss Belinda sweetened up the applesauce and Martha dusted the hot plates while Bob took Tiny Tim beside him in a tiny corner at the table. The two young Cratchits set chairs for everybody, and mounting guard upon their posts, crammed spoons into their mouths, lest they should shriek for goose before their turn came to be helped. At last the dishes were set on, and grace was said. It was succeeded by a breathless pause, as Maena, looking slowly all along the carving-knife, prepared to plunge it in the breast, but when she did, and when the long-expected gush of stuffing issued forth, one murmur of delight arose all round the board, and even Tiny Tim, excited by the two young Cratchits, beat on the table with the handle of his knife, and feebly cried "Hurrah."

There never was such a goose. Bob said he didn't believe there ever was such a goose cooked. Its tenderness and flavor, size and cheapness, were the themes of universal admiration. Eked out by applesauce and mashed potatoes, it was a sufficient dinner for the whole family; indeed, as Maena said with great delight (surveying one small atom of a bone upon the dish), they hadn't eaten it all at last. Yet every one had had enough, and the youngest Cratchits in particular, were steeped in sage and onion to the eyebrows. But now, the plates being changed by Miss Belinda, Maena left the room alone—too nervous to bear witnesses—to take the pudding up and bring it in.

Suppose it should not be done enough? Suppose it should break in turning out? Suppose somebody should have got over the wall of the back-yard, and stolen it, while they were merry with the goose—a supposition at which the two young Cratchits became livid. All sorts of horrors were supposed.

Hallo. A great deal of steam. The pudding was out of the copper. A smell like a washing-day. That was the cloth. A smell like an eating-house and a pastry cook's next door to each other, with a laundress's next door to that. That was the pudding. In half a minute Cratchit's sister-in-law entered, flushed, but smiling proudly, with the pudding, like a speckled cannon-ball, so hard and firm, blazing in half of half-a-quarter of ignited brandy, and bedight with Christmas holly stuck into the top.

"Oh, a wonderful pudding, Maena!" Bob Cratchit said, and

calmly too, that he regarded it as the greatest success achieved by his sister-in-law. "We are so fortunate to have had you come to join our family after my dear Mrs. Cratchit's death."

"My duty," murmured Maena, turning red-faced as she took her seat again. Now the weight was off her mind, she would confess she had had her doubts about the quantity of flour. Everybody had something to say about it, but nobody said or thought it was at all a small pudding for a large family. It would have been flat heresy to do so. Any Cratchit would have blushed to hint at such a thing.

❧ 26 ❧

At last the dinner was all done, the tablecloth was cleared, the hearth swept, and the fire made up. The compound in the jug being tasted, and considered perfect, apples and oranges were put upon the table, and a shovel-full of chestnuts on the fire. Then, all the Cratchit family drew round the hearth, in what Bob Cratchit called a circle, meaning half of one, and at Bob Cratchit's elbow stood the family display of glass. There were two tumblers, and a custard-cup without a handle.

"That's it?" asked Scrooge watching the pitiful little gathering. "Three glasses for the lot of them? How will they all drink from three cups?"

The spirit continued to gaze at the family gathered around the fire.

The meager cups held the hot stuff from the jug as well as golden goblets would have done, and Bob served it out with beaming looks, while the chestnuts on the fire sputtered and cracked noisily. It appeared they would *share* the cups. Then Bob proposed:

"A merry Christmas to us all, my dears. God bless us."

Which all the family re-echoed.

"God bless us, every one," said Tiny Tim, the last of all. He sat very close to his father's side upon his little stool.

Bob held his withered little hand in his, as if he loved the child, and wished to keep him by his side, and dreaded that he might be taken from him.

"Spirit," said Scrooge, with an interest he had never felt before, "talk of becoming a great vampire killer is obviously nonsense as the sister-in-law pointed out, but tell me if Tiny Tim will live. You know, to be a clerk or something equally useful like his father."

"I see a vacant seat," replied the ghost, "in the poor chimney-corner, and a crutch without an owner, carefully preserved. If these shadows remain unaltered by the future, the child will die as the aunt has suggested."

"No, no," said Scrooge. "Oh, no, kind spirit. Say he will be spared."

"If these shadows remain unaltered by the future, none other of my race," returned the ghost, "will find him here. What then? If he be like to die, he had better do it, and decrease the surplus population."

Scrooge hung his head to hear his own words quoted by the spirit, and was overcome with penitence and grief.

"Man," said the ghost, "if man you be in heart, not adamant, forbear that wicked cant until you have discovered what the surplus is, and where it is. Will you decide what men shall live, what men shall die while men and women such as Cratchit and his daughter, and the woman, Belle, are on the streets fighting to save mankind against what you conspire with?"

Scrooge shook under the intensity of the ghost's admonishment. "I do not conspire with the vampires! They . . . they have persecuted me!" He was shaking from head to toe. "The . . . the visitor previous to you, he showed me what they did. How they conspired against me! I . . . I had no choice!"

"Oh, you have had choices," boomed the ghost. "Far more than you have deserved, and yet you have chosen against your own kind again and again in favor of that golden idol the young woman spoke of so many years ago. You had choices, and for that reason, it may be, that in the sight of heaven, you are more worthless and less fit to live than millions like this poor man's child. Oh God, to hear the insect on the leaf pronouncing on the too much life among his hungry brothers in the dust."

Scrooge bent before the ghost's rebuke, and, trembling, cast his eyes upon the ground, tears in his eyes. But he raised them speedily, on hearing his own name.

"Mr. Scrooge," said Bob. "I give you Mr. Scrooge, the founder of the feast."

"The founder of the feast indeed," cried Martha, reddening. "I wish I had him here. I'd give him a piece of my mind to feast upon, and I hope he'd have a good appetite for it!"

"My dear daughter," said Bob. "The children. Christmas Day."

"It should be Christmas Day, I am sure," said she, "on which one drinks the health of such an odious, stingy, hard, unfeeling man as Mr. Scrooge. You know he is, Father. Nobody knows it better than you do, poor fellow."

"My dear," was Bob's mild answer. "Christmas Day."

"I'll drink his health for your sake and the day's," said his eldest daughter. "Not for his. Long life to him. May he not see the shadows when they swarm him in the end. A merry Christmas and a happy new year. He'll be very merry and very happy, I have no doubt."

"The shadows? Swarming me?" Scrooge turned to the ghost. "Whatever is she talking about?"

The spirit watched on, making no comment.

The children drank the toast after Martha. It was the first of their proceedings, which had no heartiness. Tiny Tim drank it last of all, but he didn't care twopence for it. Scrooge was the ogre of the family. The mention of his name cast a dark shadow on the party, which was not dispelled for a full five minutes.

After it had passed away, they were ten times merrier than before, from the mere relief of Scrooge the baleful being done with. They toasted to various people they knew, including the woman Scrooge had once been betrothed to.

"To Belle," Martha declared. "If only I can one day fight the vampires as she fights them, caring for those who risk their lives to protect us."

"To Belle," the children echoed enthusiastically, all having something good to say about her for, apparently, they all knew her well.

Bob Cratchit then told his family how he had a situation in his eye for Master Peter, which would bring in, if obtained, full five-and-sixpence weekly. The two young Cratchits laughed tremendously at the idea of Peter being a man of business, and Peter himself looked thoughtfully at the fire from between his collars, as if he were deliberating what particular investments he should favor when he came into the receipt of that bewildering income. Martha, who was a poor apprentice at a milliner's, then told them what kind of work she had to do, and how many hours she worked at a stretch, and how she meant to lie abed tomorrow morning for a good long rest, the next day being a holiday she passed at home. She told them how she had seen a countess and a lord some days before, and how the lord was as tall as Peter, at which Peter pulled up his collars so high that you couldn't have seen his head if you had been there.

All this time the chestnuts and the jug went round and round, and by-and-by they had a song, about a lost child traveling in the snow, from Tiny Tim, who had a plaintive little voice, and sang it very well indeed.

There was nothing of high mark in this. They were not a handsome family; they were not well dressed. Their shoes were far from being waterproof, their clothes were scanty, and Peter might have known, and very likely did, the inside of a pawn-broker's. But, they were happy, grateful, pleased with one another, and contented with the time. When they faded, and looked happier yet in the bright sprinklings of the spirit's torch at parting, Scrooge had his eye upon them, and especially on Tiny Tim, until the last.

✁ 27 ✁

By this time it was getting dark, and snowing pretty heavily, and as Scrooge and the spirit went along the streets, the brightness of the roaring fires in kitchens, parlors, and all sorts of rooms, was wonderful. Here, the flickering of the blaze showed preparations for a cozy dinner, with hot plates baking through and through before the fire, and deep red curtains, ready to be drawn to shut out cold and darkness. There all the children of the house were running out into the snow to meet their married sisters, brothers, cousins, uncles, aunts, and be the first to greet them. Here, again, were shadows on the window-blind of guests assembling. There a group of handsome girls, all hooded and fur-booted, and all chattering at once, tripped lightly off to some near neighbor's house, where, woe upon the single man who saw them enter—artful witches, well they knew it—in a glow.

But, if you had judged from the numbers of people on their way to friendly gatherings, you might have thought that no one was at home to give them welcome when they got there, instead of every house expecting company, and piling up its fires half-chimney high. Blessings on it, how the ghost exulted! How it bared its breadth of breast, and opened its capacious palm, and floated on, outpouring, with a generous hand, its bright and harmless mirth on everything within its reach. The very lamplighter, who ran on before, dotting the dusky street with specks of light, and who was dressed to spend the evening somewhere, laughed out loudly as the spirit passed, though little kenned the lamplighter that he had any company but Christmas.

Seeing the lamplighter, Scrooge thought back on the conversation he'd had the day before with the gentlemen seeking donations. They said a lamplighter had been murdered by the vampires and could not help wondering how his family fared today. Doubtless there would be little celebration of Christmas in that household, for deprived of a father and husband and breadwinner, the case would be so dire as to threaten the workhouse for the widow and children, down to the smallest babe in swaddling clothes.

Without a word of warning from the ghost, they stood upon a bleak and desert moor, where monstrous masses of rude stone were cast about, as though it were the burial place of giants, and water spread itself where so ever it listed, or would have done so, but for the frost that held it prisoner, and nothing grew but moss and furze, and coarse rank grass. Down in the west the setting sun had left a streak of fiery red, which glared upon the desolation for an instant, like a sullen eye, and frowning lower, lower, lower yet, was lost in the thick gloom of darkest night.

"What place is this?" asked Scrooge.

"A place where miners who labor in the bowels of the earth live," returned the spirit. "But they know me. See."

A light shone from the window of a hut, and swiftly they advanced toward it. Passing through the wall of mud and stone, they found a cheerful company assembled round a glowing fire. An old, old man and woman, with their children and their children's children, and another generation beyond that, all decked out gaily in their holiday attire. The old man, in a voice that seldom rose above the howling of the wind upon the barren waste, was singing them a Christmas song—it had been a very old song when he was a boy—and from time to time they all joined in the chorus. So surely as they raised their voices, the old man got quite blithe and loud, and so surely as they stopped, his vigor sank again.

Outside, near the window, Scrooge spotted the silhouette of a man in a dark cloak, peering inside. It was not until the feeble light from inside reflected off the man's pale face that Scrooge saw his glistening fangs.

"A vampire," Scrooge whispered, for no matter how he tried to reason with reason itself, he could no longer argue that they did not exist. "Will it kill one of them?"

"I cannot say. It will try, certainly; the beast has a hungry air about him. The family has lost two of their young men this year, this family," said the ghost. "And they still rejoice in the day, despite the dangers lurking at their very door, or rather, in this case, window."

"Mining is dangerous," Scrooge remarked. "But that is why it pays well. They know the risks."

The spirit glanced down at Scrooge. "They did not lose their men to the mines, but to the vampires. Look at it watching them, drool leaking from the corners of its twisted mouth. The vampires grow bolder with each passing year. They have been seen down in the mines. In fact, it is thought they like the hunting ground, for it is always dark below, and as you know, they cannot abide the light of the sun."

"I don't know why you tell me these things." Scrooge folded his arms over his chest. "What can I do? If my tenant is a vampire, do you suggest I go down, tap upon his door, and request that he cease feeding on the miners? He is liable to gobble me whole."

"He will not feed upon you. Not now. The queen has too much invested in you."

"I do not care for the way you say that," Scrooge muttered, unable to meet the ghost's gaze this time. "It bodes evil for me, and haven't I had enough struggles in my life that I should throw myself into the fray between men and beasts at my age?" He caught his breath. "Have we further stops, or are we bound for my bedchamber at last?"

The spirit did not tarry here, but bade Scrooge hold his robe, and passing on above the moor, sped—whither? Not to sea? To sea. To Scrooge's horror, looking back, he saw the last of the land, a frightful range of rocks, behind them, and his ears were deafened by the thundering of water, as it rolled and roared and raged among the dreadful caverns it had worn, and fiercely tried to undermine the earth.

Built upon a dismal reef of sunken rocks, some league or so from shore, on which the waters chafed and dashed, the wild year through, there stood a solitary lighthouse. Great heaps of seaweed clung to its base, and storm-birds—born of the wind one might suppose, as seaweed of the water—rose and fell about it, like the waves they skimmed.

But even here, two men who watched the light had made a fire, that through the loophole in the thick stone wall shed out a ray of brightness on the awful sea. Joining their horny hands over the rough table at which they sat, they wished each other merry Christmas in their can of grog. One of them, the elder, with his face all damaged and scarred with hard weather, as the figure-head of an old ship might be, struck up a sturdy song that was like a gale in itself.

"Hmmm," Scrooge said. "Safe enough there from vampires, I should guess."

"But vampires are not the only threat," said the spirit.

"Indeed?"

"The true threat is the inhumanity that settles upon men, men like yourself who could make a difference. Men who could fight for what is good and fair."

Scrooge frowned, but said nothing.

❧ 29 ❧

Again the ghost sped on, above the black and heaving sea—on, on—until, being far away, as he told Scrooge, from any shore, they lighted on a ship. They stood beside the helmsman at the wheel, the look-out in the bow, the officers who had the watch. They were dark, ghostly figures in their several stations, but every man among them hummed a Christmas tune, or had a Christmas thought, or spoke below his breath to his companion of some bygone Christmas Day, with homeward hopes belonging to it. And every man on board, waking or sleeping, good or bad, had had a kinder word for another on that day than on any day in the year. Each one had shared to some extent in its festivities and had remembered those he cared for at a distance, and had known that they delighted to remember him.

It was a great surprise to Scrooge, while listening to the moaning of the wind, and thinking what a solemn thing it was to move on through the lonely darkness over an unknown abyss, the threat of annihilation by vampires a possible reality. Suddenly the darkness seemed even more foreboding, for within its depths were secrets as profound as death. It was a great surprise to Scrooge, while thus engaged, to hear a hearty laugh. It was a much greater surprise to Scrooge to recognize it as his own nephew's and to find himself in a bright, dry, gleaming room, with the spirit standing smiling by his side, and looking at that same nephew with approving affability.

Scrooge was at once taken in by how pretty the room was, with simple paintings and minimal furniture, a grand fire blazing in the fireplace. But it was the Christmas tree that made the room, why, *the people* within, glow.

The tree was planted in the middle of a great round table on the far side of the room between windows that overlooked the street. The tree towered high above the heads of those inside the parlor and those who gazed at it from outside as they passed by. It was brilliantly lighted by a multitude of little tapers, and everywhere sparkled and glittered with bright objects. There were rosy-cheeked dolls hiding behind the green leaves, and there were real watches (with movable hands, at least, and an endless capacity of being wound up) dangling from innumerable twigs. There were French-polished tables, chairs, bedsteads, wardrobes, eight-day clocks, and various other articles of domestic furniture, wonderfully made in tin, perched among the boughs, as if in preparation for some fairy housekeeping. There were jolly, broad-faced little men, much more agreeable in appearance than many real men—and no wonder, for their heads took off, and showed them to be full of sugar-plums. There were fiddles and drums, tambourines, books, work-boxes, paint-boxes, sweetmeat-boxes, peep-show boxes, and all kinds of boxes. There were trinkets for the elder girls, far brighter than any grown-up gold and jewels, baskets and pincushions in all devices. There were guns, swords, and banners. There were witches standing in enchanted rings of pasteboard, to tell fortunes, humming tops, needle-cases, pen-wipers, smelling-bottles, conversation cards, bouquet holders. There was real fruit, made artificially dazzling with gold leaf: imitation apples, pears, and walnuts, crammed with surprises. There was everything, and more.

"What in heavens," Scrooge managed. "How could my nephew afford all those trappings? What will he do with them all? Preposterous. A waste!" he declared.

"All bah humbug?" questioned the spirit.

"My thought exactly," agreed Scrooge. "Such a waste of money for such a poor man."

"Ha, ha," laughed Scrooge's nephew, Fred. "Ha, ha, ha."

If you should happen, by any unlikely chance, to know a man more blest in a laugh than Scrooge's nephew, all I can say is, I should like to know him too. Introduce him to me, and I'll cultivate his acquaintance.

It is a fair, even-handed, noble adjustment of things, that while there is infection in disease and sorrow, there is nothing in the world so irresistibly contagious as laughter and good humor. When Scrooge's nephew laughed in this way, holding his sides, rolling his head, and twisting his face into the most extravagant contortions, Scrooge's niece, by marriage, Fred's wife, laughed as heartily as he. And their assembled friends being not a bit behindhand, roared out lustily.

"Ha, ha. Ha, ha, ha, ha."

"Have they taken leave of their senses?" Scrooge questioned the spirit.

"I think not," the Ghost of Christmas Present responded.

"He said that Christmas was a humbug, as I live," cried Scrooge's nephew. "He believed it, too."

"More shame for him, Fred," said Scrooge's niece, Penny, indignantly. "I hope he can say the same one day when he comes nose to nose with the vampire that will suck him dry and leave him on a doorstep, to be used as a doormat."

She was very pretty, exceedingly pretty. With a dimpled, surprised-looking, capital face, a ripe little mouth, that seemed made to be kissed—as no doubt it was. She had all kinds of good little dots about her chin, that melted into one another when she laughed, and the sunniest pair of eyes you ever saw in any little creature's head. Altogether she was what you would have called provoking, you know, but satisfactory, had the girl an adequate training in housewifery and some measure of sense.

Penny reminded Scrooge of Belle in her younger years.

"My love, not on Christmas Day," Fred admonished gently. "He's a comical old fellow," he continued. "That's the truth, and not so pleasant as he might be. However, his offenses carry their own punishment, and I have nothing to say against him."

"I'm sure he is very rich, Fred," hinted one of the female guests. "At least Charles always tells me so." She patted the arm of a young man seated beside her on the settee.

"Rich, indeed," agreed Charles. His hair and whiskers were blacker and thicker, looked at so near, than even I had given them credit for being. A squareness about the lower part of his face, and the dotted indication of the strong black beard he shaved close every day, reminded Scrooge of the wax-work that had traveled the city once. This, his regular eyebrows, and the rich white, and black, and brown, of his complexion— confound his complexion—made Scrooge think him, in spite of his misgivings, a very handsome man. No doubt the young lady on his arm thought so, too.

"And dangerous, if you ask me," continued the guest. "The way the vampires keep their eye on him. It would not surprise me if he was one of them!"

"Me?" Scrooge turned to the spirit. "He thinks me a vampire? Has he ever seen me drink blood? Has anyone? Preposterous that anyone would make such a statement!"

The spirit looked down upon Scrooge with great sorrow. "It seems that unbeknownst to you, you *have* drunk blood," he pointed out.

Scrooge hesitated, then recalling the scene from his birth and the words Queen Griselda had spoken, he made a face. "I was a babe. It was of the wet nurse's doing and none of mine. Surely that cannot be held against me!"

"There are others who have given it to you, as well," pointed out the phantom. "Would you care to have the Ghost of Christmas Past revisit and show you?"

Scrooge recoiled. "No. Certainly not." The thought was beyond his comprehension, but he had no desire for any more truths than had already been thrust upon him, and so he returned his attention to the Christmas gathering.

"So what if he is rich?" said Scrooge's nephew. "His wealth is of no use to him or anyone else, for that matter, poor soul. He doesn't do any good with it; he gives no aid to any of the VS organizations. Not ours. Not anyone's."

"It's no wonder of that," muttered the pretty girl with Charles.

"He does not give to the church or the poorhouse," Fred continued, polite enough to pretend he had not heard his guest's remark. "He doesn't even make himself comfortable with it. He hasn't the satisfaction of thinking—ha, ha, ha—that he is ever going to benefit us with it."

"I, for one, have no patience with him," observed Penny. Her three sisters, and all the other ladies, expressed the same opinion.

"Oh, I have," said Scrooge's nephew. "I am sorry for him; I couldn't be angry with him if I tried. Who suffers by his ill whims? Himself, always. Here, he takes it into his head to dislike us, and he won't come and dine with us. What's the consequence? He doesn't lose much of a dinner."

"Indeed, I think he loses a very good dinner," interrupted Scrooge's niece. Everybody else said the same, and they must be allowed to have been competent judges, because they had just had dinner; and, with the dessert upon the table, were clustered round the fire, by lamplight.

"Well, I'm very glad to hear it," said Scrooge's nephew, "because I haven't great faith in these young housekeepers," he teased the young women.

Everyone laughed. "Ha ha ha ha."

"So, what do you hear these days, Topper? I saw you quite intent in conversation with Bob Cratchit after the VSU meeting earlier in the week."

"Now Bob, there is a fine man. And to think he must endure your Uncle Ebenezer's company six days out of the week." The man called Topper shook his head. "And not a better man to have at your side in a dark alley. He works a pike well for a man his age. And his son, the one they call Tiny Tim. What a brave lad. You know, he speaks often of the Scion of the Great Culling that was prophesied to come one day. Though many a good man has come to fear it will not come to pass, the boy is certain the Scion will be born and he swears his allegiance to the Great One."

"But isn't the boy sickly?"

Topper had clearly got his eye upon Penny's sister, who spoke, for he answered that a bachelor was a wretched outcast, who had no right to express an opinion on the subject. Whereat Scrooge's niece's sister—the plump one with the lace tucker, not the one with the roses—blushed.

"Do move on to a new topic, Fred," said Scrooge's niece, clapping her hands. "He never finishes what he begins to say once he lays his gaze upon a pretty girl. He is such a ridiculous fellow."

"I . . . I am able to . . . to s . . . speak," managed Topper.

Scrooge's nephew reveled in another laugh, and as it was impossible to keep the infection off, though the plump sister tried hard to do it with aromatic vinegar, his example was unanimously followed.

Topper laughed with them, then. "Yes, yes, the boy is sickly. Some speak in whispers that he is not expected to live, for he seems to suffer more as of late. He grows paler and weaker, but even as his body seems to shrivel, I believe his heart grows truer. He knows the meaning not only of keeping the faith, but keeping good cheer."

"Unlike my husband's Uncle Ebenezer," Penny pointed out.

"Back to that matter again, is it?" said Fred, winking at his wife. "Well, the consequence of my uncle taking a dislike to us, and not making merry with us, is, as I think, that he loses some pleasant moments, which could do him no harm. I am sure he loses pleasanter companions than he can find in his own thoughts, either in his moldy old office, or his dusty chambers. I mean to give him the same chance every year, whether he likes it or not, for I pity him. He may rail at Christmas till he dies, but he can't help thinking better of it—I defy him—if he finds me going there, in good temper, year after year, and saying Uncle Scrooge, how are you. If it only puts him in the vein to leave his poor clerk fifty pounds, that's something. And I think I shook him yesterday."

It was their turn to laugh now at the notion of his shaking Scrooge. But being thoroughly good-natured, and not much caring what they laughed at, so that they laughed at any rate, he encouraged them in their merriment, and passed the bottle joyously.

After tea, they had some music. For they were a musical family, and knew what they were about, when they sung a Glee or Catch, I can assure you, especially Topper, who could growl away in the bass like a good one, and never swell the large veins in his forehead, or get red in the face over it. Scrooge's niece played well upon the harp and played among other tunes a simple little air (a mere nothing: you might learn to whistle it in two minutes), which had been familiar to the child who fetched Scrooge from the boarding-school, as he had been reminded by the Ghost of Christmas Past. When this strain of music sounded, all the things that ghost had shown him came upon his mind, he softened more and more, and thought that if he could have listened to it often, years ago, he might have cultivated the kindnesses of life for his own happiness with his own hands, without resorting to the sexton's spade that buried Jacob Marley.

Had the vampires prevented him from hearing the tunes, truly *hearing* them? Or had he not taken the time and energy to listen? It's common knowledge that many who are accused of deafness possess the physical ability to hear, but do not take the trouble to pay attention to what is said.

But Fred and Penny and their guests didn't devote the whole evening to music. After a while they played at forfeits, for it is good to be children sometimes, and never better than at Christmas, when its mighty founder was a child himself. Stop! There was first a game at blindman's bluff. Of course there was. And I no more believe Topper was really blind than I believe he had eyes in his boots. My opinion is, that it was a done thing between him and Scrooge's nephew and that the Ghost of Christmas Present knew it. The way he went after that plump sister in the lace tucker was an outrage on the credulity of human nature. Knocking down the fire-irons, tumbling over the chairs, bumping against the piano, smothering himself among the curtains, wherever she went, there went he. He always knew where the plump sister was. He wouldn't catch anybody else. If you had fallen up against him (as some of them did), on purpose, he would have made a feint of endeavoring to seize you, which would have been an affront to your understanding, and would instantly have sidled off in the direction of the plump sister. She often cried out that it wasn't fair, and it really was not. But when at last, he caught her, when, in spite of all her silken rustlings, and her rapid flutterings past him, he got her into a corner whence there was no escape, then his conduct was the most execrable. For his pretending not to know her, his pretending that it was necessary to touch her head-dress, and further to assure himself of her identity by pressing a certain ring upon her finger, and a certain chain about her neck, was vile, monstrous. No doubt she told him her opinion of it, when, another blindman being in office, they were so very confidential together, behind the curtains.

Scrooge's niece was not one of the blindman's bluff party, but was made comfortable with a large chair and a footstool, in a snug corner, where the ghost and Scrooge were close behind her. But she joined in the forfeits, and loved her love to admiration with all the letters of the alphabet. Likewise at the game of How, When, and Where, she was very great, and to the secret joy of Scrooge's nephew, beat her sisters hollow, though they were sharp girls, too, as he could have told you. There might have been twenty people there, young and old, but they all played, and so did Scrooge, for, wholly forgetting the interest he had in what was going on, that his voice made no sound in their ears, he sometimes came out with his guess quite loud, and very often guessed quite right, too; for the sharpest needle, best Whitechapel, warranted not to cut in the eye, was not sharper than Scrooge, blunt as he took it in his head to be.

The ghost was greatly pleased to find him in this mood, and looked upon him with such favor, that he begged like a boy to be allowed to stay until the guests departed. Here, there seemed no evidence of the vampires in the city and in their lives, save for the occasional mention of them, and Scrooge seemed far removed from the bitter truths piling upon his conscience. And these games . . . these games excited him and filled him with a youthful joy that he had not experienced in many a year. But to stay any longer, the spirit said, could not be done.

"Here is a new game," said Scrooge. "One half hour, Spirit, only one."

It was a game called Yes and No, where Scrooge's nephew had to think of something, and the rest must find out what; he only answering to their questions yes or no, as the case was.

The brisk fire of questioning to which he was exposed elicited from him that he was thinking of an animal, a live animal, rather a disagreeable animal, a savage animal, an animal that growled and grunted sometimes, and talked sometimes, and lived in London, and walked about the streets, and wasn't made a show of, and wasn't led by anybody, and didn't live in a menagerie, and was never killed in a market, and was not a horse, or an ass, or a cow, or a bull, or a tiger, or a dog, or a pig, or a cat, or a bear. At every fresh question that was put to him, this nephew burst into a fresh roar of laughter; and was so inexpressibly tickled, that he was obliged to get up off the sofa and stamp. At last the plump sister, falling into a similar state, cried out:

"I have found it out. I know what it is, Fred. I know what it is."

"What is it?" cried Fred.

"A vampire?" interrupted Penny.

"Not a vampire," said Fred.

"No, not a vampire," said the plump sister. "Then, it's your Uncle Scrooge."

Which it certainly was. Admiration was the universal sentiment, though some objected that the reply to "Is it a bear?" ought to have been "Yes," in as much as an answer in the negative was sufficient to have diverted their thoughts from Mr. Scrooge, supposing they had ever had any tendency that way.

"He has given us plenty of merriment, I am sure," said Fred, "and it would be ungrateful not to drink his health. Here is a glass of mulled wine ready to our hand at the moment and I say, Uncle Ebenezer."

"Well! Uncle Ebenezer," they cried.

"A merry Christmas and a happy new year to the old man, wherever he is," said Scrooge's nephew. "He wouldn't take it from me, but may he have it, nevertheless. Uncle Ebenezer."

Scrooge had imperceptibly become so gay and light of heart, that he would have pledged the unconscious company in return, and thanked them in an inaudible speech, if the ghost had given him time. But the whole scene passed off in the breath of the last word spoken by his nephew, and he and the spirit were again upon their travels.

30

Much they saw, and far they went, and many homes they visited, but always with a happy end. The spirit stood beside sick beds, and they were cheerful. In almshouse, hospital, and jail, in misery's every refuge, where vain man in his little brief authority had not made fast the door and barred the spirit out, he left his blessing, and taught Scrooge his precepts.

"They appear happy," Scrooge commented, watching over an elderly man who cared for his dying wife in a room no bigger than a broom closet. "How can they be happy with their miserable existence and vampires roaming the streets waiting to . . . to drink their blood if they are fortunate, kill them if they are not?" he asked.

"Because they have hope," said the spirit simply.

"Hope?"

"Hope in people such as these . . ."

The spirit turned and Scrooge found himself gazing down a dark street. Snow fell lightly on the shoulders of a hunch-backed old woman making her way home, her cane tapping at her side. Behind her, a man in a dark cloak followed. The old woman glanced over her shoulder and walked a little faster.

The man in the cloak's face shimmered white. Scrooge knew at once what he was.

"He gains on her," murmured Scrooge. "Can you not do something?"

The spirit watched, giving Scrooge no other choice but to do the same.

Seeming to sense the fate about to befall her, the old woman walked more quickly, her cane tapping faster on the snowy street cobbles. Scrooge felt his heart patter in his chest, and he knew the old woman's did the same. As she passed an alleyway, the man behind her in the cloak reached out to catch her shoulder.

Scrooge cringed, set on turning away, but he did not turn away, could not.

The old woman gave a cry as the man spun her around, but instead of crumpling under his force, she drew back her cane and struck the beast. Who she startled more, Scrooge or her pursuer, he could not have said.

"Quickly!" called out the old woman, whose ragged hood fell back to reveal a young man. Out of the alley tumbled two more men. The creature screeched in shock and perhaps fear, recognizing it had been drawn into a trap.

Too late! A man raised a pike much like the one the Ghost of Christmas Present carried in his scabbard, and Scrooge turned away as the vampire slayer struck home and scarlet sprayed the snow and the faces of the hunters.

"I do not want to see this," cried Scrooge, covering his eyes with his hands. "I cannot . . . I do not wish to believe. Such violence." He shuddered, imagining the blood that spilled into the snow.

"It is not all violence," said the spirit.

31

A moment later, Scrooge felt his slippers settle on floorboards and the warmth of the heat from a fire burning bright on a parlor hearth. A woman stood before the blaze, pouring cups of tea from a chipped but once rather fine china tea pot trimmed in pink roses. Four cups, chipped and yellowed with time, upon a tray matched the teapot.

"Mr. Herbert," she said kindly. It was not until she turned her face into the firelight that Scrooge recognized her.

"Belle," he murmured. "Why, she is quite pretty. She holds her age well." He had seen her only hours before (or days or years, for who knew with spirits?), but she looked different to him now. Prettier. Younger.

"Thank you so much, miss," said a man seated on a stool pulled close to the hearth. "You are too kind to have taken me in."

This was a fresh-colored young gentleman, with as good a promise of light whisker as one might wish to see, and possessed of a very velvet-like, soft-looking countenance. We do not use the latter term invidiously, but merely to denote a pair of smooth, plump, highly colored cheeks of capacious dimensions, and a mouth rather remarkable for the fresh hue of the lips than for any marked or striking expression it presented. His whole face was suffused with a crimson blush, and bore that downcast, timid, retiring look which betokens a man ill at ease with himself.

"I am only glad you were able to make your way here with your injuries."

Scrooge noticed then that the man wore his fine velvet coat slung over one shoulder, bandages protruding from beneath.

"You must take care not to move more than necessary for a few days," Belle instructed, completing the task of pouring the tea. Setting the pot on the tray on a wobbly table, she offered him a cup. "Tea, gentlemen," she called over her shoulder, in the direction of the staircase.

She looked back at the young man seated at her hearth. "Please feel free to stay as long as you like."

"Injured men come and go here, I take it?" he asked, sipping his tea. "Your address was given to me by a local vampire slayers union."

"When they must escape or hide or are injured and have no other place to go, they come to places like this. Sometimes women, too," she said, taking a padded chair across from him.

"Women?" he asked, obviously quite amazed. "Women in London fight vampires? We heard on the coast that women were taking larger roles in the battle against them, but I had no idea."

"Most of us do not fight," she said, lowering her gaze to the teacup balanced on her lap. "But some of us are braver than others."

"Well, I think you quite brave, miss," he said, beaming at her.

As Scrooge watched the exchange, he felt something in his chest that, it had been so long since he felt it, he could not, at first, identify it. "Why . . . he is half her age," he muttered, fighting the wave of jealously that was as difficult to manage as any counting-house task. "He . . . he practically flirts with her!"

"There are many men who have fallen in love with her over the years, but she has never accepted any advances," the phantom said. "She holds her heart for someone long in her past." He looked down on Scrooge.

"Me?"

The spirit smiled, but did not answer his question. "Belle has been kind to him, a stranger to the city, injured, fleeing for his life."

Male voices were heard on the staircase, in response to the call to tea, no doubt. Behind them, Ebenezer heard the sound of a child's lighter footsteps.

"Men and children?" Scrooge said, making no attempt to hide his disdain. "Is this a long-term boarding-house?"

"It is whatever is needed to support the cause of the annihilation of vampires," answered the spirit.

Three gentlemen who had come from above stairs pulled mismatched chairs closer to the burning hearth and accepted Belle's offer of tea.

"And where is Alice?" cooed Belle, glancing at the staircase where an elfin girl of no more than eight or nine stood. "Come." Belle put out a slender hand to her. "Sit upon my lap, and I will share my tea with you." She glanced at a man in his early thirties who had limped to his place before the fire. "If your father gives his approval, of course."

"After what she has been through," said the man with a tired sigh and then a smile, "my Alice may have whatever she likes. Whatever is still in my power to give her."

Belle patted her knee and the shy girl came to her, allowing Belle to draw her into an embrace. "I have a friend, a very nice friend whose name is Fred, who intends to stop by shortly with gifts for good little girls. Good girls like you, Alice." She tickled her tummy and the girl laughed. "He has all sorts of baubles, I am told; dollies, and cards, and tin horns and such. I wonder what he will bring to you."

"My nephew? He brings gifts *here?*" asked Scrooge of the ghost.

"He will deliver to houses such as this all over the city."

"The tree," said Scrooge. "The one in his parlor, so laden with toys that it looked as if it would tumble."

"Gifts for the children of the men and women displaced while fighting the vampires."

"Displaced? However are these men displaced by vampires?"

"They are a vindictive lot, vampires. When someone fights them, they resort to burning them out, or having them put out by landlords and law enforcement they hold under their dark power. Some of the men who pass through here are so well known among the vampires that they must constantly keep moving to stay alive."

"I had no idea. And Belle helps these men?"

"And their families, when they have families left. This child's mother and sister were killed by vampires near London Bridge only a few nights ago."

Against his will, Scrooge found himself gazing upon Belle again; first her pretty face and then the child's happy one. Belle whispered in little Alice's ear and shared her cup of tea with her.

"She would make a good mother," observed Scrooge. "It is unfortunate that she never married. It is too late for children now."

The spirit smiled down on him, his eyes brimming with light reflected off the blazing fire. "Who is to say?" He offered his arm. "Our time together is nearly at an end. We must hurry."

⥤ 32 ⥢

A light-headedness came over Scrooge. One moment he stood in Belle's parlor in his nightdress, the next moment in his own cold, dark, front hall. "Home?" cried Scrooge, tempted to grab the ghost's robes in thanks. "You have returned me?"

"Not yet." The ghost opened the door that led to the cellar stairs, and Scrooge found himself pulling back. A stench rose from the darkness that smelled of dirt and death. A sense of dread came over him, and his feet rooted to the floor. Not there! He would not venture there! Not even the ghost could force him to perform such an act.

"I . . . I have no wish to enter there," he said, gazing at the black hole of the doorway that seemed to hold a life of its own, suffocating and all-encompassing. "You . . . you warned me of . . . of my tenants and the tunnel below. The one you say the vampires use to make their way all over the city. Surely I cannot enter this cellar and survive."

"They cannot see us, Ebenezer."

With that, Scrooge felt himself lifted off the floor and propelled down the steps. He fought, his legs and arms flailing, but it made no difference, for the next thing he knew, he was standing on the damp dirt cellar floor, the natural illumination of his escort showing them surrounded by wine casks.

"Wine," announced Scrooge to the phantom, feeling a mild sense of relief. "I told you Mr. Wahltraud was a wine purveyor! Here are his barrels and proof of his occupation."

"Those are, indeed, wine casks. Would you care to see what he stores in these casks?" asked the ghost, fitting himself well beneath the low ceiling.

Scrooge stared at the wooden casks stored in neat, orderly rows, his mouth falling agape. "Do you mean to tell me there is *blood* in those casks?"

"Come, see how your *tenants* celebrate Christmas Day."

"Vampires celebrate Christmas?" asked Scrooge, delaying what he knew was the inevitable.

"They celebrate the Winter Solstice, today of all days, to take their minds off the good cheer of the city." The ghost stepped back, indicating a doorway that led deeper into the recesses of the cellar.

"Must I?" asked Scrooge.

"You must, and my time grows short. There is one more place we must visit before my time is gone."

"One more place?" cried Scrooge, quite close to tears. "I beg of you, Spirit—"

"This way," the phantom said.

Resolute, hands trembling at his sides, Scrooge crossed the threshold into another room, which contained nothing more than two ornate caskets: mahogany wood, black as coal, adorned with silver handles and silver filigree trim, and within white satin interiors as spotless and pristine as new-fallen snow. If it had been possible, Scrooge would have trembled harder, but was it possible for a bowl of jelly, once set in motion, to quiver more?

Where there should have been a solid wall, there was another archway. "Here ends my property, I am sure of it," Scrooge said.

The phantom lifted his hand, ushering Scrooge onward.

They entered a tunnel that was close and dark and dank, and it frightened Scrooge even more than the room with the coffins. When the tunnel split, the ghost indicated Scrooge should go left, then right, then right again and again, until Scrooge could no longer get his bearings. All he knew was that he was beneath the city in a place that was more hopeless than hell itself.

The tunnel opened without warning, and Scrooge found himself on what appeared to be a city street. But of course it was not a city street, for they were below ground, below London town.

Some ladies passed, walking to and fro, in pairs and singly. They all had skin of alabaster, all dressed in bright colors. One even carried a blue parasol, though there was no sun from which she needed protection. The street was lit by stinking pitch torches set here and there like street-lamps.

"What is this place?" asked Scrooge.

"It is where many live. It is the way they move about the city so freely."

"But . . . it looks like a city. Any city." Scrooge stared in disbelief. "How is this possible? How . . . how long have they been here?"

"Longer than you would care to know," said the spirit sadly.

The streets and shops were lighted by the torches, and as Scrooge's eye traveled down the long thoroughfare, dotted with bright flares of fire, it reminded him something (God forbid!) of Oxford Street, or Piccadilly. Here and there a flight of broad stone cellar-steps appeared, and a painted sign that directed you to the Bowling Saloon, or Ten-Pin Alley; Ten-Pins being a game of mingled chance and skill, invented when the legislature passed an act forbidding Nine-Pins. At other downward flights of steps were other signs, marking the whereabouts of oyster-cellars and all kinds of caters of fish, or flesh, or fowl.

"Vampires eat food?" asked Scrooge.

"No, but the men and women who work for them do. Much of this is to entice them," explained the ghost. "And you must admit, it could be enticing, considering the squalor some live in above ground. It is very like London."

What was different than the streets above was how quiet it was here. There were no itinerant bands, no wind or stringed instruments. Not one. There were no punches, dancing dogs, jugglers, conjurers, or orchestrinas. Scrooge saw only one barrel-organ and a dancing monkey—sportive by nature, but fast fading into a dull, lumpish monkey. Beyond that, nothing lively, not so much as a white mouse in a twirling cage. He wanted to ask why the vampires had no such entertainment, but fearing the answer, did not ask.

Scrooge saw, as he and the spirit walked unnoticed by the pedestrians, that there was a lecture-room across the way. There was a counting house, a store, even a barroom. The latter, he could see through these windows, was pretty full. He heard the clinking sound of hammers breaking lumps of ice, and the cool gurgling of the pounded bits, as, in the process of mixing, they were poured from glass to glass!

Inside, there were men sucking on cigars, vampire and human. Humans were swallowing strong drinks, their hats and legs in every possible variety of twist, all obviously enjoying themselves. These were not vapid, waterish amusements, but good, strong stuff, dealing in round abuse and blackguard names, pulling off the roofs of private houses, as the Halting Devil did in Spain. Scrooge surmised that there was pimping and pandering for all degrees of vicious taste, and gorging with coined lies the most voracious maw, imputing to every man in public life the coarsest and the vilest motives; scaring away from the stabbed and prostrate body-politic, any Samaritan of clear conscience (could there even be a Samaritan down here?) and good deeds and setting on, with yell and whistle and the clapping of foul hands, the vilest vermin and worst birds of prey.

The ghost prodded Scrooge forward and they passed a wilderness of a hotel with stores about its base, like some Continental theater, or the London Opera House shorn of its colonnade. As he walked, Scrooge noticed that he had seen no beggars in the streets, but of other kinds of strollers, plenty. Despite the smiles upon the passersby's faces, he sensed that poverty, wretchedness, and vice were still rife enough here. The king and queen of the vampires had not saved the humans from their wretched lives, only changed the scenery.

The street grew darker, narrower, and there were fewer burning torches.

"The older part of their city," the ghost explained.

"Who lives here?" asked Scrooge.

"The minions, when they can no longer live above ground."

"They make them vampires?"

"No, but the blood they take changes them. They become more sensitive to the light. They acquire a taste for the blood that must be satisfied, and so they do the vampires' bidding to get it. There are rules. They must have permission from vampires to take blood from humans."

This older section of the place where the vampires' minions dwelled was one of narrow ways, diverging to the right and left, and reeking everywhere with dirt and filth. Such lives led here bore the same fruits as the slums of London. The coarse and bloated faces at the doors had counterparts on the streets above, and all the wide world over. Debauchery had made the very houses old. The rotten beams were tumbling down, and the patched and broken windows seemed to scowl dimly, like eyes that had been hurt in drunken frays.

"Enough," Scrooge cried, covering his face with his hands. "Please, Spirit. Have I not seen enough?"

"This way," said the Ghost of Christmas Present.

They took a short alley and the underground walls grew close around them again until it seemed that they were in the same tunnels as when they had first entered. Ahead, standing in a doorway, on guard, no doubt (though who would dare trespasses save for spirits and their unwilling captives, Scrooge did not know) was a wrinkled hideous figure with deeply sunk and bloodshot eyes and an immensely long cadaverous face, shadowed by jagged and matted locks of coarse black hair. He wore a kind of tunic of a dull bluish color, which, Scrooge observed regarding it attentively, was clasped or ornamented down the front with coffin handles. His legs, too, were encased in coffin plates as though in armor; and over his left shoulder he wore a short dusky cloak, which seemed made of a remnant of some pall. He took no notice of the ghost and Scrooge, of course, but was intently eyeing the far side of the vaulted-ceilinged room.

The underground room was enormous, cavern-like, and apparently served as a dining facility this night, for there were at least two dozen large tables of pale-faced guests and a raised dais on the far side of the room where King Wahltraud and his lady, Queen Griselda, held court.

"I've seen enough!" Scrooge cried, suddenly afraid, because until that moment he had not allowed himself to truly believe his tenants were vampires, or that these creatures had controlled his life. He had allowed them to control his life. "Please, O Spirit, believe me when I say it is not necessary that you keep me here a moment longer. If you say my tenants are vampires, then vampires they are, and I will see them evicted come morning."

The spirit did not respond.

"Are . . . are these all vampires?" Scrooge dared, taking note that some of the diners were as pale-faced as their host and hostess, while others seemed . . . more earthly.

"Many are, but some are their minions. If you were to look closely, I believe there are others here you might recognize."

"No, I see no one I recognize, nor anyone I wish to recognize," Scrooge assured the ghost.

"What of him?"

Scrooge took a sharp breath, staring at a round-faced man with a broad nose and rosy cheeks. "My butcher?" he murmured. "Harry Chop, from whom my serving wench has fetched sweetbreads and kidneys for my own table? My butcher?"

"And there."

A young, pock-faced woman drank from a silver tumbler. "The girl who sells sweetmeats on the corner?" Scrooge asked in shock. "I know her. I have passed her every morning for two years at least, and nothing of her ruined countenance proclaimed that she possessed any more diabolical traits than others of her station in life."

"And what of him?" asked the spirit, sounding impatient, though Scrooge could not tell if it was with the present scene or his present company, meaning Scrooge.

It took him a moment to figure out who the ghost was referring to, but eventually, Scrooge laid his gaze upon none other than his employee, Lucius Disgut. He recognized his beady eyes and rat-like nose at once. "Not Disgut. It cannot be." His trusted man, Lucius? Impossible! This was beyond belief.

"Why can it not be?" asked the spirit, sounding as if his patience had returned.

"Why, because . . ." Scrooge could think of nothing to say. If the butcher and the sweetmeat girl were vampire minions, who was to say who else was one of them? The rector of St. Michael's-Upon-Fields? Lord Dumbworthy, the earl of Witherspoon? Her majesty herself?

"When did the clerk come to you?"

"The week Marley died. I remember it distinctly because . . ." Scrooge felt a lump the size of a hefty piece of coal rise in his throat, and he swallowed hard. "He came with references from Mr. Wahltraud," he managed to finish.

Scrooge thought before he spoke again. "Cratchit, he . . . he is one of the slayers. Does he realize he works with a man who could be plotting to do him harm, even kill him?"

"Members of the VSU know they encounter dangers each and every day. It's part of their sacrifice to mankind. But to answer your question, I am quite sure Mr. Cratchit knows where Mr. Disgut's allegiances lie."

Thinking of nothing else to say, Scrooge took in the room once again. Tall tapers burned low on the tables: the meal was obviously over but overly large platters still lay here and there, platters so immense they could have well held, dared he think, a human.

I must put here, fair and brave reader, that had I been Scrooge, I would have run from this place as fast as my feet could have carried me, by now. But by now, I would have also seen the sin of my acts and begged for any aid the spirit could have offered in the area of redemption. But Scrooge was a man well set in his ways, a man not easily swayed . . . except by vampires.

There was music, a harp and fiddle, which played from somewhere Scrooge could not see. The tune being played was lively enough, but he took note that none of the guests danced, or appeared particularly gay.

"You say they celebrate the Winter Solstice," Scrooge murmured, noting the long faces of the king and queen and their guests. Those in the room conversed, but there was none of the light-heartedness Scrooge had seen in the other places the ghost had taken him that night. Even the poorest of poor seemed more enthused than these men and women, who appeared well fed and housed and garbed in the finest clothing, albeit of sober cut and color, but fine stuff all the same. "It does not appear much like a celebration to me. From the talk we have heard, from what we have seen tonight, it seems that the vampires would have much reason for making merry, the way they have wreaked havoc in London." He studied the king and queen of the vampires, feeling at least a little confident that he was, at present, safe from them. "They do not seem so threatening tonight. Look at how they slouch in their mighty chairs, how they speak softly, their gazes flitting here and there. I would think they would be more jovial than the humans we have seen this night."

"It is the spirit of the humans on this night that steals the joy from the vampires," the Ghost of Christmas Present explained, "and saps them of their strength. If every day could be Christmas Day, the vampires would die out in no time at all."

"Every day, Christmas Day," Scrooge snorted. He had intended to follow his comment with a "bah, humbug," but could not bring himself to speak the words. The sight of the vampires and their minions in this chamber below the city had brought so many emotions to Scrooge's heart, emotions he barely recognized, that he could not express them. Would not, for fear he might crumble. "Please, Spirit," he said, "tell me this is the last place we will visit tonight. Tell me I may walk through these tunnels and find my way to my bed."

"My time is, indeed, almost expired, but there is one place we must revisit."

"No more, please." Scrooge put his hands together. "Must I beg?"

"It will do you no good. Touch my robe."

"Must I?" inquired Scrooge.

"Would you prefer I left you here?"

"For the love of mercy, no! Do not leave me in this den of bloodsuckers, I beseech you!" Scrooge grabbed the phantom's robe, and in the blink of an eye and a swirl of snow, they were back at Cratchit's house again, though this time it was much later. Children slept on pallets on the floor in front of the fireplace, and Bob Cratchit snored softly on a bed of rags beside the table upon which they had shared their great Christmas Day feast. The only light burning was from the candle the sister-in-law, Maena, carried up the wobbling staircase.

"Follow her," the spirit instructed.

Scrooge did as ordered, for if there was one thing he had learned this night, it was that there was no need to waste one's breath arguing with those of the spirit world. They passed a closet-sized chamber where another pallet was made up; Maena's room, no doubt. But she kept going up until they reached the attic space where the Cratchit boys slept.

Scrooge stood in the doorway, watching with something akin to a smile on his face as the boys' dear aunt picked her way across the sleeping bodies to reach Tiny Tim, who slept on a raised pallet against the wall. "Why, she's tucking him in. How . . ." The word "sweet" was on Scrooge's mind but he could not find the strength to say it.

The spirit made no reply.

Maena reached Tiny Tim, set down her candlestick, and grasped the edge of the ragtag blanket wrapped around the boy, but instead of drawing it higher upon his chin, she drew it back.

"What the devil?" muttered Scrooge. "Can she not feel the chill in this room? Look, the water has frozen in the cup beside his bedding."

The candlelight revealed an open, weeping wound on the boy's calf.

"Is . . . is she tending his wound?" Scrooge asked, but even as he spoke the words, he took a step back, then in horror watched as the woman who was supposed to be caring for Cratchit's children leaned over and pressed her mouth to the wound, making a sucking sound. When she lifted her head, her smiling lips were covered in the child's blood. She then took a glass vial from a pocket and began to fill it with the boy's blood.

"He will not survive because of her," Scrooge said, in dull shock, as much to himself as to the ghost. "Not if the present is not altered." He took one last look at the treacherous woman and turned to the ghost, placing his hand upon the spirit's sleeve. They slipped out of the house and Scrooge found himself on a dark, snowy street.

It was a long night, if it were only a night, but Scrooge had his doubts of this, because the Christmas holidays appeared to be condensed into the space of time they passed together. It was strange, too, that while Scrooge remained unaltered in his outward form, the ghost grew older, clearly older. Scrooge had observed this change, but never spoke of it until now when, looking at the spirit as they stood together in an open place, he noticed that its hair was gray.

"Are spirits' lives so short?" asked Scrooge.

"My life upon this globe is very brief," replied the ghost. "It ends tonight."

"Tonight?" cried Scrooge. "That hardly seems fair, when vampires can live forever if they are not decapitated, or run through with a pike or however it is the slayers do it."

"Tonight at midnight. Hark! The time is drawing near."

The chimes were ringing the three quarters past eleven at that moment.

"Forgive me if I am not justified in what I ask," said Scrooge, looking intently at the spirit's robe, "but I see something strange, and not belonging to yourself, protruding from your skirts. Is it a foot or a claw?"

"It might be a claw, for the flesh there is upon it," was the spirit's sorrowful reply. "Look here."

"Please tell me you do not conceal vampires within your cloak." No more, he prayed. His delicate nature could take no more shocking revelations.

"They are not vampires." From the folds of its robe, it brought two human children, wretched, abject, frightful, hideous, miserable. They knelt down at its feet, and clung upon the outside of its garment.

"Oh, man, look here. Look, look, down here," exclaimed the ghost.

They were a boy and a girl: yellow, meager, ragged, scowling, wolfish, but prostrate, too, in their humility. Where graceful youth should have filled their features out, and touched them with its freshest tints, a stale and shriveled hand, like that of age, had pinched and twisted them, and pulled them into shreds. Where angels might have sat enthroned, devils lurked and glared out menacing. No change, no degradation, no perversion of humanity, in any grade, through all the mysteries of wonderful creation, have monsters half so horrible and dread existed.

Scrooge started back, appalled. Having them shown to him in this way, he tried to say they were fine children, but the words choked themselves, rather than be parties to a lie of such enormous magnitude.

"Spirit, have the vampires done this to these poor children?" Scrooge could say no more.

"Mankind has done this to these children," said the spirit, looking down upon them. "And they cling to me, appealing from their fathers. This boy is Ignorance. This girl is Want. Beware them both, and all of their degree, but most of all beware this boy, for on his brow I see that written which is Doom, unless the writing is erased."

"But . . . but what can I do? What can any of us do? If . . . if the vampires have controlled me, they have controlled others like me, have they not?" he asked shakily. "We cannot stop them. We cannot prevent this. Mankind is not responsible for—"

"Deny your responsibility," shouted the spirit, stretching out its hand toward the city. "Slander those who tell it to ye. Admit it for your factious purposes, and make it worse. And abide the end."

"Have they no refuge or resource?" cried Scrooge.

"Are there no prisons?" said the spirit, turning on him for the last time with his own words. "Are there no workhouses?" The bell struck twelve.

Scrooge looked about him for the ghost, and saw it not. As the last stroke ceased to vibrate, he remembered the prediction of old Jacob Marley, and lifting up his eyes, beheld a solemn phantom, draped and hooded, coming, like a mist along the ground, toward him.

STAVE 4

THE LAST OF THE SPIRITS

❧ 33 ❧

The phantom slowly, gravely, silently approached. When it came, Scrooge bent down upon his knee, for in the very air through which this spirit moved it seemed to scatter gloom and mystery.

It was shrouded in a deep black garment, which concealed its head, its face, its form, and left nothing of it visible save one outstretched hand. But for this it would have been difficult to detach its figure from the night, and separate it from the darkness by which it was surrounded.

He felt that it was tall and stately when it came beside him, and that its mysterious presence filled him with a solemn dread. He knew no more, for the spirit neither spoke nor moved.

"I am in the presence of the Ghost of Christmas Yet To Come," said Scrooge.

The spirit answered not, but pointed onward with its hand.

"You are about to show me shadows of the things that have not happened, but will happen in the time before us," Scrooge pursued. "Is that so, Spirit?"

The upper portion of the garment was contracted for an instant in its folds, as if the spirit had inclined its head. That was the only answer he received.

Although well used to ghostly company by this time, Scrooge feared the silent shape so greatly that his legs trembled beneath him, and he found that he could hardly stand when he prepared to follow it. The spirit paused a moment, as observing his condition, and giving him time to recover.

But Scrooge was all the worse for this. It thrilled him with a vague uncertain horror to know that behind the dusky shroud, there were ghostly eyes intently fixed upon him, while he, though he stretched his own to the utmost, could see nothing but a spectral hand and one great heap of black. This was somehow worse than the notion of vampires watching him, controlling those around him, all these years, their fangs protruding, dripping with human blood.

Is it not thus with all mortal humans . . . that we fear the unknown even more than we fear the monsters we have seen with our own eyes?

"Ghost of Christmas Yet to Come," he exclaimed. "I fear you more than any specter I have seen. But as I know now that your purpose is to do me good, and as I hope to live to be another man from what I was, I am prepared to bear your company, and do it with a thankful heart. After all I have seen, I fear these vampires as perhaps no one else fears them, for they seem to have particular interest in me." He sighed, looked down at his trembling feet thrust into his slippers, and then looked up again. "Will you not speak to me?"

It gave him no reply. The hand was pointed straight before them.

"Lead on, then," said Scrooge with resignation. "Lead on. The night is waning fast, and it is precious time to me, I suspect. Lead on, Spirit."

The phantom moved away as it had come toward him.

Scrooge followed in the shadow of its dress, which bore him up, he thought, and carried him along.

They scarcely seemed to enter the city, for the city rather seemed to spring up about them, and encompass them of its own act. Scrooge found himself on a familiar street, his very own, just before dawn when there was that strange light that was neither day nor night, following a tall figure in a handsome black cloak. He knew the man he followed, but could not quite place him from his perspective, walking ten feet behind.

At a gate off the alley that ran along Scrooge's house, the cloaked figure encountered no less a person than Mr. Martins, the parochial undertaker. Scrooge knew him from his dealings with him seven years before, when Marley died. Strange that he should be here at this time and place, and Scrooge did not dare to wonder which of his neighbors might be the object of Mr. Martins's attention. Scrooge wondered if it might be one of the vampires who'd rented his cellar rooms, but that seemed unlikely, as he'd never heard of an undertaker being called to dispose of a vampire. What they did with their dead, he did not know, did not care to know, and in truth, wondered if the beasties did ever die of natural causes. As far as he could tell from what he had gleaned this night, the only way to kill one was with a pike through the heart—as he had seen on that street while being escorted by the Ghost of Christmas Present.

Mr. Martins was a tall, gaunt, large-jointed man, attired in a suit of threadbare black, with darned cotton stockings of the same color, and shoes to answer. His features were not naturally intended to wear a smiling aspect, but he was in general rather given to professional jocosity. His step was elastic, and his face betokened inward pleasantry, as he advanced to a cloaked man and shook him cordially by the hand.

"I have taken the measure of a man who died last night, sir," said the undertaker.

"You'll make your fortune, Mr. Martins."

"Think so?" said the undertaker in a tone which half admitted and half disputed the probability of the event. "The prices allowed by the board are very small." He thrust his thumb and forefinger into a snuffbox, which was an ingenious little model of a patent coffin. "And then there's always the matter of actually collecting. You cannot send a dead man to debtor's prison."

"True enough." The stranger, his back still to Scrooge, tapped the undertaker on the shoulder, in a friendly manner, with his cane.

"And the coffins are not cheap, not even the poorly made ones," added the undertaker with precisely as near an approach to a laugh as a man of his occupation ought to indulge in.

"I think you are paid well enough."

"Well, well," Mr. Martins said at length, "there's no denying that, I suppose, since the new system of feeding has come in. The coffins are something narrower and more shallow than they used to be, but we must have some profit, sir. Well-seasoned timber is an expensive article, sir, and all the iron handles come, by canal, from Birmingham."

"Well, well," the cloaked figure imitated the undertaker, "every trade has its drawbacks. Even mine." He chuckled. "A fair profit is, of course, allowable."

"Of course, of course," replied the undertaker, "and if I don't get a profit upon this or that particular article, why, I make it up in the long run, you see—he! he! he!"

"Just so," said the man in the cloak.

"Though I must say," continued the undertaker, resuming the current observations which the man had interrupted, "that I have to contend against one very great disadvantage, which is that all the stout people go off the quickest. The people who have been better off, and have paid rates for many years, are the first to sink when they come into the house, and let me tell you, sir, that three or four inches over one's calculation makes a great hole in one's profits, especially when one has a family to provide for, sir."

"What, there is no way to fit the remains into a narrower container?"

"I have tried, sir, of that, I assure you, and the results are usually, but not always, less than one would hope."

"Turned them sideways, did you?"

"In a manner of speaking, but as I did say, that is rarely satisfying, as what bulk is squeezed up in one area tends to flow into another. And if all fails and a coffin must be altered, the price is costly. Most people do not remember that I, too, have a large family to support, with many mouths to feed, and many hands extended for charity. I tell you, it is enough to keep me from my sleep many nights, with the fear that a particular client will not be secured in a standard coffin, and I will be left the poorer by the transaction."

"Well, I can promise you that in *this* instance, you will be paid well, for your skill and your discretion. All I ask for now is that you wrap the body and hold it. Do not begin the embalming practice, for I doubt it will be necessary."

"Hold the body?" questioned the undertaker uneasily. "Unusual, at best, but not unheard of. And for what purpose are you requesting that I store the remains?"

"A coffin may not be necessary." The cloaked man's tone was short as he passed a small bag of jingling coins to the undertaker. "Hold the body, without questions or comment, until I or one of mine contact you."

The undertaker shifted his weight from one foot to the other. "Will it be long? With this weather he will keep a few days, but should we have a warm day—"

"It will not be long. . . ."

The undertaker weighed the bag in his bare hand and then quickly slipped it inside his coat. "Yes, sir." He turned on his heels and hurried away. "A good day to you, Mr. Wahltraud."

Wahltraud? Scrooge turned to question the ghost, but in that blink of an eye, the undertaker, Wahltraud, and the alley were gone. Scrooge and the Ghost of Christmas Yet to Come were still in London, but now in the heart of it. They were at the 'Change, amongst the merchants who hurried up and down, and chinked the money in their pockets, and conversed in groups, and looked at their watches, and trifled thoughtfully with their great gold seals and so forth, as Scrooge had seen them often. It was here where stocks were traded and fortunes found and lost.

The spirit stopped beside a little knot of businessmen. Observing that the spirit pointed its hand to them, Scrooge advanced to listen to their talk.

"No," said a great fat man with a monstrous chin. "I don't know much about it, either way. I only know he's dead. My wife heard it from the baker on the corner this morning."

"When did he die?" inquired another.

"Last night, I believe."

"Why, what was the matter with him?" asked a third, taking

a vast quantity of snuff out of a very large snuffbox. "I thought he'd never die. Some said he would live forever." He chuckled.

"Whatever do you mean?" said the fat one. "It's one and the same, is it not?"

"I think not," said his companion, giving him a jab in his monstrous abdomen, "if you know what I mean. There are rumors . . . that he was never one of us, but one of *them.*"

"I don't believe it! He was too sour. I've vampires next door to me, two tailors. They're quite pleasant so long as you keep your neck covered. They pay their rent on time, speak pleasantly, and I believe they keep the riff-raff off my doorstep. Beggars and other such undesirables seem to sense where they haunt, and avoid them when possible. My lady wife does worry so about the value of our home being lost due to the vampires' presence, but I'd far rather have them than some of the country-bred, puffed-up trash that passes for gentry in this city."

"I'm not certain I believe you about the value of tailors for neighbors, vampire or human, but either way, he's still dead," said the one with the snuff, with a yawn. He had another pinch of snuff in his hand, but gradually let it drop from between his fingers to the floor, then smoothed it out with his foot, looking down at it the while.

"What has he done with all his money, that's what I'd like to know," inquired a newcomer, a red-faced gentleman with a pendulous excrescence on the end of his nose that shook like the gills of a turkey-cock.

"I haven't heard," said the man with the large chin, yawning again. "Left it to his relations, perhaps. I heard he had a nephew. He hasn't left it to me. That's all I know."

This pleasantry was received with a general laugh.

"It's likely to be a very cheap funeral," said the same speaker, "for upon my life I don't know of anybody to go to it. I suppose we should make up a party and volunteer."

"I don't mind going if a lunch is provided, and only humans

are invited," observed the gentleman with the excrescence on his nose. "But I must be fed, and not fed upon." He chuckled at his own jest and another laugh rose from the group.

"Well, I am the most disinterested among you, after all," said the first speaker, "for I never wear black gloves, and I never eat lunch. But I'll offer to go, if anybody else will. When I come to think of it, I'm not at all sure that I wasn't his most particular friend, for we used to stop and speak whenever we met. Good day." He tipped his hat and moved away.

Speakers and listeners strolled away, and mixed with other groups. Scrooge knew most of the men by acquaintance, at least, and looked toward the spirit for an explanation.

The phantom glided on into the street. Its finger pointed to two persons meeting. Scrooge listened again, thinking that the explanation might lie there.

He knew these men perfectly. They were men of business, very wealthy, and of great importance. He had made a point always of standing well in their esteem, that is, strictly in a business point of view.

"How are you?" said one, blowing a cloud of fragrant smoke out of his nose.

"Well enough," returned the other, a man of short stature with a tall hat. "Taken up tobacco, have you?"

"My wife says it keeps the vampires away."

"My wife says the same and has taken up the pipe herself. I don't know where they get such notions, women. Jebediah Cronkie's coachman smoked a pipe the whole day long, every day for seventy years, and it didn't keep the beasties from stealing him off the coach bench while waiting for Jebediah at the public house. Left his pipe, they did, and not a morsel more. Never seen again. He's just now found a new coachman."

"Pity. Good coachmen are not abundantly available."

"Some say the vampires have taken to hiring the good ones

at a higher stipend, which, if true, would be an outrage. My neighbor's son-in-law saw two coaches pass his very door last Wednesday evening, conveyances full of vampires making quite merry. The curtains at the windows were thick, black, of course, but the driver and the footmen were as human as you and me. My neighbor's son-in-law was certain that he'd seen those very coaches, the coachmen, and the footmen in attendance of Viscount Wiggleybottom, not a week past, and swore the viscount's crest still remained visible, though painted over with lamp black, on the door. There should be a law against that kind of buying up the servants and coaches of gentry."

"Well," said the short man, "I'd make no bones about that. It's neither right nor decent that good coachmen should be overpaid and made to think they are better than the common sort. Most coachmen, for all their snap and polish, have horse dung on the soles of their boots, do they not?" He fumbled in his pocket for a handkerchief and blew his nose in a loud, trumpeting manner. "But, that's neither here nor there, is it? As you say, Old Scratch has got his own at last, hey?"

"So I am told." The first man inhaled and blew a fine ring of smoke. "Cold, isn't it?"

"Seasonable for Christmas time. You're not a skater, I suppose?"

"No. No, but my wife was, in her younger years, before the nine children and the sweets. Not that it's safe to skate after sunset anymore, not with the you-know-whats lurking around every corner." He tipped his hat. "Well, good morning to you, sir."

"Good morning."

Not another word. That was their meeting, their conversation, and their parting.

Scrooge was at first inclined to be surprised that the spirit should attach importance to conversations apparently so triv-

ial, but feeling assured that they must have some hidden purpose, he set himself to consider what it was likely to be. They
could scarcely be supposed to have any bearing on the death of
Jacob, his old partner, for that was past, and this ghost's
province was the future. Nor could he think of anyone immediately connected with himself, to whom he could apply them.
But not doubting that to whomsoever they applied they had
some latent moral for his own improvement, he resolved to
treasure up every word he heard, and everything he saw, and
especially to observe the shadow of himself when it appeared.
Scrooge had an expectation that the conduct of his future self
would give him the clue he missed, and would render the solu-
tion of these riddles easy.

He looked about in that very place for his own image, but
another man stood in his accustomed corner, and though the
clock pointed to his usual time of day for being there, no matter how he searched, he saw no likeness of himself among the
multitudes that poured in through the porch. Whatever could
have detained him, he wondered. Not his tenants, he hoped, for
though the Ghost of Christmas Present had suggested Queen
Griselda would not suck him dry of his blood and kill him,
having had too much time invested at this point, his confidence
in the ghost's word on this matter was not entirely solid. Not
seeing himself at the stock exchange gave him little surprise, for
he had been resolving in his mind a change of life, and thought
and hoped he saw his new-born resolutions carried out in this.

Thoughts swirled in Scrooge's head that must be considered,
first of all being that some opportunity for profit might have
presented itself, and although he did not consider himself a man
of sudden impulse, he had been known to act swiftly when the
right moment and the right investment presented itself. And
secondly, would he know himself if he observed himself about
his daily routine, for he was not a man wont to spend any

amount of time admiring his visage in a mirror—indeed, just the opposite, and who among us sees ourselves as others see us?

Quiet and dark, beside him stood the phantom, with its outstretched hand. When he roused himself from his thoughtful quest, he fancied from the turn of the hand, and its situation in reference to himself, that the unseen eyes were looking at him keenly. It made him shudder, and feel very cold.

≈ 35 ≈

They left the busy scene and Scrooge found himself, at once (how did they do it? the spirits, he wondered), on his own doorstep facing the very door where he had seen the face of Jacob Marley that very night. Scrooge turned to question the spirit of the purpose of the return to his home so early in their journey together (for surely the spirit meant to show him more than a few men chatting at the 'Change), but the door swung open of its own accord and he entered. The door to the cellar opened next, and though Scrooge would have liked to have protested entering the vampire's lair for a second time in one night, he felt himself propelled down the flight of stairs.

Together, he and the dark, silent phantom made their way through winding tunnels, all the while growing more and more alarmed as they drew near what he felt might be the presence of the beastly bloodsuckers, until Scrooge heard the sound of fiddle play. "A celebration?" he asked the phantom. "Do such creatures as these enjoy simple pastimes such as music and song?" *And if they did, would it be of mournful quality or something more restful?*

The phantom, of course, gave no reply.

Scrooge found himself in the same vaulted chamber where the previous spirit had brought him, only the atmosphere was quite different, on this occasion, on this *future* occasion. The previous pall had lifted and the king and queen, though on their dais as before, were far more animated than when last Scrooge visited. Mrs. Wahltraud was decked out in the finest and most fashionable gown, and her husband, Mr. Wahltraud, was equally attired in a new suit cut and sewn by some skilled tailor, perhaps even the ones Scrooge had heard mentioned earlier in the 'Change by the gentlemen discussing a coming funeral. The toothed host and hostess wore matching identical capes of the dearest-priced black velvet, a length of which cost more than a prudent man would wish to spend in furnishing a parlor.

The dining tables in the room had been pushed to the outer edges of the earthen wall, making room for two girls who danced merrily together to the sound of music and laughter. With dozens of folk looking on (some pale-faced, some not), the two girls, quite unconstrained and careless, danced in the freedom and gaiety of their hearts. The girls, at least upon first glance, appeared quite human to Scrooge and not beasties at all, which was odd when he thought of it, for what human females would dare to come to this place and conduct themselves in such a careful manner unless they were under some terrible spell, but as hard as he studied them, he could detect no hint of glaze in their eyes or slackness in their features.

Despite the close proximity of the vampires Scrooge so feared, he found it charming to see how these girls danced for themselves, despite the number of spectators, including the king and queen. The young girls, while very glad to please the crowd, seemed to dance to please themselves (or at least you would have supposed so from the smiles upon their faces), and he could no more help admiring, than they could help dancing.

How they did dance! And Scrooge could not help but wonder how they had come to be in the vampires' den, for they did not appear to be there against their will. But what human would enter a vampire's lair of his or her own accord? Scrooge would certainly not have been there for a second visit in the same night, had he been given the opportunity to choose, and he most certainly would not be there with his current escort, an apparition as frightening as the man and woman on the dais. Could these pretty, light-hearted girls be minions like his wet nurse, Mrs. Grottweil, and his clerk, Disgut?

The girls who performed for the king and queen did not dance like opera dancers. Not at all. And not like Madame Anybody's finished pupils. Not the least. It was not quadrille dancing, nor minuet dancing, nor even country-dance dancing. It was neither in the old style, nor the new style, nor the French style, nor the English style, though it may have been, by accident, a trifle in the Spanish style, which was a free and joyous one, deriving a delightful air of off-hand inspiration, from the chirping little castanets, nor was it the crude style recently brought from the Americas and finding followers among the higher clergy, which as far as Scrooge's opinion, and he did not consider himself an expert on the art of dance, but knew what he liked and what he did not. The new style consisted of jumping up and down and howling gibberish to the sound of primitive drums, all the while waving wooden axes and wearing feathered head-dresses.

The merry maidens danced among the spectators and sometimes the dining tables, and down the center of the room before King Wahltraud and Queen Griselda and back again. They twirled each other lightly round and round; the influence of their airy motion seemed to spread and spread, like an expanding circle in the water.

At last, the younger of the dancing girls, out of breath, and laughing gaily, threw herself upon the floor before the dais. The other leaned against an ivory-faced man wearing a green velvet coat, riding boots, and tiny bows in his hair. The music, a harp and fiddle played by two ghoulish-looking men, left off with a flourish, as if it boasted of its freshness, though the truth is, it had gone at such a pace, and worked itself to such a pitch of competition with the dancing, that it never could have held on, half a minute longer. The crowd raised a hum and murmur of applause, and then, in keeping with the cheer, Queen Griselda rose to her feet, clapping her slender, pale hands, encrusted with rings set with priceless gemstones, most of which, by coincidence or deliberate choosing, were blood-red rubies.

When Scrooge had last seen her in Christmas Present, minutes, hours, years ago, perhaps, the vampiress had been dressed in heavy black crepe to match her countenance, but today she wore a printed gown of the most beautiful colors money could buy beneath her black velvet cape, blue stockings, and fine leather shoes tied with blue silk ribbons. Her black hair fell down her back in thick waves, pinned in place with a sparkling crown of diamonds and rubies.

"Thank you so much, so much, indeed, all of you," she cried regally, demonstrating an easy grace. "And of course you, my dearest husband, my sovereign king, I thank you most of all for the coming of this day." She inclined her head toward King Wahltraud, who sat upon his throne, bearing his own crown, one even larger and more magnificent than hers, and a smile of satisfaction upon his face.

"This night has been many years in the making, and many of you have been instrumental in my success."

"Has he agreed?" shouted a short man with stout legs.

"Yes, is he ours?" called another.

"Tonight will be the final step in our journey, a mere formality," the beautiful queen assured her subjects.

"A toast," someone shouted.

"A toast," chimed others.

"You promised us a toast, Your Highness."

Scrooge recognized the voice and turned to see his clerk, Lucius Disgut, peek from behind a pillar.

"And so I did." She opened her arms to her subjects, then glanced over her shoulder. "Would you care to do the honor, my love?"

"It is yours, my love, for this is your accomplishment, not mine," responded the king with an equally regal eloquence.

The queen leaned over her king and kissed his lips lightly. The crowd cheered, and some of the younger men began to stomp and whistle. Disgut came from behind the pillar, and Scrooge had a mind to march over and dismiss him from his employment at that very moment, but that, of course, was not possible. This was an event that would take place in the future; as in the scenes of Christmas past and present, those who surrounded him were obviously unaware of his presence. Disgut's presence, however, made Scrooge no less angry.

What happened next, Scrooge was not entirely sure, for the scene seemed to burst all at once with too many things occurring at the very same instant, so frightening, so shocking, that he could not comprehend what he was seeing. One moment, the young girl who had danced was seated at the queen's feet, the very next, Griselda had caught her by the throat, lifted her lithe body up, and sunk protruding fangs into the girl's flesh.

The victim screamed, and her scream was echoed by her sister's. The older of the two girls had enough sense to try to escape, but not the capability. The queen's subjects fell upon the second dancer like rat terriers upon a rodent. Scrooge could have sworn he heard barking; most assuredly he heard grunting cries of delight, even as the girls struggled and cried out, fighting for their lives. Disgut was upon the very top of the heap, ripping the older girl's flesh and howling with pleasure.

Blood spattered and Scrooge turned away, his specter escort the lesser of the evils at the moment. "Spirit!" he cried, fallen to the cold, earthy ground and covering his face. "Take me away. I beg of you!"

Perhaps the ghost took pity on Scrooge; perhaps he was only following his own pre-ordained schedule (did such a thing exist among spirits?). Scrooge did not attempt to think he understood or even cared to; all he knew was that he was somewhere beneath the city one moment, on a familiar street in the daylight the next.

Still shaking, Scrooge slowly rose from his knees, staring at his hands, at his nightdress, certain they must be covered in blood. There was no evidence of blood, but in his head, Scrooge could still hear the young girls' screams.

"Take me where you must," he murmured to the phantom that stood over him, "but for pity's sake, take me far from that scene of evil."

They went into an obscure part of the town where Scrooge had never penetrated before, although he recognized its situation, and its bad repute. The ways were foul and narrow, the shops and houses wretched, the people half-naked, drunken, slipshod, ugly. Alleys and archways, like so many cesspools, disgorged their offenses of smell, and dirt, and life, upon the straggling streets, and the whole quarter reeked with crime, with filth, and misery. This place, at first glance, was worse than the tunnels beneath the city, infested by the vampires.

Far in this den of infamous resort, there was a low-browed, beetling shop, below a pent-house roof, where iron, old rags, bottles, bones, and greasy offal, were bought. Upon the floor within were piled up heaps of rusty keys, nails, chains, hinges, files, scales, weights, and refuse iron of all kinds. Secrets that few would like to scrutinize were bred and hidden in mountains of unseemly rags, masses of corrupted fat, and sepulchers of bones. Sitting in among the wares he dealt in, by a charcoal stove made of old bricks, was a gray-haired rascal, nearly seventy years of age, who had screened himself from the cold air without by a frowzy curtaining of miscellaneous tatters hung upon a line, and smoked his pipe in all the luxury of calm retirement.

Scrooge and the phantom came into the presence of this man, just as a woman with a heavy bundle, a boy at her side, slunk into the shop. But she had scarcely entered when another woman, similarly laden, came in, too. The second woman was closely followed by a man in faded black who was no less startled by the sight of them than they were of him. After a short period of blank astonishment in which the old man with the pipe had joined them, they all three burst into laughter.

"Let the laundress be the first," cried she who had entered first.

"B . . . be the f . . . f . . . first," repeated the boy.

"My son and I will be the second, and let the undertaker's man be the third. Look here, Old Joe, here's a chance. If we haven't all three met here without meaning it."

"W . . . w . . . without m . . . m . . . meaning it," said the boy.

Scrooge recognized the voice of the first woman, then the face of the boy who trotted behind her. "That's my housekeeper!" he exclaimed to no one in particular, for the spirit did not seem to be interested in anything he had to say. "And her son!"

"You couldn't have met in a better place," said the one she called Old Joe, removing his pipe from his mouth. "Come into the parlor. You were made free of it long ago, you know, and the other two ain't strangers. Stop till I shut the door of the shop. Ah! How it shrieks. There ain't such a rusty bit of metal in the place as its own hinges, I believe, and I'm sure there's no such old bones here, as mine. Ha, ha! We're all suitable to our calling, we're well matched. Come into the parlor. Come into the parlor."

The parlor was the space behind the screen of rags, and smelled as bad as any sewer Scrooge had ever had the misfortune of encountering. The old man raked the fire together with an old stair-rod, and having trimmed his smoky lamp (for it was so dark inside the hovel despite the light of day outside) with the stem of his pipe, put it in his mouth again.

While he did this, Gelda, Scrooge's shiftless housekeeper, threw her bundle on the floor, and sat down in a flaunting manner on a stool. She pointed for her son to drop to the floor as if to protect their possessions, and crossing her elbows on her knees, she looked with a bold defiance at the other two.

"What odds then. What odds, Mrs. Dilber?" said the housekeeper.

"W . . . w . . . what o . . . o . . . odds," echoed the son, drool dribbling from his crooked mouth.

"Every person has a right to take care of themselves," said Gelda. "He always did."

"A . . . a . . . always d . . . did."

"That's true, indeed," said the laundress. "No man more so."

"Why then, don't stand staring as if you was afraid, woman. Who's the wiser? The vampires, they care not. They've better to do tonight, I can promise you. No blood here, and no souls worth having, and that's all they seek. None such as we need fear them. We must stick together, the likes of us. We're not going to pick holes in each other's coats, I suppose."

"I . . . I s . . . suppose," reiterated the boy.

"An annoying habit," commented Scrooge to the spirit. "The boy, repeating what his mother says. But I suppose he cannot help himself," he added thoughtfully.

"No, indeed," said the laundress and the man together.

"We should hope not," continued the laundress. "Got what they want, I s'pose."

"Very well, then," cried the housekeeper. "That's enough. Who's the worse for the loss of a few things like these? Not a dead man, I suppose."

"D . . . dead man, I . . . I s . . . s . . . suppose."

"No, indeed," said Mrs. Dilber, laughing. She ignored the boy, for apparently she knew of his affliction and tolerated it well.

"It's not like he had need to keep them after he was dead, a wicked old screw," pursued Gelda. "Why wasn't he natural in his lifetime? If he had been, he'd have had somebody to look after him when he was struck with Death, instead of lying gasping out his last there, alone by himself."

"I heard he was engaged to be married once," put in the undertaker's man.

"I don't believe it. Not that one. He was too sour. Too mean."

"T . . . t . . . too m . . . m . . . mean," offered the boy.

His mother wiped his mouth with the cuff of her sleeve.

"It's the truest word that ever was spoke, Tag, boy," said Mrs. Dilber with a nod of her chin. "It's a judgment on him. Him bein' left to die alone in his own puddle!"

"I'd rather have the life sucked out of me by the vampire that lives under the eaves than die that way," said Old Joe thoughtfully, "or even the tall thin one that do hide in the chimney. But I guess you'd not feel the same, workin' for 'em the way you do." He looked pointedly at Gelda.

"Not my fault!" the housekeeper snapped. "It was that or give 'im my Tag. And us, we don't have more than a sip here or there. Not like some."

"N . . . not l . . . like s . . . s . . . some."

"I only wish it was a little heavier judgment," continued the housekeeper. "And it should have been, you may depend upon it, if I could have laid my hands on anything else. Open that bundle, Old Joe, and let me know the value of it. Speak out plain. I'm not afraid to be the first, nor afraid for them to see it. We know pretty well that we were helping ourselves, before we met here, I believe. It's no sin. Open the bundle, Joe."

"The b . . . b . . . bundle, J . . . J . . . Joe."

But the gallantry of her friends would not allow this, and the man in faded black, mounting the breach first, produced his plunder. It was not extensive. A seal or two, a pencil-case, a pair of sleeve-buttons, and a brooch of no great value, were all. They were severally examined and appraised by Old Joe, who chalked the sums he was disposed to give for each, upon the wall and added them up into a total when he found there was nothing more to come.

"That's your account," said Joe. "And I wouldn't give another sixpence if I was hung and fed upon for not doing it. Who's next?"

Mrs. Dilber was next. Sheets and towels, a little wearing apparel, two old-fashioned silver teaspoons, a pair of sugar-tongs, and a few boots. Her account was stated on the wall in the same manner.

"I always give too much to ladies. It's a weakness of mine, and that's the way I ruin myself," said Old Joe. "That's your account. If you asked me for another penny, and made it an open question, I'd repent of being so liberal and knock off half-a-crown."

"And now undo my bundle, Joe," urged Gelda.

"J . . . J . . . Joe," cried the boy enthusiastically. Again, the string of drool.

Joe went down on his knees for the greater convenience of opening the bundle, and having unfastened a great many knots, dragged out a large and heavy roll of some dark stuff. "What do you call this?" he asked. "Bed-curtains?"

"Ah," returned Scrooge's housekeeper, laughing and leaning forward on her crossed arms. "Bed-curtains."

"B . . . b . . . bed-curtains!"

"You don't mean to say you took them down, rings and all, with him lying there?" said Joe with a slap to his thigh.

"Yes, I do," she replied. "The master said 'take what you want, 'twas owed to you.' Why not?"

"W . . . why n . . . n . . . not?"

"You were born to make your fortune," said Joe, "and you'll certainly do it."

"I certainly shan't hold my hand when I can get anything in it by reaching it out, for the sake of such a man as he was, I promise you, Joe," returned Gelda coolly. "It's his fault I had to do the vampires' biddin' in the first place. Don't drop that oil upon the blankets, now, and ruin 'em."

"R . . . ruin 'em!"

Gelda smiled at her boy and patted his head.

"His blankets, too?" asked Joe.

"Whose else's do you think?" replied the housekeeper. "He isn't likely to take cold without them, I dare say."

"D . . . dare s . . . say."

"I hope he didn't die of anything catching. Eh?" said Old Joe, stopping in his work, and looking up.

"Don't you be afraid of that," returned the woman. "I ain't

so fond of his company that I'd loiter about him for such things, if he did. Ah. You may look through that shirt till your eyes ache, but you won't find a hole in it, nor a threadbare place. It's the best he had, and a fine one, too. They'd have wasted it, if it hadn't been for me."

"B . . . been f . . . for Mum!" the boy volunteered.

"What do you call wasting of it?" asked Old Joe.

"Putting it on him to be buried in, to be sure," replied Gelda with a laugh. "Somebody was fool enough to do it, but I took it off again. If calico ain't good enough for such a purpose, it ain't good enough for anything. It's quite as becoming to the body. He can't look uglier than he did in that one."

The boy opened his mouth to speak and his mother clamped her hand over it, drool and all, and Scrooge, for one, was thankful.

"Told to leave 'im, you know," said the undertaker's man.

"Leave him?" asked Old Joe. "Whatcha mean?"

"Mr. Martin, my employer, he said I wasn't to begin the embalming."

Old Joe scowled. "Not embalm him?"

"Why ever not?" demanded Gelda.

"N . . . not?" squeaked Tag from beneath his mother's hand.

"Not my part to ask," replied the undertaker's man. "Though I have my suspicions who gave the word."

Scrooge listened to this dialogue in horror. As they sat grouped about their spoil, in the scanty light afforded by the old man's lamp, he viewed them with a detestation and disgust, which could hardly have been greater, as though they were the demons, marketing the corpse itself.

"Ha, ha," laughed the housekeeper when Old Joe, producing a flannel bag with money in it, spilled out their gains upon the ground. "This is the end of it, you see. He frightened every one away from him when he was alive, to profit us when he was dead. Ha, ha, ha."

"Haaaa haaaa," the boy garbled under his mother's gag.

"Spirit," said Scrooge, shuddering from head to foot as he watched his own housekeeper, watched all of them cackle. "I see, I see. The case of this unhappy man might be my own. My life leads that way, now. Merciful Heaven, who is this they speak of?"

❧ 37 ❧

He recoiled in terror, for the scene had changed, and now he almost touched a bed, a bare, uncurtained bed on which, beneath a ragged sheet, there lay a something covered up, which, though it was dumb, announced itself in awful language.

The room was very dark, too dark to be observed with any accuracy, though Scrooge glanced round it in obedience to a secret impulse, anxious to know what kind of room it was. A pale light, rising in the outer air, fell straight upon the bed and on it, plundered and bereft, unwatched, unwept, uncared for, was the body of this man.

On the fringes of the room stood people, hazy and without form, though surely people. Men and women he recognized from the scene below stairs where the two girls had been attacked. The people did not see Scrooge, of course; they were too intent upon talking to each other, or perhaps not really there.

"Will you go tonight?" came a voice.

"We're not invited."

"Not invited?"

The voices seemed to come from everywhere, not just from the walls where the people stood, but from the ceiling and floor as well.

"A private ceremony."

"After all I've done for her! It is outrageous!"

"And you will say that to the queen?"

Others chimed in, voicing equal sentiments, until the singular voices created one, like the great hum of summer insects.

Scrooge glanced toward the phantom. Its steady hand was pointed to the head. The cover was so carelessly adjusted that the slightest raising of it, the motion of a finger upon Scrooge's part, would have disclosed the face. He thought of it, felt how easy it would be to do, and longed to do it; but had no more power to withdraw the veil than to dismiss the specter at his side.

Oh cold, cold, rigid, dreadful Death, set up thine altar here, and dress it with such terrors as thou hast at thy command, for this is thy dominion. But of the loved, revered, and honored head, thou canst not turn one hair to thy dread purposes, or make one feature odious. It is not that the hand is heavy and will fall down when released. It is not that the heart and pulse are still, but that the hand was open, generous, and true, the heart brave, warm, and tender, and the pulse a man's. Strike, Shadow, strike. And see his good deeds springing from the wound, to sow the world with life immortal.

No voice pronounced these words in Scrooge's ears. They were not the words of the men and women he had seen below and above his stairs, and yet he heard them when he looked upon the bed. He thought, if this man could be raised up now, what would be his foremost thoughts? Avarice, hard-dealing, griping cares? They have brought him to a rich end, truly.

He lay, in the dark empty house, with not a man, a woman, or a child, to say that he was kind to me in this or that, and for the memory of one kind word I will be kind to him. A cat was tearing at the door, and there was a sound of gnawing rats beneath the hearth-stone. The dancing girls, surely dead by now, cried out, and the ghouls that had fallen upon them howled their pleasure. What they wanted in the room of death, and why they were so restless and disturbed, Scrooge did not dare to think.

"Spirit," he said, shaking in his slippers, his nightcap falling over his forehead. "This is a fearful place. In leaving it, I shall not leave its lesson, trust me. I beg of you, take me from these demons that will suck the life's blood from mankind. Let us go."

Still the ghost pointed with an unmoved finger to the head.

"I understand you," Scrooge returned, "and I would do it, if I could. But I have not the power, Spirit. I have not the power."

Again it seemed to look upon him.

Scrooge placed his hands together, threading his fingers as if in prayer.

As I would have been, dear reader . . . in prayer, that is! Can you imagine the terror evoked in him, by spirit and vampire alike?

"If there is any person in the town who feels emotion caused by this man's death," said Scrooge, quite agonized, "show that person to me, Spirit, I beseech you."

❧ 38 ❧

The phantom spread its dark robe before him for a moment, like a wing, and withdrawing it, revealed a room by daylight, where a mother and her children were.

She was expecting someone, and with anxious eagerness, for she walked up and down the room, started at every sound, looked out from the window, glanced at the clock, tried, but in vain, to work with her needle, and could hardly bear the voices of the children in their play.

At length the long-expected knock was heard. She hurried to the door, and met her husband, a man whose face was care-worn and depressed, though he was young. There was a re-markable expression in it now, a kind of serious delight of which he felt ashamed, and which he struggled to repress.

"I know this man," said Scrooge. "Do I not? He is somehow familiar, and yet I cannot recall his name."

The man sat down to the dinner that had been boarding for him by the fire, and when she asked him faintly what news (which was not until after a long silence), he appeared embar-rassed how to answer.

"Is it good," she said, "or bad?"—to help him.

"Bad," he answered.

"We are quite ruined, then."

"No. There is hope yet, Caroline."

"If he relents," she said, amazed, "there is. Nothing is past hope, if such a miracle has happened."

"He is past relenting," said her husband. "He is dead."

She was a mild and patient creature if her face spoke truth, but she was thankful in her soul to hear it, and she said so, with clasped hands. She prayed forgiveness the next moment, and was sorry, but the first was the emotion of her heart.

"What the half-drunken housekeeper whom I told you of last night, said to me, when I tried to see him and obtain a week's delay, and what I thought was a mere excuse to avoid me, turns out to have been quite true. He was not only very ill, but dying, then."

"To whom will our debt be transferred? Not vampires, I pray. Mrs. Mutter's sister's debt was transferred to a vampire on Fleet Street, and he and his missus take blood from her each week for the interest owed. I cannot imagine how he will demand the principal."

"I don't know who it will be transferred to. Not vampire, I pray, although they do say that their foul fangs sink deep into the underbelly of the city and into the highest citadel, even to the palace itself. But before that time we shall be ready with the money, and even though we were not, it would be a bad fortune indeed to find so merciless a creditor, even a vampire, in his successor. We may sleep tonight with light hearts, Caroline."

Yes. Soften it as they would, their hearts were lighter. The children's faces, hushed and clustered round to hear what they so little understood, were brighter, and it was a happier house for this man's death. The only emotion that the ghost could show him, caused by the event, was one of pleasure.

And then, just at Scrooge turned away, he recalled suddenly

from where he recognized the man. "I know him, I do!" he told the spirit excitedly. Then his face fell and his pleasure of the moment went with it. "I spoke with him today."

The phantom waited, and though Scrooge could not see his face beneath the black hood, he felt the specter's black eyes upon him, boring into him.

"I . . ." Scrooge hung his head, tears filling his eyes. "His . . . his name is William . . . William something. William Dodd," he recalled, wiping at his eyes. "I threatened to send him on his way to debtor's prison if he did not make payment upon his bill to me."

The phantom continued to stare.

"O Spirit, let me see some tenderness connected with a death," said Scrooge. "Or . . . or that dark chamber, which we left just now, will be forever present to me."

The ghost conducted him through several streets familiar to his feet, and as they went along, Scrooge looked here and there to find himself, but nowhere was he to be seen. They entered poor Bob Cratchit's house, the dwelling he had visited before, and found the aunt and the children seated round the fire.

Quiet. Very quiet. The noisy little Cratchits were as still as statues in one corner, and sat looking up at Peter, who had a book before him. Cratchit's sister-in-law and her nieces were engaged in sewing. But surely they were very quiet.

"And he took a child, and set him in the midst of them." Peter hesitated. "And so the Great Scion will not have—"

Where had Scrooge heard those words? He had not dreamed them. The boy must have read them out, as he and the spirit crossed the threshold. Why did he not go on?

Because young Peter's voice choked and would not spill forth.

The aunt, Maena, laid her work upon the table and glanced at one of the girls. "Enough tears for him," she said impatiently.

"The color hurts my eyes," said the one called Martha.

Scrooge wondered what had become of her employment, but did not ask, for who was there to question? The specter would not answer him, and the Cratchits were unaware of his presence.

"Ah, poor Tiny Tim," said another.

"They're better now again," said Martha, blinking the moisture from her eyes. "It makes them weak by candle-light, and I wouldn't show weak eyes to my father when he comes home, for the world. It must be near his time."

"Past it rather," Peter answered, shutting up his book and wiping at his eyes. "But I think he has walked a little slower than he used to, these few last evenings, Martha."

They were very quiet again. At last Martha said, and in a steady, cheerful voice, that only faltered once, "I have known him to walk with—I have known him to walk with Tiny Tim upon his shoulder, very fast indeed, even on the nights they were not followed by bloodsuckers seeking fresh prey."

"And so have I," cried Peter. "Often."

"And so have I," exclaimed another. So had all.

"But he was very light to carry," Martha resumed, intent upon her work. "And his father loved him so, that it was no trouble. No trouble at all."

"No trouble at all," repeated several Cratchits.

"Enough with this maudlin talk!" Cratchit's sister-in-law threw down her sewing and rose from her chair. "You would think a child had never died! I've news for you all. They die every day. It is not so great an event. It is not as if he was an only child." She stomped from the room to climb the staircase.

"She has not been very understanding," whispered one of the Cratchit children.

"I do not think Aunt Maena feels the same loss we do," observed Peter, watching his aunt take her leave. There was a suspicious tone to his voice. "She was the one who cared for him, and yet how is it that she did not notice how ill he was?"

"Hush such talk!" Martha whispered. "There's Father at the door. You wouldn't want him to hear."

She hurried out to meet him, and Bob in his comforter—he had need of it, poor fellow—came in. His tea was ready for him on the hob, and they all tried to help him at once, pouring his tea and tucking his ragged comforter around him. Then two young Cratchits got upon his knees and laid, each child a little cheek, against his face, as if they said, "Don't mind it, Father. Don't be grieved."

Bob was very cheerful with them, and spoke pleasantly to all the family. He looked at the work upon the table, and praised the industry and speed of Martha and the girls. They would be done long before Sunday, he said.

"Sunday. You went today, then, Robert," said his eldest daughter, Martha.

"Yes, my dear," returned Bob. "I wish you could have gone. It would have done you good to see how green a place it is. But you'll see it often. I promised him that I would walk there on a Sunday. My little, little child," cried Bob, into his cup of tea. "My little child to whom we had all weighed such great hopes upon."

He broke down all at once. He couldn't help it.

"There, there, Father," whispered Martha, getting to her feet to lean over him and wrap her arm around his thin shoulders. "It's not your fault. You're not to blame."

"But everyone at the VSU, they were certain our Tim would grow up to be second to the Scion. And now—" He sobbed into his hands.

"Perhaps I can be the Scion's man, Father," offered Peter.

"I fear this means the prophecy will never be fulfilled," muttered Bob into his hands, not seeming to know, any longer, that his children were even there. "Gone is the hope. Gone is the hope," he repeated. Then he leaped from his chair near the hearth and hurried up the stairs, leaving behind his comforter.

Scrooge and the spirit followed.

Bob Cratchit entered the room above, which was lighted cheerfully, and hung with Christmas. There was a chair set close beside the child's body already laid out for his burial, and there were signs of someone having been there, lately. Poor Bob sat down in it, and when he had thought a little and composed himself, he kissed the little face. He sat there for several minutes to compose himself, kissed the child again, and returned below to join his family.

They drew about the fire, and talked, the girls working still. There was no sign of Maena. Bob told his family of the extraordinary kindness of Mr. Scrooge's nephew, whom he knew well from the Vampire Slayers Union, and who, meeting him in the street that day, and seeing that he looked a little—"just a little down you know," said Bob, inquired what had happened to distress him. "On which," said Bob, "for he is the pleasantest-spoken gentleman you ever heard, I told him. 'I am heartily sorry for it, Mr. Cratchit,' he said, 'and heartily sorry for your good family.' By-the-by, how he ever knew that, I don't know."

"Knew what, Father?" questioned Martha.

"Why, that you were a good family," replied Bob.

"Everybody knows that," said Peter, attempting to make a feeble jest.

"Very well observed, my boy," cried Bob. "I hope they do. 'Heartily sorry,' he said, 'for your good family. If I can be of service to you in any way,' he said, giving me his card, 'that's where I live. Pray come to me.' Now, it wasn't," said Bob, "for the sake of anything he might be able to do for us, so much as for his kind way, that this was quite delightful. He knew Tiny Tim well from the union meets, and I suspect that in his heart he will miss him as we all will. Not just because of the future we hoped he might bring, but for the person he was today."

"I'm sure Mr. Scrooge's nephew's a good soul," said Martha.

"You have said that he often spoke to you in the counting house."

"A good soul, a fine man. You would be surer of it, my dear," returned Bob, "if you saw and spoke to him. I shouldn't be at all surprised—mark what I say—if he got Peter a better situation."

"Only hear that, Peter," said the eldest daughter.

"And then," cried one of the girls, "Peter will be keeping company with someone, and setting up for himself."

"Get along with you," retorted Peter, grinning.

"It's just as likely as not," said Bob. "One of these days, though there's plenty of time for that, my dear. But however and when ever we part from one another, I am sure we shall none of us forget poor Tiny Tim—shall we—or this first parting that there was among us."

"Never, Father," cried they all.

"And I know," said Bob, "I know, my dears, that when we recollect how patient and how mild he was, although he was a little, little child, we shall not quarrel easily among ourselves, and forget poor Tiny Tim in doing it."

"No, never, Father," they all cried again.

"I am very happy," said little Bob, putting on a brave smile. "I am very happy to have you all."

Martha kissed him on his cheek, then the little girls kissed him, then the boys threw themselves to him, and Peter and himself shook hands. Spirit of Tiny Tim, thy childish essence was from God.

"Specter," said Scrooge, dabbing at his eyes. "Something informs me that our parting moment is at hand. I know it, but I know not how. Tell me what man that was whom we saw lying dead."

❧ 40 ❧

The Ghost of Christmas Yet To Come conveyed him, as be-fore—though at a different time, he thought, indeed, there seemed no order in these latter visions, save that they were in the future—into the resorts of businessmen, but showed him not himself. Indeed, the spirit did not stay for anything, but went straight on, as to the end just now desired, until besought by Scrooge to tarry for a moment.

"This court," said Scrooge, "through which we hurry now, is where my place of occupation is, and has been for a length of time. I see the house. Let me behold what I shall be, in days to come."

The spirit stopped; the hand was pointed elsewhere.

"The house is yonder," Scrooge exclaimed. "That which is Marley's but is now mine, vampire cellar and all. Why do you point away?"

The inexorable finger underwent no change.

Scrooge hastened to the window of his office, and looked in. It was an office still, but not his. The furniture was not the same, and the figure in the chair was not himself. The phantom pointed as before.

He joined it once again, and wondering why and whither he had gone, accompanied it until they reached an iron gate. He paused to look round before entering.

A churchyard. Here, then, the wretched man whose name he had now to learn, lay underneath the ground. It was a worthy place. Walled in by houses, overrun by grass and weeds, the growth of vegetation's death, not life choked up with too much burying, fat with repleted appetite. A worthy place.

The spirit stood among the graves and pointed down to one. Scrooge advanced toward it, trembling. The phantom was exactly as it had been, but he dreaded that he saw new meaning in its solemn shape.

"Before I draw nearer to that stone to which you point," said Scrooge, "answer me one question. Are these the shadows of the things that *will* be, or are they shadows of things that *may* be, only?"

Still the ghost pointed downward to the grave by which it stood.

"Men's courses will foreshadow certain ends, to which, if persevered in, they must lead," said Scrooge. "But if the courses be departed from, the ends will change. Say it is thus with what you show me."

The spirit was immovable as ever.

Scrooge crept toward it, trembling as he went, and following the finger, read upon the stone of the neglected grave his own name, Ebenezer Scrooge.

"Am I that man who lay upon the bed?" he cried, falling upon his knees, his nightdress tangled around his bony limbs.

The finger pointed from the grave to him, and back again.

"No, Spirit. Oh no, no."

The finger still was there.

Then a figure appeared at Scrooge's feet, a woman thrown

prostrate upon the grave, her arms spread wide. She sobbed, making great gulping sounds, struggling to take each breath, she was so overcome by emotion. "Ebenezer," she cried. "My Ebenezer. I cannot believe you are lost. I cannot believe we could not save you and now you are doomed to walk the earth as Jacob walks it, enrobed in those awful chains. It's my fault. My fault you were not saved!"

She turned her face, pressing her cheek to the ground, and Scrooge knew her at once. It was Belle! It was his Belle, and she cried for him! For his death!

"Belle . . . ," Scrooge murmured, wishing he could reach out to her, knowing he could not. "It is not your burden," he told her, a sob rising up in his throat for, at that moment, he was as wrought over Belle's broken heart as he was his own doomed fate. "It is my fault, dear Belle. Mine and mine alone. Please do not cry. Do not mourn for me, for I cannot stand it. To know you loved me all these years, and I was blind. So blind."

"How will I go on, knowing you are gone," she went on. "Knowing I failed you?"

"You see," exclaimed Ebenezer. "There is someone who weeps for my death. Don't you see, Spirit—" He looked up to where the spirit had been, but it was gone. In its place stood Wahltraud, King of the Vampires, and his Queen Griselda.

Ebenezer cried out in fear and stumbled to his feet, for these two frightened him more than would a dozen copies of Ghosts of Christmas Yet to Come.

Belle faded from his vision.

"What are you doing here?" Scrooge demanded, shaking in his slippers. "Can you not even give me peace in my death?"

Somehow he felt his present body becoming one with his future self. The lines seemed to blur, not just between the future and the present, but with the past as well. He didn't quite understand what was happening, but the entire evening had been without complete understanding, had it not?

The vampire queen smiled and glided toward him, a truly beautiful and frightening creature. "It does not have to be this way," she said in a voice as silky as the lining of any good coffin. She turned to Wahltraud and he smoothed her hair, petting her as if she were a kitten. "Do you wish to tell him or shall I, my dear?"

"Oh, you must tell him, my love," crooned Wahltraud, still stroking her. "He is, after all, your pet."

She smiled up at him, a smile that revealed long, ivory fangs, and then she returned her attention to Scrooge, her voice taking an edge. "You heard what she said, that one? Regarding your fate?" She gestured with a slender, pale hand. "You will be doomed to walk the earth eternally, neither dead nor alive, dragging those dreadful chains, agonizing over each link, regretting what cannot be altered."

Scrooge threaded his fingers together, gripping his hands. "My fate is to be the same as Jacob Marley's," he said. "Worse."

"Worse by many stone," the queen assured him with a smile.

"A terrible fate," intoned the king.

Scrooge shook his head in disbelief, his eyes closed. He wanted to tell them this was all their fault, the king's and queen's . . . the vampires'. But he knew the truth. Time and time again while they might have offered temptation or tribulation, it was he who had made the final choice. No one had ever physically forced his hand.

"A wretched fate, indeed," said the queen. "But one you can still avoid."

Scrooge looked up, his hands still clenched in prayer. "I . . . I can? You mean these events can still be altered?" He glanced back at the spirit, who was fading with every passing moment, and somehow Scrooge knew that once the ghost was gone, Scrooge's fate would be sealed. "How?" he begged, turning back toward the vampires.

I hesitate to interrupt, dear reader, at such a pivotal moment in this tale, but I must question why, after all Scrooge had witnessed, he would turn to Queen Griselda and King Wahltraud. Were you Ebenezer Scrooge, would you not place your trust in the spirit (no matter how frightening he might seem) sent to guide you, rather than the vampires that have spent your full life contributing to your undoing?

I apologize for my digression. Back to the story. . . .

"Tell me how," Scrooge insisted. "How may I alter my fate?"

The queen smiled at her king, then smiled down upon Scrooge, for she seemed taller than he at this moment. "You can join us," she said in the sweetest voice, a voice that could mesmerize a man. Enchant him. Even entice.

"Join you?" questioned Scrooge.

"Become one of us and live for all eternity. You would have great autonomy. You would be left to count your gold, make as much of it as you like, take advantage of as many as you like." She smiled sweetly. "It would be a good life, Ebenezer. No chains, no howling, no wandering the earth."

Ebenezer looked into her black eyes. "And in return for this reprieve?" he asked, for nothing was ever free.

Queen Griselda glanced over her shoulder, smiled at the king, and then looked back at Ebenezer. "All you must do is bring me the blood of one little human." She held up a finger.

"One?" Scrooge whispered, horrified.

"Bring me the blood of your Belle, and you will live forever, Ebenezer Scrooge."

"Nooooooo!"

Ebenezer heard the scream, and for a moment, he did not know from where it came. The he realized his own mouth was agape and the terrifying sound was coming from within. Out of the corner of his eye, he caught a glimpse of the fading robe of the Ghost of Christmas Yet to Come, and he flung himself into the dark mist that was the specter, his last hope.

"Spirit," he cried, tightly clutching at its robe, his eyes screwed shut. "Hear me. I am not the man I was. I will not be the man I must have been but for this intercourse. Why show me this, if I am past all hope?"

For the first time the hand appeared to shake.

The vision of the king and queen was beginning to fade. Ebenezer could still hear Queen Griselda's voice, but it sounded far off. She was shouting at him, demanding his attention, but he ignored her. The more he ignored her, the faster she faded.

"Good Spirit," Scrooge pursued, as down upon the ground he fell before it, "your nature intercedes for me, and pities me. Assure me that I yet may change these shadows you have shown me, by an altered life. That I am not forced to chose between two variations of the undead."

The kind hand trembled.

"Give me a chance and I will honor Christmas in my heart, and try to keep it all the year. I will live in the past, the present, and the future. The spirits of all three shall strive within me. I will not shut out the lessons that they teach. I will never again be controlled by the vampires," he declared, and the vision of them vanished. "I will rise against them with my fellow man until they are no more. Oh, tell me I may sponge away the writing on this stone."

In his agony, he caught the spectral hand. It sought to free itself, but he was strong in his entreaty, and detained it. The spirit, stronger yet, repulsed him.

Holding up his hands in a last prayer to have his fate reversed, he saw an alteration in the phantom's hood and dress. It shrunk, collapsed, and dwindled down into a bedpost.

STAVE 5

THE END OF IT

∽ 42 ∽

Yes! and the bedpost was his own. The bed was his own, the room was his own. Best and happiest of all, the time before him was his own, to make amends in!

"I will live in the past, the present, and the future," Scrooge repeated, as he scrambled out of bed. "And I shall be a champion of mankind. I will see an end to the vampires! I will smite them head and foot. I will dedicate my life to doing good and ridding Great Britain of the bloodsuckers. The spirits of all three shall strive within me—past, present, and future—and their words within me will give me the strength to carry a pike upon my shoulder. Oh Jacob Marley! Oh my dearest Belle who sent him! Heaven, and the Christmas time be praised for this. I say it on my knees, my dearest Belle, my beloved, on my knees."

He was so fluttered and so glowing with his good intentions that his broken voice would scarcely answer to his call. He had been sobbing violently in his conflict with the spirit, and his face was wet with tears.

"They are not torn down," cried Scrooge, folding one of his bed-curtains in his arms and then burying his face in the heavy fabric. "They are not torn down, rings and all. They are here— I am here—the shadows of the things that would have been, may be dispelled. They will be. I know they will."

He released the curtains, throwing out his arms to turn in a circle, not caring that his nightdress tangled around his feet, nearly tripping him. "What to do first! So many choices. So many!"

His hands were busy with his garments, turning them inside out, putting them on upside down, tearing them, mislaying them, grabbing a pillow and setting it upon his head, laughing, dancing, making his clothing and linens parties to every kind of merry extravagance of spirit.

"So many potential opportunities that I don't know what to do," cried Scrooge, laughing and crying in the same breath. "I am as light as a feather, I am as happy as an angel, I am as merry as a schoolboy. I am as giddy as a drunken man. A merry Christmas to everybody—everyone who does not drink of the life's blood of his fellow man. A happy new year to all the humans in this world. Hallo here." His voice seemed to echo in the dingy, high-ceilinged chamber. "Whoop. Hallo."

He frisked into the sitting room, and stood there, perfectly winded.

"There's the saucepan of gruel upon the hob that Gelda made me," cried Scrooge, starting off again, and going round the fireplace. "Oh, what to do about Gelda? Do I keep her on and snatch her from the vampires' grip?" Would it even be possible? Once a human became a vampire's minion (for surely she was one), could he or she be turned around, or was Gelda already lost to mankind? What if she, like Scrooge, had been taken advantage of, manipulated by the beasties? Didn't she deserve another chance? And the boy? What to do with that poor boy of hers, for surely he could not be held responsible for his mother dallying with vampires! Surely, there must be some redemption for the hapless pair, some way to snatch them from the fangs of the evil ones. And if there was, he would discover it. "I will save you," he cried, "even you, Gelda, and your pitiful boy, even him, so help me Christmas!"

Scrooge spun in a circle, the motion and his jumble of thoughts making him dizzy. His mind was racing at an incredible speed, his heart still pounding. "Here's the door, by which the ghost of Jacob Marley entered. There's the corner where the Ghost of Christmas Present sat. There's the window where I saw the wandering spirits. It's all right, it's all true, it all happened. Ha ha ha!"

Really, for a man who had been out of practice for so many years, it was a splendid laugh, a most illustrious laugh. The father of a long, long line of brilliant laughs trapped for so long in darkness and misery now let out to the light of day and all the merrier for it.

"I don't know what day of the month it is," said Scrooge. "I don't know how long I've been among the spirits. I don't know anything. I'm quite a baby. Never mind. I don't care. I'd rather be a baby." He thrust out his arms and spun as he had not since he was a little child. "Hallo. Whoop. Hallo here!"

He was checked in his transports by the churches ringing out the lustiest peals he had ever heard. Clash, clang, hammer; ding, dong, bell. Bell, dong, ding; hammer, clang, clash. Oh, glorious, glorious bells, happy, happy day of joy, wonderful, glorious, happy day of his true birth.

Running to the window, he opened it, and put out his head. No fog, no mist. It was clear, bright, jovial, stirring, cold, cold, piping for the blood to dance to. (Blood? He did not want to even think of blood. Not yet! There would be plenty of time for that, would there not? Plenty of time, thanks to the spirits!) Sun upon his face, he breathed in the frosty air; it burned his lungs and made him choke and laugh at the same time. Oh golden sunlight! Heavenly sky! Sweet fresh air and merry bells. Oh, glorious. Glorious.

But he could not stand here in his window in his night-clothes with so much to accomplish, could he? This was not a day to be wasted, not an hour, not a minute, not a heartbeat—he must be about the business of living and caring for his neighbors and fellow men.

"What's today?" cried Scrooge, calling downward to a boy in Sunday clothes, who perhaps had loitered in to look about him.

"Eh?" returned the boy, with all his might of wonder.

Scrooge plucked off his nightcap and ran his fingers through his hair, or what was left of it! "What's today, my fine fellow?" he asked.

"Today?" replied the boy, seeming as shocked by Scrooge's appearance as one would be by a vampire shouting the same question from an upper-story window. "Why, Christmas Day."

"It's Christmas Day," said Scrooge to himself as he balled up his nightcap and tossed it over his shoulder. "Then I haven't missed it. The spirits have done it all in one night. They can do anything they like. Of course they can. Of course they can." Scrooge began to make plans in his head, his thoughts jumping from one matter to the next. So much to do! "Hallo, my fine fellow!"

"Hallo," returned the boy, taking a step back. If Scrooge flew down from the windowsill, the boy probably reasoned he still had a good chance at making an escape.

"Do you know the poulterer's, in the next street?"

The boy wrinkled his nose. "The one the vampires just took over, sir?"

"The one the vampires just took over?" Scrooge repeated to himself. "Certainly not! Certainly not."

How had he missed such an occurrence when this young lad had knowledge of it? Blind, because he had been blind, of course! For years he'd gone through life with his eyes closed, thinking only of making his fortune, thinking only the thoughts that the evil ones had planted in his mind, but no more. From this day on he was as free as a bird.

"Not that one, lad. Better not that one. What about on the next street over? Barnakins, it's called, I believe."

"I should hope I did know that one," replied the lad.

"An intelligent boy," remarked Scrooge. "A remarkable boy." He looked down to him. "Do you know whether they've sold the prize turkey that was hanging up there? Not the little prize turkey. The big one."

"What, the one as big as me?" returned the boy, gesturing with his arms opened wide.

"What a delightful boy," said Scrooge, trying to make some semblance of his hair with his fingers, for surely it was standing on end after removing his nightcap. "Yes, that's the one," he hollered down.

"It's hanging there now," replied the boy.

"Is it?" said Scrooge. "Go and buy it, then!"

"Vampires addled your brain?" exclaimed the lad, only half in jest.

"No, no. Well, yes, actually."

The lad stared up at him with a queer look on his face.

"No, of course not," said Scrooge, not wanting to scare the boy and not sure how to explain himself. How could he explain to this lad what he did not understand himself? "I am in earnest in the matter of the turkey. Go and buy it, and tell them to bring it here, that I may give them the direction where to take it. Come back with the man, and I'll give you a shilling. Come back with him in less than five minutes and I'll give you half-a-crown!"

The boy was off like a shot. He must have had a steady hand at a trigger who could have got a shot off half so fast.

"Delightful boy, smart and sturdy lad, the pride of his

mother's house, I'm sure," Scrooge cried and laughed aloud again.

"I'll send it to Bob Cratchit's," murmured Scrooge, rubbing his hands, and splitting with another peal of laughter. "He shan't know who sends it. It's twice the size of Tiny Tim. Imagine his sister-in-law trying to cook that up." (It occurred to him that Maena would have to be dealt with, as well, if he was to protect Tiny Tim, but he would have to speak to Bob on that matter, and tomorrow would be soon enough.) Thinking of the turkey again, he could only imagine Maena's complaints as she was forced to haul it to the cook shop, for she could never roast such a bird in the Cratchits' inadequate kitchen. He giggled at the thought of Maena trudging to the cook shop with that massive bird.

The hand in which he wrote his clerk's address was not a steady one, but write it he did, somehow, and went downstairs to open the street door, ready for the coming of the poulterer's man. As he stood there, waiting his arrival, the knocker caught his eye.

"I shall love it, as long as I live," cried Scrooge, patting it with his hand. "I scarcely ever looked at it before. What an honest expression it has in its face. It's a wonderful knocker."

His gaze shifted to the door that led into his cellar and the vampires' lair. His first impulse—though still in his nightclothes—was to grab something resembling a pike and race down the stairs impaling the first vampire he encountered, not stopping until the beasties were obliterated, or they obliterated him. But of course that was not wise, not wise at all. He needed a plan. He needed assistance. He had an idea who to seek in this matter, but he had to set his priorities this first day of his new life, and there was someone he had to see before he made plans to bring down the King and Queen of Vampires.

And ah, here was the turkey! He spotted the poulterer's

man, lugging the dressed fowl up the walk, huffing and puffing with the exertion of it. Behind him ran the lad who had served as messenger.

"Hallo," cried Scrooge with a wave of his hand and a little, "Whoop! How are you? Merry Christmas."

"Brought your turkey, sir," announced the bearer.

And a fine turkey it was! It never could have stood upon its legs, that bird. It would have snapped them short off in a minute, like sticks of sealing-wax. In fact, the poulterer's man looked as if *his* legs might snap under the burden. His limbs wobbled, his face perspired, and he was as red as a pot of cranberry jelly.

"Why, it's impossible to carry that to Camden Town," said Scrooge from the threshold, concerned for the man's health. "You must have a cab."

The chuckle with which he said this, and the chuckle with which he paid for the turkey, and the chuckle with which he paid for the cab, and the chuckle with which he recompensed the boy, were only to be exceeded by the chuckle with which he sat down breathless in his chair again, and chuckled till he cried.

Seeing the poultry bearer and the boy off, Scrooge bounded up the stairs again. He had to be on his way, for he had many stops to make, but first he had to dress, and sharp he wanted to look. His sharpest ever for what his intentions were!

Shaving was not an easy task, for his hand continued to shake very much, and shaving requires attention, even when you don't dance while you are at it. But if he had cut the end of his nose off, he would have put a piece of sticking-plaster over it, and been quite satisfied. As Scrooge shaved, twisting his chin this way and that, he was amazed to see that there was no fear in the man's eyes who looked back at him. No fear at all! No fear of the vampires he knew crawled in the cellar below, or perhaps slept in their coffins at that very moment. No fear of the call he would make first on that day. If he had any sense, he would be more afraid of the second than the first, but he felt none of the dread, only the excitement of possibility. Had the spirits of the previous night frightened all the fear out of him? He did not know, but the thought made him laugh aloud. To frighten one's fear. Really!

Scrooge dressed himself all in his best in a green serge waistcoat and matching frock coat, with a fresh linen shirt and smart four-in-hand necktie, and at last got out into the streets. The people were by this time pouring forth, as he had seen them with the Ghost of Christmas Present. Walking with his hands behind him, Scrooge regarded every one with a delighted smile. He looked so irresistibly pleasant, in a word, that three or four good-humored fellows said, "Good morning, sir. A merry Christmas to you." And Scrooge said often afterward, that of all the blithe sounds he had ever heard, those were the blithest in his ears.

He had not gone far, when coming on toward him he beheld the portly gentleman who had walked into his counting house the day before, and said, "Scrooge and Marley's, I believe." It sent a pang across Scrooge's heart to think how this old gentleman would look upon him when they met, but he knew what path lay straight before him, and he took it.

"My dear sir," said Scrooge, quickening his pace, and taking the old gentleman by both his hands. "How do you do? I hope you succeeded yesterday. It was very kind of you to collect for the poor. A merry Christmas to you and yours, sir."

"Mr. Scrooge," the man said. Shock followed recognition. He offered his hand, but not without suspicion in his eyes.

"Yes," said Scrooge jovially. "Ha ha. That is my name, and I fear it may not be pleasant to you. Allow me to ask your pardon. And will you have the goodness to allow me to make a donation of . . ." Here, Scrooge whispered in his ear.

"Lord bless me," cried the gentleman, as if his breath were taken away. He looked Scrooge right in the eyes. "My dear Mr. Scrooge, are you serious?"

"If you please," said Scrooge with a grin, for it felt quite grand, really, to offer such a sum. And the words slipped so easily from his lips, as if he had spent his entire life dwelling in generosity. "Not a farthing less. A great many back payments are included in it, I assure you. Will you do me that favor? Please say you will."

"My dear sir," said the other, shaking hands with him. "I don't know what to say to such munificence. I don't know what to do."

"Don't say or do anything, please," retorted Scrooge, pumping his hand again. He leaned close. "Most of all, please don't drag me into the alley and sink your fangs into me and drink my blood, for I've a busy day planned." He laughed.

The man did not see the humor of Scrooge's comment, but, instead, seemed rather horrified. "Mr. Scrooge, I am not a vampire," he said with such repulsion that Scrooge quite believed him.

"Well, good for you, because if you were, I might have to take that walking stick from you and pierce your heart! And I've absolutely no idea how to do such a thing, and I fear I'd make a mess of it." He gave another merry laugh. "Now, come and see me in my office, and we will talk. I have some thoughts on keeping some of those men and women out of the poorhouse and getting rid of some of these vampires at the same time. It just makes good business sense, you know, to give good men and women work and rid the city of pestilence at the same time. Will you come and see me?"

"I will," cried the old gentleman. And it was clear he meant to do it.

"Thank you," said Scrooge as he walked away, tipping his

hat again and again. "I am much obliged to you. I thank you fifty times. A hundred. Bless you."

He went to church, and then made his way to a white house with a roof of three gables and an old arched door. He had passed here only the night before, but had seen it in an entirely different light then. Now it was a haven, not just for those who fought for the cause, but he hoped for himself. He prayed the invitation extended for so many years was still open.

❧ 43 ❧

Scrooge screwed up his nerve with only a little hesitation and knocked. Behind the door, he heard a woman's footsteps, light and full of . . . hope, he thought, and his heart swelled with possibilities. Then the door opened and there she was.

"Ebenezer," she said in obvious shock. She wore a dress with a small domed skirt that had not been fashionable in a very long time (women's skirts had grown bigger over the years!), but the blue of the faded bodice matched her eyes most exquisitely, and he took note that unlike the hair on his own pate (what was left of it), she was not in the least bit gray. Hadn't she been gray at the temples only last night?

But it didn't matter. He wouldn't have cared if she were an old woman bent over a cane.

"Belle," he said, her name tasting as sweet on his lips as fresh strawberries in the springtime. Though it had been many years, perhaps decades, since he had sampled fresh strawberries in the spring, even though they had once been his most favorite. The vampires? Were they responsible? Did Queen Griselda even control what fruit he put into his mouth? If they had, they were in for a terrible shock, the evil beasties, for he'd eat strawberries by the basket, fresh and sweet, and sparkling with morning dew and heaped all over with Devonshire cream and the best white sugar whenever they were in season.

"Ebenezer . . . you're here." The frown lines on her forehead smoothed, and she appeared to grow younger before his very eyes until she nearly seemed the girl of twenty he had once known. "The ghost of Jacob came to see you, didn't he? He did it," she managed, tears springing in her eyes. "I hoped. I prayed, but I did not even know if it was possible."

"Jacob did come to me as a ghost—and many others—and to you I owe my thanks. He told me it was you who sent him, so I owe you my life, Belle. I don't know how you managed it. How you or Jacob or any of the spirits—"

"Spirits?" she asked, her eyes growing wide. "You see spirits, Ebenezer?"

He smiled, his own eyes welling up. "I've so much to tell you, but first I must beg your forgiveness. " He took her hand and she let him, and he kissed it once, twice, and then again. Her skin was as smooth as he remembered. "Please forgive me for the foolish, unseeing, uncaring man I have been."

"Ebenezer, there is no need for you to—"

"No, there is need. I must say it. I must make amends with you and so many others, before I can start my work fighting the vampires that I know you have been fighting all these years. But I must start with you," he said firmly. He still held her hand.

"What you must *start* with is breakfast," she told him, giving him quite a saucy look. "That's why you came, isn't it? To break your fast on this fine Christmas Day?"

Her smile was infectious. "Yes . . . yes, I suppose I did. But I must make my apologies, and I have so much to tell you, Belle. The spirits, they showed me so many things I did not know."

A man appeared over her shoulder. "Is everything all right here, Belle?"

It was the same man Scrooge recognized from his visit here the night before with the Ghost of Christmas Present. It was the man with the limp. The man whose little girl's name was Alice.

"Everything is fine, John."

"How is that delightful little girl of yours?" inquired Scrooge. "Such a pretty girl." He looked to Belle. "Such a pretty child, and so sweet. So well-behaved a child I do not believe I have ever seen!"

"I'm sorry, sir. But do I know you?" asked the man called John, his gaze narrowing suspiciously. (And why shouldn't he be suspicious, considering all he had been through as of late?)

"John, this is my old friend Ebenezer. Ebenezer, John," she introduced. "We tend not to use last names," she explained to Scrooge. "It's safer this way."

Scrooge was itching to ask the whys of such a statement. He had so many questions about the Vampire Slayers Union and its members and was quite eager to join them as a member, giving whatever aid he could, financial and otherwise, but he knew he must be patient and gain their trust, first. So instead of asking questions, he thrust out his hand. "It is a pleasure to meet you firsthand, sir, for we have not actually met. I only know of you," he explained. "I am an admirer of yours. You are quite well known in slayer circles, I do believe."

John looked at Belle questioningly as he accepted the handshake, but she only smiled. "Come now, gentlemen. Inside with you both."

John left them on the doorstep, but Scrooge remained where he was. "I have so much to tell you, Belle. I want to be a part of your life again. I want your cause to be my cause." He suddenly felt shy as he looked down on her, wondering if there could be any possibility a man like him could have a woman like her. "I want you to give me another chance. *Us* another chance."

"Oh, Ebenezer!" She threw her arms around him. "I cannot tell you how many times I dreamed of this moment. Now, come inside and join me and my guests, and we will talk later. There are many at my table this morning, but there is always room for another."

Belle grasped a handful of her skirt in each hand and turned. "Come along, Ebenezer, or the sausages will grow cold and the porridge gluey."

Her order left him with no choice but to follow, and gleefully he did so.

Hours later, Scrooge set out with Belle on his arm and they walked about the streets, and watched the people hurrying to and fro. He was so enthralled by the people around him that he patted children on the head, questioned beggars, and looked down into the kitchens of houses, and up to the windows, and found that everything could yield him pleasure. He had never dreamed that any walk—that anything—could give him so much happiness. And what made him happiest of all was having Belle at his side again after all these years.

"I cannot believe you're here," Scrooge said to Belle as he nodded to this man and that woman on the street.

"But I've always lived in London," she teased, looking quite striking in an old blue bonnet. (Scrooge had wanted to buy her a new dress and coat and bonnet today, but she had insisted there would be time for that another day. Besides, with so many in need, she was not certain she wanted a new bonnet. Imagine that, reader! A woman who doesn't want a new bonnet. Of course, that made Scrooge all the more eager to buy her one.)

"You know what I mean." Scrooge flipped a beggar a coin. Realizing his sack was nearly empty, he wondered if they would have to return to his house and grab another bag from beneath the loose brick on the hearth in his bedchamber. Who would have believed that he could find such joy by sharing the silver that had lain so long in darkness, for he had never felt so free or rich as he did today. "I mean I cannot believe that you are willing, after the things I have done, to you and to others, to walk with me in public. Are you not afraid?"

"Whatever of?" she asked, smoothing the sleeve of his great-coat.

"Of the vampires," he said, lowering his voice. They passed an old woman leaning against a door to catch her breath and he pressed a coin into her palm.

"God bless ye!" she called after him, staring in disbelief at the money she now held. "Merry Christmas!"

"And a merry Christmas to you," Scrooge threw over his shoulder. "Are you not afraid the vampire king and queen will come after me, seeing that I am a changed man, and try to sway me, perhaps harming you?"

"I'm not afraid, Ebenezer," she said, looking into his eyes. "They draw much of their strength from the humans who deny their existence. They were able to control so much around you because you could not see it. And we are protected."

"Protected?" he questioned.

"I . . . Because of my ability to see and communicate with spirits, I possess a certain strength against the vampires." She laid her cheek upon his sleeve. "And now that you allow me, I can protect you."

"Will . . . will this protection allow me to fight the vampires?"

She laughed, music in his ears. "I think you need a few lessons in the proper use of a pike from your clerk first, and there will still be danger for you, but if you continue to walk in the light you walk in today, I have faith you will live a long life, Ebenezer, and give aid to many people."

"With you at my side."

"With me at your side," she agreed.

They walked another half block, giving out several more pennies before he spoke again. "You spoke of lessons from my clerk." He looked down at her. "You meant Cratchit, not Disgut, did you not?"

"I meant Bob, yes." She looked away, smiling at a woman leading two rosy-cheeked children by the hands.

"You know Bob Cratchit?"

Again the smile. "Quite well. He's an active member of the local VS union and a fine man." Her pretty smile turned into a frown. "It was a very sad thing when his wife was killed. She died protecting her children."

Scrooge also felt a sadness, not because he had known Mrs. Cratchit as Belle had, but a sadness for his lack of proper response when Cratchit had lost his wife and a sadness for the sorry man he'd been to be so unfeeling.

"You know," Belle said. "Lucius Disgut is a very bad man. A dangerous man. The VSU has been keeping track of him for some time. He is protected by the king and queen."

"And me inadvertently," he put in.

"Now, now, that cannot be helped. You must move forward and not look back. Looking back will only allow the vampires to move closer to you again, to control you again."

"I've so much to learn," Scrooge said.

"But I will help you," she insisted, smiling again.

"But I will have you." He glanced at the door off the street which was their intended destination. "And here we are." He hesitated. "What if he does not welcome me?" Scrooge asked. "What if it is too late?"

"It's not too late," she murmured.

Scrooge knocked and the door was quickly answered. "Is

your master at home, my dear?" said Scrooge to the girl with nutmeg brown eyes. Nice girl. Very nice, indeed. No sign whatsoever of vampire control. On the walk here Belle had given Scrooge some lessons on how to spot a vampire, one of their minions, or someone who had been somewhat manipulated by the vampires. This girl was not one of them; her skin was bright pink, no fangs, no smears of blood on her face, and she looked well-fed, by her employer, probably. He could catch glimpses of her rosy throat, and it was not wrapped all about and covered to hide the fang marks; indeed, it was a lovely neck and a lovely head on top of it, an altogether merry girl of good spirit. The vampires, Belle had explained, tended to prey upon those in the greatest need.

"Yes, sir, he is at home," said the girl.

"Where is he, my love?" asked Scrooge.

"He's in the dining room, sir, along with mistress. I'll show you upstairs, if you please. Let me take your coats and hats."

Scrooge helped Belle with her cloak and bonnet, then removed his own outer garments and handed the whole pile to the petite maidservant. "Do you need help?" he asked, quite afraid he had overburdened her.

She laughed, peeking over the high pile of woolens, one blue ribbon of Belle's bonnet tickling her nose. "No, sir. Thank you, sir. I can show you the way." She staggered forward.

"That won't be necessary," said Scrooge, with his hand already on the dining-room lock. "He knows us. We'll go in ourselves, my dear."

Offering his arm to Belle again, he turned the doorknob gently, and sidled his face in, round the door. They were looking at the table (which was spread out in great array), for these young housekeepers were always nervous on such points, and like to see that everything is right.

"Fred," said Scrooge, surprised by the nervous gurgle he felt in his stomach. What if his nephew turned him away? What if, after all these years, the young man, his brave sister's son, had had enough abuse? What would Scrooge do then? He did not even want to consider the matter.

He stepped into the dining room.

Dear heart alive, how his niece, Penny, started! Scrooge had forgotten, for the moment, about her sitting in the corner with the footstool, or he wouldn't have done it, on any account.

"Why bless my soul," cried Fred, in obvious and genuine shock. He rose from his chair at the head of the table. "Who's that?" he cried, though he most certainly knew who it was.

"It's I. Your Uncle Scrooge. I have come to spend the afternoon with you. Will you let me in, Fred? I have brought my betrothed, with whom I believe you are well acquainted. Better acquainted right now, I might say, than I. I hope you don't mind my taking the liberty of bringing her with me, but the truth is, I could not stand to leave her . . . and I thought perhaps you would show an old fool a little kindness if I hid behind a pretty woman."

"Your betrothed?" squealed Penny in a most delightfully feminine manner. "You are betrothed, Belle? To Uncle Ebenezer?" Her tone of voice suggested "why ever would you agree to such a thing?" but the smile on Belle's face seemed to sway her.

"Then congratulations! Come, tell us all about it." The two women, hand in hand, walked away to join the other female guests and giggle.

It was a mercy Fred didn't shake his arm off. Scrooge was feeling at home and feeling like a true member of the family in five minutes. Nothing could have been heartier. His niece looked just the same. So did Topper. So did the plump sister. So did everyone.

"Uncle Ebenezer, I cannot believe it's you." Fred finally let go of Scrooge's hand, then reached out and gave it another four or five shakes. "And what is this talk of your betrothal?" He glanced at Belle, surrounded by the other women.

Though Belle was older than the female guests present by nearly an entire generation, Scrooge thought she was the prettiest one there. Even prettier than his pretty niece, but of course he kept that to himself.

"I know you must wonder what has brought me here with this smile upon my lips and this woman at my side," Scrooge told his nephew, drawing him to a corner to have some measure of privacy before they joined the merry-making.

"I wonder," said Fred, grasping his uncle's shoulders. "But it's not necessary that you tell me. I'm happy that you've come and that you're a changed man." He looked into his eyes. "And you are a changed man, aren't you, Uncle? I can see it on your face."

"That I am. I apologize for my behavior all these years. It is no excuse, but it appears I have been under others' influence for many years. Many years," he repeated.

"Others' influence?" The party around the dining table was beginning to break up and the guests were moving to the parlor, but Fred's attention remained on his uncle. "Whatever do you mean?"

"Vampires, dear Fred." Scrooge feared his nephew might scoff, or think him making excuses, but it was important to him that he be entirely honest. "I fear . . . no, I am certain that vampires have been swaying me since a very early age. It is a long story, which I promise to share with you in entirety, but it's Christmas Day." He grinned. "And we should join your guests. There will be time for talk tomorrow and the day after, and the day after that, I do hope."

"Well said. I just still cannot believe you're here." Fred shook Scrooge's hand, stepped back, stepped forward and embraced him, and stepped back yet again. "We're going to play games. Would you like to join us?"

"I hoped we would not miss the games!" Scrooge said with enthusiasm.

"Excellent." Fred clasped his hands. "But be forewarned; Belle is very good."

"I would like to play, particularly that game Yes and No."

"You know it, do you?" Fred asked. "Excellent. But I can promise you Belle shall beat us all at that one." He hesitated. "You say you're engaged to be married? Just like that? Might I ask?"

Scrooge snapped his fingers. Enjoying the sound it made so greatly, he did it again. "Just like that."

"And when will you wed?"

"As soon as she will have me," Scrooge declared, unable to wipe the foolish grin from his face. He still could not believe that Belle loved him. That she had waited all these years for him. That she had kept faith in him long after he had lost faith in himself. "Do not look so surprised. It has been a rather long engagement." He chuckled, and Fred chuckled with him.

"Well, congratulations. I am glad you have come to your senses. A wife is a wonderful gift that every man should experience. If you hurry, there's even still time for children, Uncle." Fred winked.

"Children?" Scrooge felt his cheeks grow warm as he remembered, for the first time, the prophecy Queen Griselda had spoken of. Surely it was not possible . . . not at their age . . . was it? He looked to Fred, but his nephew only grinned.

"After you." Fred held open the door.

"Delighted." Scrooge started through the doorway, intent upon the sound of the merry-making in the next room, but then halted. "On thing, before it slips from my mind in the midst of the fun. I'd like you to do me one favor. Tomorrow morning, early. It's imperative that we move quickly."

"Anything," said Fred.

Scrooge lowered his voice so that Belle and the other women could not hear, because he did not want to worry them or, worse, frighten them. Fred listened to his uncle, offered comment, and the two men after five minutes of talk shook on their agreement.

"Fred? Uncle Ebenezer? Are you coming?" sang Penny.

"Come along, Ebenezer," called Belle. "You and Fred will have time to talk vampire business later. It's Christmas Day, and I do not want to even think of them!"

Scrooge entered the parlor and went to stand behind his Belle, who was seated on the same settee he had seen the previous night when escorted by the Ghost of Christmas Present. The Christmas tree, heavily laden with gifts for the children in the city whose parents were uprooted slayers, stood just where it had before, in a place of honor in the big window. "What a beautiful tree. What a magnificent tree! Might I go with you later, nephew, when you deliver the playthings?"

Fred looked at him oddly. "Of . . . of course you may." He glanced at Belle as if to ask how his uncle knew where the toys were bound, then back at Scrooge. "Anyone is welcome, so long as you understand we cannot divulge to anyone where the safe houses lie."

"I would never divulge such information." Scrooge drew his finger across his sealed lips. "Never."

"So, what shall we play first?" asked Penny. "Blindman's bluff or Yes or No? You choose, Uncle Ebenezer, for you are our guest of honor."

And so he did choose. First they played blindman's bluff, then Yes or No, then a host of other games and Yes or No again at Scrooge's request. It was every bit as much fun as he thought it would be. It was a wonderful party, wonderful games, wonderful unanimity, wonderful happiness.

✎ 45 ✎

Scrooge was early upon the street the next morning, tipping his hat and calling greetings to any other early risers. He spoke to coachmen and bankers alike, a fishmonger and a charwoman on her way to work. At the appointed time, he met his nephew on a street corner in front of a dressmaker's shop (still closed at this early hour) only a few blocks from the building that read "Scrooge and Marley."

"Uncle Ebenezer!" Fred was precisely on time, and once again pumped Scrooge's hand again and again.

"Nephew."

Fred flipped up the collar of his wool greatcoat to cut the wind, for it whipped fiercely around the corner, blowing snow from what had fallen during the night. "Are you certain you want to do this?"

"You said yesterday that the VSU has been trying to trap him for some time."

"Yes, that's true," Fred agreed. "He's a sly one. Travels mostly in a group with vampires protecting him. Six months ago, one of our men thought he had him cornered in a root cellar three blocks north. Turned out to be a trap."

"Disgut killed him?" Scrooge asked, horrified that he had been paying this creature wages all these years. Spotting a man leading a pig on a rope on the opposite side of the street, he tipped his hat. "Good morning, sir."

The shabbily dressed man with the pig looked behind him to see if, perhaps, Scrooge called to another man. Realizing he hadn't, he broke into a wide, toothy grin. "Mr. Scrooge. A good morning to you!" His broad forehead crinkled. "Are you well, sir?"

"Quite well! Quite well, thank you. Have a good day!"

Fred waited until the man had passed to continue the conversation with his uncle. "We're unsure what happened to our friend. He never reported in again. Disgut probably offered him as a sacrifice to the streets below."

"You know about the streets below?" Scrooge asked, eyes wide.

"*You* do?" asked Fred. "How?"

"As I said yesterday, it is a long story." Scrooge grasped his nephew's arm. "This must be done. Today. And then we enter my cellar. I want the entrance bricked up. If we're lucky, perhaps we will even catch the king and queen in their coffins. I could make good use of the pike there, don't you think?"

Fred looked up one side of the street and down the other. It was already becoming busier. Shutters were swinging open. Carts and carriages were passing on the street. "I'm not saying we don't want Disgut badly, but this is dangerous business. There was a great deal of activity last night. Some of the vampires were seen fleeing the city." He hesitated. "Our spies tell us it has something to do with you."

"With me?" Scrooge pretended to be surprised. Actually, he wasn't, but he and Bella had a long discussion last night in her parlor before he had bid her farewell, and they had agreed that to protect those they cared about, he would not reveal the full explanation of his *change of heart*. "Well, I have no idea how I would affect them, but I'm offering this opportunity to see London spared from Disgut's treachery any longer. I do not want another man woman or child to die at his hand."

"That is good-hearted and brave of you, Uncle Ebenezer. I just want to be certain you understand the risks. Even if you do not actively fight, they could go after you. They very likely will when they learn that you will be funding the unions."

"I understand risks." He opened his arms wide and smiled. "I'm a businessman. Now lead the way. I must be at the office before Cratchit arrives." Unable to control himself, he chuckled. "I've plans for Bob Cratchit!"

"This way, then." Fred led Scrooge to the door of a ham and beef shop that had not yet opened for the day. He approached the shop, walked right up to the door and entered, ignoring the Closed signage. Scrooge followed. They went through several rooms, past a family having breakfast at their table, and out the back door and through a tiny, barren yard. They climbed through a hole in a fence, and went down another alley.

At a painted green door that barely hung on its hinges it was so old, Fred knocked twice, paused, then knocked three times, paused, and knocked once.

Scrooge gazed around the muddy plot while they waited quite close to a refuse pile. Here there were shattered chairs, rotted crates, and the rusty rings of an old barrel. A spotted mutt dug in the wet earth near a broken earthen pot. Scrooge looked back at the door questioningly. "Have we the right place?"

"We've the right place, all right." His nephew smiled.

A moment later, a shutter banged open overhead and a young woman with a head of fiery red hair and the most beguiling green eyes popped her head out. She was pulling on a little white cap. "Hold a minute! One of the children will let you in. Good morning to you," she called, making eye contact with Scrooge.

"Good morning to you," he returned, tipping his hat.

The shutter banged shut, and a few moments later there was the grating sound of a key turning a lock. The hinges creaked as the door swung open, and a lad of six or seven with hair the same color as the woman's greeted them cheerfully.

"Morning, sirs! They're in the cellar. All assembled. Quite a turnout for early." His eyes were the same color as the woman's. "Could I get ye some tea?"

"Thank you, Charles, but no. I know the way." Fred led Scrooge past the child.

"What a bright boy, a bright boy, indeed," Scrooge said as he heard the door barred and locked behind them.

Fred led his uncle down a narrow hall, past a small parlor that while shabby with age was lit brightly by a fire. At a narrow door at the end of the hall, he issued the same series of knocks. "Precautions are always necessary," he explained as they waited. "We have spies, but they have more of them. Last month, we caught one of the minions pretending to be a fishmonger whose wife had been killed by a vampire. Had he made it inside these walls or any of the other meeting places of the VSU, it could have been devastating to our cause."

The tiny door opened and another red-haired lad, a few years older than the front door keep, led them down a rickety staircase. The open cellar, occupied by a least a dozen men, smelled of damp earth, rich tobacco, and hot mulled cider, of all things.

"Hot drink to warm your insides before ye go back out?" asked the lad.

Fred smiled and mussed up his mop of red hair with his hand. "No thank you, William."

"Off with you, Wills. Stand your post upstairs at the door."

A man of perhaps twenty, with the same red hair, gave the order.

"Beatty," Fred introduced, pointing to the eldest of the redheads. He then introduced his uncle to all the men: a baker, lamplighter, a businessman like himself, even a member of Parliament. The members of the VSU who had come that morning were from all walks of English life; some were rich, some were poor, some old, some young. Perhaps they had more difference than similarities, but the common body that drew them together was their determination to fight the vampires unto death. To save humanity.

The meeting did not last long, for all understood the importance of surprise if they were to catch Disgut. Fred feared that once he entered Scrooge and Marley, it would not take him long to see the change in Ebenezer Scrooge and become suspicious.

In less than half an hour's time, Scrooge was back on the street, alone this time. Fred had wanted to accompany him, for fear for his uncle's safety, but the members of the union, and Scrooge, agreed that nothing should appear different that morning than any other morning.

❧ 46 ❧

So, Scrooge arrived early to his place of business, hoping to catch Bob Cratchit coming late. Praying Disgut would be later. (For he always seemed to arrive after Bob, no matter the time. Had he been following him all these years?) That was the thing he had set his heart upon.

And he did it; yes, he did. The clock struck nine. No Bob. A quarter past. No Bob. He was a full eighteen minutes and a half behind his time. Scrooge sat with his door wide open, that he might see him come into the tank.

His hat was off, before he opened the door; his ragged, dirty comforter that served as his greatcoat, too. He was on his stool in a jiffy, driving away with his pen, as if he were trying to over-take nine o'clock.

"Hallo," growled Scrooge from behind his desk, in his ac-customed voice, or as near as he could feign it. "What do you mean by coming here at this time of day?"

"I am very sorry, sir," said Bob. "I am behind my time. My . . . my sister-in-law, who has cared for my children since my wife passed on, left last night in the middle of the night in a great hurry. She said she had had enough of badly behaved children, but they are not badly behaved."

Scrooge thought about what Fred had said about vampires and minions fleeing the city. He wondered if Maena had somehow gotten word that she was in danger of being discovered. What if Disgut had been warned as well? He returned his attention to his employee, clearing his voice. "You are quite behind your time," repeated Scrooge. "Yes. I think you are. Step this way, sir, if you please."

"It's only once a year, sir," pleaded Bob, walking into the rear office. "It shall not be repeated. I was making rather merry yesterday, sir. And then my sister-in-law—"

"Now, I'll tell you what, my friend," said Scrooge. He waved him in, for he did not want Bob to be a part of what would soon happen. "I am not going to stand this sort of thing any longer. And therefore," he continued, leaping from his stool, and giving Bob such a dig in the waistcoat that he staggered backward, nearly falling, "and therefore I am about to raise your salary!"

Bob trembled, and got a little nearer to his employer. He had a momentary idea of knocking Scrooge down, holding him, and calling to the people in the court for help and a straitwaistcoat. "Sir?"

"A merry Christmas, Bob," said Scrooge, with an earnestness that could not be mistaken, as he clapped him on the back. "A merrier Christmas, Bob, my good fellow, than I have given you for many a year. I'll raise your salary, and endeavor to assist your struggling family, and we will discuss your affairs this very afternoon, over a Christmas bowl of smoking bishop punch, Bob."

"Raise my salary?" Again Bob staggered. "You mean to share a bowl of punch with me?"

"That I do." Scrooge lowered his voice. "I want to discuss my membership in the VSU, and then there's the matter of my wedding." He threw up his hands. "We've so much to speak of." Scrooge heard a sound at the front door, and laid his hand on Cratchit's shoulder, pushing him toward the rear entrance. You see, he did not want Bob there for Disgut's undoing, just in case it did not turn out well. "But first you must make up the fires, which means you must buy another coal-scuttle before you dot another i, Bob Cratchit!"

"You want me to buy coal?"

"I do." Scrooge pushed several coins into his hand and even opened the door for him. "Now go along with you."

"Cratchit?" Disgut called from the tank. "Cratchit, are you here?"

With Bob out the rear door, Scrooge made his way out front. "Disgut," he said, eyeing the front door. He thought he saw movement outside the window, but he could not be sure. A black cloak? Was it the vampires come to Disgut's rescue, or the VSU? He couldn't be sure, and he felt a tingle of fear down his spine. But not enough fear to set him off his righteous path.

"Where is Cratchit?" asked Disgut suspiciously. He took a step backward toward the door.

"Why . . ." Scrooge stalled as he eyed an iron poker, used to stir the coals of the fire, leaning against the wall. He could not let Disgut get away, and though he was certain his clerk was a minion and not an actual vampire, he had no intention of testing his theory. "I . . . I fired him," he grumbled, moving sideways toward the would-be weapon. Fred had warned that he should do nothing; that his only task was to lead the slayers to Disgut, but Scrooge was partially responsible for this man's evil doings, and he felt it his responsibility to see his end, or die trying.

Scrooge thought of Belle as he moved closer to the wall.

"Fired him?" Disgut asked, his rat-like eyes narrowing behind his glasses. "Why ever for?"

"Late." Scrooge slid one foot across the floor. It was difficult for a man his age, used to inactivity, to be stealthy.

"But I was late," suggested Disgut.

Scrooge now stood in front of the poker, blocking its view from the minion. He casually tucked his hands behind his back and leaned forward, putting on his sternest face. "I could not fire you both the same week!" he shouted. "Now could I? I pay you less."

Disgut's scowl turned into an evil smirk. "I see."

"Do you?" Scrooge grasped the metal poker with both hands and drew it over his head, throwing himself forward. As he swung the heavy weapon, he did not see Disgut's pointy nose or pale cheeks. He saw the two pretty girls who had danced for the King and Queen of the Vampires—who *would* dance for them if the future was not altered. He did not hear Disgut's cry of shock that turned to pain. He heard the laughter of the dancers just before the vampires descended upon them. Before Disgut bathed himself in their blood. All which would come to pass if Scrooge didn't stop it.

As the metal poker sank into the minion's chest, the front door flew open and the slayers poured in carrying long pikes and heavy clubs. Scrooge barely felt the arms of his nephew around his shoulders as Fred pulled him back from the carnage.

"Uncle Ebenezer," Fred cried. "Are you all right? We sent men to your cellars, and the king and queen have fled. We feared they had come after you."

"I am well. Safe. Better than safe and well." Scrooge buried his face in his nephew's lapel. "Thank you, Fred. Thank you for not losing faith in me."

"Do not thank me, Uncle Ebenezer," Fred whispered. "It was my mother's faith that has carried us both."

"I will not let you down, I swear it." Scrooge wiped at the tears in his eyes as he gazed into his nephew's face. "Not you or Belle or Bob, or any of the VSU members. I will be true to you to my very end."

❧ 47 ❧

Scrooge was better than his word. He did it all, and infinitely more. To Tiny Tim, who did not die, he was a second father. He became as good a friend, as good a master, and as good a man, as the good old city knew, or any other good old city, town, or borough, in the good old world. He not only supported the vampire slayers local union, but unions far and near. He attended every meeting and was the first to offer coin when need was voiced. He never told anyone but Belle of the things he saw that night with the ghosts of Christmas. He saw no need to share the pain that he would carry for the rest of his life—life was about joy to him now, and he wanted to spare others when he could.

Some people laughed to see the alteration in Ebenezer Scrooge, but he let them laugh, and little heeded them, for he was wise enough to know that nothing ever happened on this globe, for good, at which some people did not have their fill of laughter in the outset. And knowing that such as these would be blind anyway, he thought it quite as well that they should wrinkle up their eyes in grins, as have the malady in less attractive forms. His own heart laughed and that was quite enough for him.

A few months after his encounter with the spirits, Scrooge married his Belle, and nine short months later, bells rang in the city as a miracle took place. The prophesy of the birth of the Scion of the Great Culling was fulfilled. Scrooge attended the birth of his son, and he felt no shame in his tears as he took his swaddled son from his rosy-cheeked wife and held him to his heart.

At the same moment as Scrooge held his son for the first time, a woman far away screamed.

Queen Griselda, dressed in a tattered gown, her pale face sunken with hunger, fell to her knees. "No," she cried, reaching out in the dark emptiness of the cave she had taken shelter in. "It cannot be! The Scion of the Great Culling has been born! Ebenezer Scrooge has fathered the man who will see the end of us." Tears ran down her cheeks as she raked her long, dirty nails over her face.

One of the few minions she had left tried to comfort her. "It's not true. It cannot be true," the starving man insisted.

"It is true. You might as well run a pike through my heart now," she moaned. "First my Wahltraud murdered in his own coffin, and now this. It's the end of the world," she keened, throwing herself again and again into the dirt. "The end of the world."

And so, while it may not have been the very end for Queen Griselda and the vampires, it was most certainly the beginning of the end, for the prophecy had come true. Ebenezer Scrooge, once the namesake for skinflint, miser and general sourpuss had, against all odds, become the man his mother had hoped he would be. He had no further intercourse with spirits, but lived upon the Total Abstinence Principle, ever afterward, and it was always said of him, that he knew how to keep Christmas well, if any man alive possessed the knowledge. May that be truly said of us, and all of us! And so, as Tiny Tim observed, God bless Us, Every One!

Scrooge stayed true to his word and was the husband Belle wanted him to be and the father to his son, the Scion, he deserved. The Scion of the Great Culling grew to adulthood with Tiny Tim as his right-hand man, and together, with slayers all over the world, the vampires were nearly wiped out.

Nearly, I say, dear reader, for I must warn you, on a cold and blustery night, when the snow falls, you must still keep your eye out for Queen Griselda and her minions. For such as she and her loathsome kind will always creep about seeking weakness of character, sloth, and greed, and if she sniffs it out, she will slip into your house, hide in the shadows, and wait for the time when she may sink her fangs deep into your throat and drink your life's blood to the last drop. . . .

Did you miss Sarah Gray's first vampire-infused classic?

What if the enigmatic hero of one of our most timeless love stories was part vampire? The answer lies in this haunting retelling of the classic tale of Catherine and Heathcliff, kindred spirits bound by a turbulent—and now forbidden—passion . . .

When a young orphan named Heathcliff is brought to Wuthering Heights by the manor's owner, Mr. Earnshaw, rumors abound. Yet the truth is more complicated than anyone could guess. Heathcliff's mother was a member of a gypsy band that roamed the English countryside, slaying vampires to keep citizens safe. But his father was a vampire. Now, even as Heathcliff gallantly fights the monsters who roam the moors in order to protect beautiful, spirited Catherine Earnshaw, he is torn by compassion for his victims—and by his own dark thirst.

Though Catherine loves Heathcliff, she fears the vampire in him, and is tempted by the privileged lifestyle their neighbors, the Lintons, enjoy. Forced to choose between wealthy, refined Edgar Linton and the brooding, increasingly dangerous Heathcliff, she makes a fateful decision. And soon Heathcliff, too, must choose—between his hunger, and the woman he will love for all eternity . . .

Keep reading for a taste of WUTHERING BITES. . . .

❧ 1 ❧

1801

I've just returned from a visit with my landlord—the solitary neighbor, rumor has it, is a vampire. It is truly a pity, really, this infestation of unholy bloodsuckers, because this is certainly a beautiful country, the moors of England. I do not think I could have picked a place more solitary or removed from the stir of society. It is a perfect misanthrope's heaven . . . at least it will be so long as I do not have the misfortune of being bitten by said neighbor—or any of the other unnatural beasties that roam the countryside.

I think Mr. Heathcliff and I are a suitable pair to share this desolation. A capital fellow! I do not think he realized how my heart warmed to him when I beheld his suspicious black eyes as I rode up. Who knows? Maybe we are both the subject of unfounded rumor and he has been warned that I am vampire!

As he stared at me, I asked, "Mr. Heathcliff?"

He nodded.

"Mr. Lockwood, your tenant, sir." *And most unquestionably*

not a vampire, I thought, but did not say. "I do myself the honor of calling as soon as possible after my arrival. I hope I did not inconvenience you when I persevered to solicit occupation of Thrushcross Grange. I—"

"I do not allow anyone to inconvenience me if I can prevent it," he interrupted. "Walk in!"

His last words seemed expressed with the sentiment *May your flesh be sucked dry* and the hair rose on the back of my neck. But despite the inkling of fear for wonder if the rumors about him could possibly be true, I was curious enough of his reserved nature to follow his bidding.

"Joseph, take Mr. Lockwood's horse," he ordered as we entered the court.

Joseph was an old man, though hale and sinewy. His skin was paler than the palest moon and his eyes red, rimmed in dark shadows. Around his neck, he wore a long scarf that he tied high beneath his ear, a peculiar accessory, indeed, for a manservant.

"The Lord help us!" he whined, taking my horse. Why we needed the Lord's help I was unsure, but I dared not speculate.

Wuthering Heights is the name of Mr. Heathcliff's dwelling, though I have heard that all in the countryside refer to it as Wuthering *Bites.* A poor, unimaginative jest, I know. "Wuthering" is an adjective referring to the atmospheric tumult to which the house is exposed in stormy weather. By the look of the excessive slant of a few stunted firs and tangled briars at the end of the house, I can only guess at the power of the north wind that must blow over the edge. Happily, the architect had the foresight to build the structure strong; the narrow windows are set deep in the wall and the corner is defended by large, jutting stones.

Before I passed the threshold into the house, I paused to admire the grotesque carving lavished over the front of the principal door. Among crumbling griffins and what appeared to be cloaked figures, their faces obscured, I detected the date "1500" and the name "Hareton Earnshaw." Curiosity tempted me to ask about the history of the place from my surly, pale-skinned, black-haired owner, but his curt attitude at the door suggested he wished a speedy entrance or complete departure, so I hurried after him.

Without a lobby or passage, one step took us into the family sitting room. They called it "the house." It included the parlor and the kitchen in the back, from where I could distinguish a chatter of tongues and a clatter of culinary utensils. At one end of the parlor stood the massive fireplace, flanked by ranks of pewter dishes that reflected both light and heat, interspersed with jugs and tankards. On a vast oak dresser was a frame of wood laden with oat cakes and clusters of legs of beef, mutton, and ham.

They say vampires take no nourishment but blood, so the sight of the feast encouraged me. Surely the sign of abundant foodstuffs was proof enough that the master was no such creature! . . . Unless the spread was meant to disarm and persuade me that all here was as it should be in a decent household.

Above the chimney were sundry villainous old guns, a couple of horse pistols, and three gaudily painted canisters on the ledge. The floor was smooth, white stone unsoiled, I noted, by bloodstains; the chairs, high-back, primitive structures painted green. In the arch under the dresser was a huge liver-colored bitch pointer, surrounded by a swarm of squealing puppies, and more dogs haunted other recesses.

The parlor and furniture would have been nothing extraordinary for a simple northern farmer among these hills and moors, but Mr. Heathcliff formed a contrast to his abode. Despite his dark-haired, dark-eyed gypsy looks, in dress and manners he seems a gentleman country squire. By his appearance, some might suspect a degree of underbred pride; gypsies are known for such arrogance, and I wonder if he could be one of them. Since the infestation of the vampires, the gypsy vampire slayers have become bold in their haughtiness. With some right, as it is their skill and courage that keep the beasties from devouring all of us and taking over our fair country. But I am running too fast, bestowing attributes on Mr. Heathcliff that might be unfounded.

I took a seat at the end of the hearthstone opposite my landlord and filled up the interval of silence by attempting to caress the pointer bitch that had left her pups and was sneaking wolfishly to the back of my legs.

My caress provoked a long, guttural snarl. At closer glance, I saw that this creature was half again as large as one of her kind, with great ivory fangs and a fierce eye. Her throat, I noted, was protected by a thick leather collar studded with spikes, no doubt to keep her from being drained of blood by a vampire.

"You better let the dog alone," growled Mr. Heathcliff, punctuating his words with a punch of his foot. "She's not a pet!"

He strode to a side door and shouted again. "Joseph!"

The old man mumbled indistinctly from the depths of the cellar but gave no suggestion of ascending, so his master went down, leaving me with the monstrous bitch and a pair of sheepdogs.

Not anxious to come in contact with their fangs—or anyone's, for that matter—I sat still. Unfortunately, I indulged myself by making a face at the dog, and she broke into a fury and leapt for my throat. I hastened to put the dining table between us, this action rousing the whole pack. Half a dozen four-footed fiends of various sizes and ages issued from their hidden dens and I felt my heels and coat-laps subjects of assault. I parried off the larger dogs as effectually as I could with a fireplace poker, but was forced to call for assistance from the household when a yipping terrier slipped beneath my guard and latched onto my knee. He was hedgehog small but keen of tooth, and I felt each tiny dagger dig into my flesh until warm drops of blood ran down my boot.

Mr. Heathcliff and his henchman climbed the steps, slow as molasses running off a block of ice. Fortunately, an inhabitant of the kitchen came running; a lusty dame with tucked-up gown, bare arms, and flushed cheeks rushed into the midst of us, flourishing a frying pan, and used the weapon to such purpose that the storm magically subsided, leaving her heaving like a sea after a high wind when her master entered the scene.

"What the devil is the matter?" he asked, eyeing me in a manner I could barely endure after such inhospitable treatment.

"What the devil, indeed," I muttered, collapsing into a chair, trying to pry the still-clinging terrier from my wounded knee. "A herd of possessed swine has better manners than those animals of yours, sir. You might as well leave a stranger in a hive of vampires!"

He put a bottle of spirits down in front of me. "The hounds do right to be vigilant. We all do, considering what roams the moors. A glass of wine?"

"No, thank you." The terrier released my knee long enough to bite my thumb and went back to the knee with undisguised glee.

"Not bitten, are you?"

"By the son of Lucifer!" I replied, trying to shake the little dog off. "If blood loss be any measure—"

"Vampire bitten," Heathcliff corrected.

I could not suppress a shudder, as I knew the meaning of the phrase was far broader these days than it had once been. "If I had been, I would have set my silver dagger on the biter," I responded, laying my hand on its sheath at my waist, my meaning equally broader than it might once have been.

In these times of roaming vampires, both gentlemen and

gentlewomen had taken to carrying weapons to fend the beasties off. Pure silver made up for the small size of the dagger and my lack of vampire fighting skills, I was assured by the salesman when I made the purchase in London. Well worth the extraordinary cost, I was promised.

The vicious terrier continued to rend my poor knee until the kitchen wench with her flushed cheeks and noble frying pan put her fingers to her lips and emitted a sharp whistle. The canine fury's pointed ears perked up and his gaze fixed on the skinned rabbit the dame dangled from one hand. With one final nip, the dog unclenched its jaw and dove for the rabbit. She sliced off the head and tossed it, bringing all the hounds to full cry and chase. The small devil that had so harried me reached the meat a paw's length ahead of the pointer bitch and carried his prize to the top of a sideboard and hence to a lofty shelf to devour the bunny head, to the sorrow of those companions left supperless.

Heathcliff's countenance relaxed into a grin, surprising me. "A noble beast. A first-rate terrier. I've lost count of his bloodsucker kills. Of course, his mother was a badger, his father a noble hunter of vermin. Still, I doubt you've seen the like in your travels."

"No, I can't say I have." I unwound my second-best stock from my neck and used it to stanch the worst of the bleeding.

"Come, come, you are flurried, Mr. Lockwood. You look pale."

The massive pointer bitch had crept closer to lap up the droplets on the floor around my boots. "I have lost blood," I pointed out.

"Naught but a spoon or two. Nothing to grouse about. Take a little wine. Welcome guests are so rare in this house that I and my dogs hardly know how to receive them. To your health, sir!"

I bowed, beginning to realize it would be foolish to sit and sulk over the misbehavior of a few curs and unwilling to yield my host further amusement at my expense.

He—probably persuaded by the realization he should not offend a good tenant—relaxed a little and introduced a subject of interest to me, my present state of retirement. I found him very intelligent, and before I went home, I volunteered another visit tomorrow. He evidently, however, wished no further intrusion and expressed such.

It is astonishing how sociable I feel myself compared to him.

❦ 2 ❧

The next afternoon set in so misty and cold that I had half a mind to spend it by my study fire instead of wading through mud, risking my life in tempting the demons that course the moors—to Wuthering Heights.

Walking down the hall with this lazy intention, I spotted a serving girl on her knees and stepped into the room thinking I might greet her. Settled in front of the fireplace, she was surrounded by brushes and coal scuttles and raising an infernal dust as she extinguished flames with heaps of cinders. When she looked up, startled by my intrusion on her work, I noticed two distinguishing puncture marks on her pale neck. The spectacle drove me back through the doorway, and she watched with the oddest little smile on her face.

I resolved to place a chair in front of my bedchamber door at night and keep a vigilant eye on this saucy jade. It was well-known that maidens of the lower sort often traded virtue for the thrill of sexual congress with the fanged ones. Male vampires were said to possess extraordinary physical attributes such as to render foolish females incapable of moral judgment.

Who knew if she was an innocent seized on her way home from church or a lusty wench who sought her own downfall among the beasts? In any case, she would bear watching, and if I sensed anything amiss, she would find herself dismissed without a letter of recommendation. She might be happier dancing half naked and exposing her slender throat in some vampire-friendly tavern than emptying chamber pots in an honest man's house.

Without lingering, I took my hat and made the four-mile walk to Wuthering Heights. Fortunately, on my journey, I encountered no sign of cloaked and bloodthirsty predators. In fact, I had not seen one since my arrival. Just as I made my way to the garden gate, however, I thought I spied what seemed to be shadows of the enemy through the first feathery flakes of a snow-shower.

On that bleak hill-top, the earth was hard with black frost and the air made me shiver through every limb as I blinked, unsure if the shadows were real or mirage. Vampire or swaying grass? Unwilling to wait out the answer, I ran up the causeway and knocked for admittance, keeping a look over my shoulder.

When there came no immediate answer from within save for the howl of dogs, I grasped the latch and shook it vehemently. Vinegar-faced Joseph projected his head from a round window of the barn.

"What ye want?" he shouted, adjusting the scarf around his neck. "Go round if ye want the master."

"Is there no one to open the door?" I responded, looking again over my shoulder. Yes, something was definitely there . . . and there! I recalled the poor maid's wound and went on faster. "Open to me, Joseph, for pity's sake! 'Tis not safe for man untrained in vampire repelling to stand out in this weather."

"There's nobody but the missus, and she'll not open the door. Not for King Georgie himself."

"Why?" I peered up at him, shivering inside my coat. "Can't you tell her who I am?"

The head vanished and I was left in the snow, which had begun to drive thickly. I had the sense that I was being watched, a feeling so strong that I feared to turn and look over my shoulder. I had just seized the door handle to give another try when a young man shouldering a pitchfork appeared in the yard behind. He hailed me to follow him, and I, glad for flesh and bone of any human kind, trailed after him through a washhouse and a paved area containing a coal shed, pump, and pigeon cote. I gave a sigh of relief as we arrived in the warm, cheery apartment and I was formally received.

The room glowed delightfully with the radiance of an immense fire built from coal, peat, and wood. Near the table, laid for a plentiful meal, I was pleased to observe the "missus," whose existence I had not previously suspected.

I bowed and waited for her to offer me a seat, quite relieved to have arrived unscathed. Leaned back in her chair, she looked at me, remaining motionless and mute.

"Rough weather and beasties lurking!" I remarked. "I'm afraid, Mrs. Heathcliff, I had to work hard to make myself heard at the door. It was a near thing."

She never opened her mouth and I glanced at her neck, wondering if, like the maid at Thrushcross, she had fallen victim to one of the vampires I thought I had seen in the snowing mist. She kept her eyes on me in a cool, regardless manner. I saw no bite marks, but that was no guarantee; women in particular were good at hiding them when they wished to.

"Sit down," said the young man gruffly. "He'll be in soon."

I obeyed, keeping one eye on Mrs. Heathcliff while calling the villain canine, Juno, the pointer bitch, who moved the extreme tip of her tail in token of owning my acquaintance. To my relief, the tiny terror was nowhere in sight.

"A beautiful animal," I commenced. "Do you intend parting with the pups, madam?"

"They are not mine," said the hostess, more unkindly than

Heathcliff himself could have replied. "You should not have come. It is not safe." She rose, reaching for the mantel for two of the painted canisters. "Vampires are thick on these moors on such sunless days."

As if one needed reminding. . . .

Her position before was sheltered from the light; now, I had a distinct view of her figure and countenance. She was slender and barely past girlhood, an admirable form and the most exquisite little face I have ever had the pleasure of beholding. With flaxen ringlets hanging loose on her delicate neck, she had small features that, had they been in agreeable expression, would have been irresistible. Fortunately for my susceptible heart, the only sentiment they evoked hovered somewhere between scorn and a kind of desperation.

The canisters were almost out of reach, and I made a motion to aid her.

"I can get them myself," she snapped.

"I beg your pardon?"

"Were you asked to tea?" she demanded, tying an apron over her neat black frock and standing with a spoonful of leaf poised over the pot.

I detected the sharp scent of garlic, a common ingredient in English teas, as of late. It is said to ward off vampires; they detest it. Some, like my housekeeper, have even taken to wearing garlic on their persons—a foolish notion, I think. "I'll be glad to have a cup," I said. *Perhaps two, if it will get me home with the eight imperial pints of blood I possessed when I left Thrushcross Grange today,* I thought.

"Were you invited?" she repeated.

"No." I half smiled. "You're proper to ask, though. No telling what sort of strangers will try to make their way into your home these days. A cousin of mine told me that only last week a vampire pretending to be an old acquaintance tried to invite himself into my cousin's household for tea."

She flung the tea back, spoon and all, and returned to her chair in a pout, her under-lip pushed out, like a child's ready to cry.

Meanwhile, the young man had slung on a decidedly shabby upper garment, stained with blood. I wondered if, like many young men in the country, he was training to fight the dark devils. I nearly asked him myself, but then he looked at me from the corner of his eyes as if there were some mortal feud unavenged between us, and I swallowed my question. His thick brown curls were rough and uncultivated, his whiskers encroaching bearishly over his cheeks, and his hands were embrowned like those of a common laborer. Yet I began to wonder if he was a servant or not. His dress and speech were entirely devoid of the superiority one could observe in Mr. and Mrs. Heathcliff, but his bearing was free, almost haughty, and he showed no respect to the lady of the house.

In absence of clear proof of his place in the household, I deemed it best to abstain from noticing his curious behavior; five minutes later, the entrance of Heathcliff relieved me from my uncomfortable state.

"You see, sir, I've returned as promised," I exclaimed. "But I fear I shall be weather-bound. I trust you can afford me shelter." Then I cleared my throat, feeling it my duty to warn him. "Are you aware of the creatures that presently linger on your property?"

"Afford you shelter? For the night?" he said, seeming to ignore my reference to a possible vampire infestation, the more pressing issue of the conversation, I thought.

"I wonder you should select a snow-storm to ramble about in. Do you know that you run the risk of being murdered in the marshes? People far more familiar than you with these moors often miss the road on such a day and are never seen again."

So he was aware. . . . "If staying here would be an imposition, perhaps I can get a guard from among your lads to escort me home, and he might stay at the Grange until morning. With weapons, perhaps? I fear I'm not so good with a sword." I laid my hand on the tiny silver dagger I wore on my belt. Little protection should a swarm descend upon me. Perhaps I should reconsider the benefits of a garlic necklace. Who was I to question wiser heads who had known and feared vampires for generations?

"No, I could not."

"Indeed?" I drew back, surprised by his reply. "You would turn me out to certain death?"

"Are you going to make the tea?" demanded he of the shabby coat.

"Is he going to have any?" she asked, appealing to Heathcliff. "I see no need to waste good tea if he's to walk out into the moors and be drained of every drop of—"

"Get it ready!" Heathcliff uttered so savagely that I felt no longer inclined to call him a capital fellow. I wondered if I needed to consider the rumors again. Had I stepped from fang to fang?

When the tea preparations were finished, he invited me to join the others around the table. There was an austere silence while I watched Mrs. Heathcliff make a separate pot of tea from a second container for Mr. Heathcliff. I wanted to sniff it for garlic, fearing it contained naught, but I dared not. Instead, we all digested our meal: a dry wedge of cheese that bore teeth marks of mice, a crock of jellied eels, hardtack at least as old as Joseph, and a splendid length of blood sausage.

Afraid I had caused the cloud of grim silence, I thought I should make an effort to dispel it, and after a false start, I began. "It is strange," I said between swallowing the last of one cup of tea and receiving another. Heathcliff, I noted, took food on his plate and added sugar to his tea, but he neither drank nor ate. "Odd," I continued, "how custom can mold our tastes and ideas. Many could not imagine the existence of so isolated a society, surrounded by hostile hives of vampires, Mr. Heathcliff. Yet I venture to say, that surrounded by your family and your amiable lady—"

"My amiable lady!" he interrupted with an almost diabolical sneer.

For a moment, I feared he would bare fangs.

"Where is she, my amiable lady?"

"Mrs. Heathcliff, your wife, I mean."

"So you suggest her spirit has taken the post of ministering angel and guardian of Wuthering Heights, even when her body is drained of blood and gone? Is that it? She watches us from the grave?"

Perceiving my blunder, I attempted to correct it. I should have seen that there was too great a disparity of years between them. He was forty. She looked no more than seventeen. Then it flashed upon me. The clown in the bloody coat was her husband. Heathcliff, junior, of course.

"Mrs. Heathcliff is my daughter-in-law," said Heathcliff, corroborating my surmise. He turned as he spoke, a look of hatred in his eyes as he gazed at her.

"Ah, certainly," I stumbled on, turning to my neighbor. "I see now; you are the favored possessor of the beauteous lady."

This was worse than before; the youth grew crimson and clenched his fist and I began to have second thoughts as to whose blood it was upon his coat. Rather than a vampire's, did it belong to the last neighbor who came for tea?

"Poor conjecture, again, sir!" observed my host. "Neither of us have the privilege of owning your fair lady. Her husband is deceased."

"And this young man is . . ."

"Not my son, assuredly!"

"My name is Hareton Earnshaw," growled the young man.

"I meant no disrespect," I said, noting the dignity with

which he announced himself. Perhaps he was a vampire slayer, a good one, and thus the conceit.

Earnshaw fixed his eye on me longer than I cared to return the stare for fear I might be tempted to box his ear, and then he would be tempted to run me through with a sword meant to impale blacker hearts than mine.

The business of eating being concluded, and no one uttering another word of sociable conversation, I glanced out a window to examine the weather and take in the sights, worldly or otherwise.

I saw before me the dark night coming in prematurely, sky and hills mingled in bitter wind and suffocating snow. It was a perfect haven for vampires in search of heat and nourishment of human blood!

"I don't think it possible for me to get home now, with or without a guard," I exclaimed. "The roads are buried already, and I could scarcely distinguish a foot in front of me. I could walk right into the arms of one of those beasts and not know it until their hellish fangs pierced my throat."

"Hareton, drive the sheep into the barn porch. They'll be fed upon if left in the fold all night," Heathcliff said. "I don't care to go out again tonight and we've lost two this week, already."

"And what must I do?" I rose with irritation. How was it that my host was so protective of the blood of sheep and not a paying tenant? "How am I to get home safely?"

There was no reply to my question as Mrs. Heathcliff leaned over the fireplace, restoring the tea canisters to their place, and Joseph entered with a pail of porridge of sheep bones and hooves to feed the dogs.

"I wonder how ye can stand there in idleness, when all of them gone out!" Joseph cried. "But you'll never mend yer ill ways, but go right to the devil, like yer mother before ye!"

For a moment, I thought this piece of eloquence was addressed to me, and enraged, I stepped toward the aged rascal, my hand upon my tiny dagger with the intention of piercing him.

Mrs. Heathcliff, however, checked me by her answer.

"You scandalous old hypocrite!" she replied. "Are you not afraid of being tossed among the bloodsuckers? I warn you not to provoke me, or I'll turn you out of this house myself and then we will see how far you get."

"Wicked! Wicked!" Joseph declared. "May the Lord deliver me from evil."

"Too late for that." She pointed to the window. "Be off, or I'll hang you by your thumbs from the outer wall and let them feed on you until you are fully drained. They will do it if he lets them, and let them he might. You know I speak the truth!"

The woman put a malignity into her beautiful eyes, and Joseph drew back in sincere horror and hurried out.

I didn't know quite what she meant by all of that, but wanting to be on my way, I pleaded, "Mrs. Heathcliff, could you point out some landmarks to guide me home?"

"Take the road you came," she answered, dropping into her chair. "It is as sound advice as I can give."

"Then if you hear of me being discovered dead in a bog or pit of snow, sucked dry of my fluids, your conscience won't whisper that it is partly your fault?"

"Certainly not. Do you expect me to provide you safe passage, wielding my sword?" she mocked.

As if women carried swords!

"Surely there are men here in training who can fend off if not kill, should the necessity arise," I questioned.

"Who are these *men in training*? There is himself, Earnshaw, Zillah, Joseph, and I, and I guarantee you the master of this abode would not step across the lane to save your neck."

"Are there no trained boys at the farm? Living in such an isolated place, surely—"

"No trained boys. Just us."

"What of Joseph? He knows the way."

"Not Joseph!" Her head snapped up. "Not after dark. Nay, you do not want Joseph after dark. Trust me, good sir."

Her remark was odd, but I was entirely too vexed to consider her meaning. "Then, welcome or not, I am compelled to stay."

"That you must settle with your host. I have nothing to do with it."

"I hope it will be a lesson to you, to make no more rash journeys on these hills, without first finding your own guard," cried Heathcliff's stern voice from the kitchen entrance. "As to staying here, I don't keep accommodations for visitors; you must share a bed with Hareton."

"I can sleep on a chair in this room," I replied.

"No, no. A stranger is a stranger, be he rich or poor. It will not suit me to permit anyone to roam my home in the middle of the night!"

My patience was at end. In disgust, I pushed past him into the yard, running against Earnshaw in my haste. It was so dark I could not see the means of exit, but I smelled the blood upon his coat, thick and cloying.

At first, the young man appeared about to befriend me.

"I'll go with him as far as the park," Hareton said. "Past the worst of them."

"And you'll go with him to hell!" Heathcliff flung back. "You are not up to the fight of such numbers. You never will be! And who is to look after the horses, then, eh?"

I drew myself up indignantly. "A man's life is of more consequence than those of horses."

Heathcliff did not seem to hear me, for he was still upon the boy. "They will not kill you, you know; they will make you one of them!"

"Well, somebody must go," murmured Mrs. Heathcliff, more

kindly than I expected. "For this is poor hospitality to a neighbor and tenant."

"Not at your command!" retorted Hareton.

"Then I hope his pale ghost will haunt you; and I hope Mr. Heathcliff will never get another human tenant, till the Grange is a ruin and swarming with the devils!" she answered sharply.

Joseph, toward whom I had been steering, muttered something under his breath. He sat within earshot, milking the cows by the light of a lantern, which I seized unceremoniously. Calling out that I would send it back on the morrow, I rushed to the nearest door.

"Master, he's thieving the lantern!" shouted the ancient.

On opening the little door, two cloaked vampires flew at my throat, bearing me down and extinguishing the light. As I flailed on the ground, trying to protect my neck, I heard a mingled guffaw from Heathcliff and Hareton.

Fortunately, the creatures seemed more bent on taunting me and tearing at my clothing than devouring me alive. *Well-fed vampires at Wuthering Heights?*

But, oh, the stench of the creatures! When recounting a tale of attack and escape, victims fail to mention the foul scent of rotting flesh, putrid blood, and black, wet humus that wafts from them. "Help me!" I managed. Tucking in a ball to further protect my jugular, I was forced to lie till the malignant master of the abode pleased to deliver me. One bark of Heathcliff's voice and the beasts leapt off me and disappeared into the snow-driven swirl of darkness, curls of smoke, gone as fast as they had come. Then, hatless and trembling with a mixture of fear and wrath, I ordered the miscreants to let me out—on their peril to keep me one minute longer.

The vehemence of my agitation brought on copious bleeding at the nose, and still Heathcliff laughed, and still I scolded, made bold by my first true escape from death. I don't know what would have concluded the scene had there not been one person at hand rather more rational than myself, and more benevolent than my entertainer. This was Zillah, the stout housewife, who entered the room to inquire into the nature of the uproar.

"Are you going to allow folk to be murdered on our very door-stones? Look at the lad, he's fair choking! Wisht, wisht!" She waved to me. "Come in, and I'll see to that. There now, hold ye still."

With these words she splashed a pint of icy water into my face and pulled me into the kitchen. Mr. Heathcliff followed, his accidental merriment expiring quickly in his habitual moroseness.

I was dizzy and faint, realizing I had not even drawn my dagger to defend myself. What man was I! In this state, I was compelled to accept lodgings under Heathcliff's roof. He told Zillah to give me a glass of brandy, and then passed on to the inner room, whereby I was somewhat revived and ushered to bed.